Fays of the Seas
and Other Fantasies

Fays of the Seas
and Other Fantasies

Edited, introduced and translated by
Brian Stableford

A Black Coat Press Book

ISBN 978-1-64932-054-4. First Printing. April 2021. Published by Black Coat Press, an imprint of Hollywood Comics.com, LLC, P.O. Box 17270, Encino, CA 91416. All rights reserved. Printed in the United States of America.

TABLE OF CONTENTS

Introduction

This anthology is a supplement to a series that culminated in *Tales of Enchantment and Disenchantment, A History of Faerie with an exemplary anthology of Tales*. The introduction to that volume summarized the history of the French genre of published *contes de fées*, from its problematic origin in the final decade of the seventeenth century, through its rapid suppression by the royal censors—presumably under the influence of the Church—who refused licit publication to all but a handful of such works after 1697, but could not prevent the gradual rise of a tide of illicit publications that eventually engendered a "contraband renaissance" of the genre in the mid-eighteenth century. That resistance to suppression persisted, in a desultory fashion, until the Revolution of 1789, by which time the genre was effectively extinct, save for few fugitive examples. There was a further renaissance in the late nineteenth century, and the exemplary anthology included nine tales published between the Revolution and the Great War of 1914-18, but its coverage of that era was rather tokenistic and lacking in detail The present volume attempts to make up for that omission.

The initial suppression of the genre was very successful, to the remarkable extent that those commentators who knew that it had happened were very wary of saying so explicitly, and their diplomacy eventually resulted in the fact being largely forgotten, warping the recorded history of the genre considerably. The one writer who had dabbled in the production of *contes de fées* without incurring determined censorship, Charles Perrault, thus came to assume, in retrospect, an altogether unwarranted reputation for originality and quality. Insofar as his tales deal with the imagery of *contes de fées*—half of those in his original collection do not, drawing from other imaginative sources—they consist almost entirely of material recycled from oral narrations by Madame d'Aulnoy, Mademoiselle de L'Héritier and the Comtesse de Murat that Perrault had heard in salons at Versailles, only a handful of which had been allowed to reach print before 1697. That history became sufficiently blurred that the majority of modern reference books suggest that Madame d'Aulnoy's tales, which eventually became the perceived backbone of the authentic genre, were published when they were prepared for publication, in 1697-8, although no hard evidence survives that they were ever printed during her lifetime—she died in 1705—and they owe their belated fame entirely to illicit posthumous printings.

One of the effects of Perrault's grossly-overestimated contribution to the perceived genesis of the genre was that the conceptualization of a *conte de fées* became somewhat confused, and that confusion was augmented when the term was mistranslated into English as "fairy tale." The *fées* that Madame d'Aulnoy and her fellow salon writers adapted from Medieval French romance were human enchantresses; the archetype that provided their generic name was a character who figured in numerous romances under slightly various names, including Mourgue la Faye, and who became known in English versions of Arthurian romance as Morgan le Fay. The English language already had a genre of "fairy poetry" long before the salon writers defined their genre, in which "fairies" were imagined to be supernatural beings, akin to Germanic elves, Greco-Roman nymphs and other kinds of nature spirits rather than the enchantresses of French romance.

That separation might seem simple enough, but some confusion had entered into it from the very beginning; Mourgue la Faye and her kin were always slightly ambiguous figures, and the English literary tradition was deeply confused by one of its associated masterpieces, Edmund Spenser's *The Faerie Queene*, whose queen is not a fairy, but the queen of a land of Faerie—with is to say, a land of Enchantment. Many commentators have pointed out over the years that there are no fairies in *The Faerie Queene*, although there are enchantresses identical to the fays of French romance. Partly thanks to translations of Perrault—only a few of whose tales feature *fées*, and are rather unclear as to what, exactly, *fées* are supposed to be—the English tradition of "fairy tales" has developed in such a fashion that there is no particular expectation that such tales will actually contain fairies, or how those fairies ought to be conceived if they do.

Because of the persecution in France of the original authors of *contes de fées*, and the consequent elevation of Perrault to an altogether undeserved celebrity, the perception of French works inevitably began a process of evolution parallel to that in England. By the time the 1789 Revolution had operated its cultural transformation, the slate, although not entirely wiped clean, had had so much of its original script rendered illegible that the few writers interested in the potential literary employments of *fées* were starting almost from scratch, with an imagistic heritage that was both muddled and muddied. It is therefore not surprising that the stories in the present sampler—which are arranged in chronological order of publication—characterize their "*fées*" in different ways and frequently adapt them to narrative purposes very different from those embraced by Madame d'Aulnoy and her associates in the writers' workshops of late seventeenth-century Paris. Many refer back to Perrault, but tend to do so in a slightly embarrassed fashion, very mindful of the fact that Perrault's tales, unlike Madame d'Aulnoy's, were designed for reading to children. The *fées* of nineteenth century compositions are, by definition, agents of enchantment, but there is little consensus among the authors as to the context of hypothetical magic within which those agents are placed.

The 1789 Revolution put an end to the royal censors, and greatly reduced the power that had been exerted on the pattern of licit publication by the Church, but it did not put an end to censorship as such, and it left much of the Church's moral influence intact, dented but by no means broken. The removal of the specific yoke did not leave the field of publication completely free, by any means, and the notion persisted that *contes de fées* and other kinds of "fairy tales" were essentially disreputable, and that those that already existed belonged to a past that might be remembered with a hint of nostalgia but could not be renewed. The reason for the legal suppression of *contes de fées* became historically invisible, but its aftereffects persisted.

The ostensible justification for the refusal of royal warrants for the publication of *contes de fées*, for all but a handful of titles that enjoyed specific royal protection, was that the salon writers who invented *contes de fées* had deliberately employed a context of enchantment that was pagan; the imaginary history in which they elected to set their stories did not contain a Christian Church. One of the reasons that Perrault escaped persecution was that he deliberately introduced one; in "La Belle au bois dormant," unlike the stories by Madame d'Aulnoy from which its elements are stolen, the marriage ceremony is performed by a priest, whereas marriages in authentic *contes de fées* tend to be performed by "druids."

The reason for that conspiratorial decision was that the salon writers wanted to avoid the dangerous accusation that the magic featured in their stores was inherently diabolical; although the seventeenth-century "witch-craze" had almost petered out, people accused of witchcraft—especially women—were still being prosecuted and punished, sometimes capitally. Although the *contes de fées* written for the Parisian salons of the 1690s do feature occasional evil fays, for melodramatic purposes, the great majority of their fays are benevolent, and their magic is often inherently virtuous. The attempt to sidestep possible accusations of diabolism by establishing a context of enchantment devoid of the Devil misfired, however, because eliminating the Devil tacitly eliminated a specifically Christian God, substituting hypothetical virtuous deities which, in the eyes of Churchmen, could not help but offend the first Commandment.

The persecution of the original coterie of authors of *contes de fées*, which went as far as imprisonment and banishment, was not fully reproduced in later eras, when penalties rarely went much further than refusal of licit publication, but that did not mean that disapproval disappeared, or even diminished; a few of the writers of the contraband renaissance made a point of introducing an explicit and ostentatious piety into their tales, but many were determined not to do so, gladly embracing the anticlericalism of the radical Enlightenment. *Fées* seemed useful and appealing to some writers precisely because they offered an alternative vocabulary of virtue for employment in moral tales. In the more substantial *contes de fées* of the contraband renaissance, *fées* not only retain an independent moral order, but often have a formal moral organization. Thus, the enchanted world of the authentic version of "La Belle et la Bête," by Madame de Villeneuve, features an elaborate government of fées, complete with a legal Code, a parliament and a supreme court, although the adulterated plagiarism by Jeanne-Marie Leprince de Beaumont—for which she obtained authorized publication by inserting it into an exceedingly pious volume replete with Bible stories—carefully removed that material. The adulterated version is the one that remains familiar, few modern readers even being aware of the existence of the authentic version.

The original writers of *contes de fées* really were antipathetic to the Church, not because they were diabolists but because they were feminists, resentful of the Church's central role in the oppression of women. Their conceptualization of *fées* as powerful women who support a moral order that is not only independent of but superior to the one championed by the Church was never likely to win tolerance from the pious, even though it was far from unknown for virtuous Churchmen to dabble in the production of fantastic apologues employing pagan agents of enchantment for exemplary purposes, licensed by the fact that the classic works employed to teach Latin, still the language of the rites of the French Church in that era, had mostly been written before the Christianization of the Roman Empire.

Their implicit paganism was not the only intellectual battleground on which *contes de fées* were attacked, however. In

11

spite of the well-known principle that the enemy of my enemy is my friend, the principal ideological enemies of doctrinaire Churchmen—those philosophers of the Enlightenment who embraced a tacit agnosticism, because it was dangerous to express an explicit atheism—sometimes opposed all tales of enchantment, stubbornly bracketing literary fantasies with religious fantasies as so much unjustified nonsense. In terms of conventional belief, the accusation that *fées* were inherently heretical seemed to many pre- and post-Revolutionary thinkers to be far less serious than the notion that, as instruments of the imagination, they were puerile and rather silly.

None of the inventors of *contes de fées*, of course, could actually believe in the agents of enchantment that they depicted, although some of them thought that a few of their readers still could—then, as now, many parents actually tried to persuade young children of the reality of a special coterie of such agents, just as priests try to persuade laymen of the reality of their favored set, for reasons of moral terrorism as well as comforting reassurance. All of the salon writers felt forced to defend their use of such motifs against the supposition of puerility as well as the suspicion of heresy. All of them did so on the grounds that it was, in fact, the criticism of their narrative strategy that was stupid (although they normally put it more diplomatically than that), and that the literary employment of hypothetical agents of enchantment did not imply belief in their actual possibility—that fiction routinely functions on a more sophisticated intellectual level, even when it is designed for children. The writers of the contraband renaissance, who had to mount a resistance to explicit, if unadvertised, censorship as well as to simple-minded disapproval, had to work very hard indeed in supporting their apologetic arguments. It is not surprising that many of them became masters of scathing satire and vitriolic sarcasm—and not surprising, either, that they were vastly outnumbered by those "realists" who avoided the unequal struggle against formal and informal censorship and kept their literary imagination under a very tight and scrupulously polite rein.

The nineteenth-century writers who inherited that legacy of disapproval found themselves in a situation that some of them found profoundly uncomfortable. Most post-Revolutionary writers and readers took it for granted that *contes de fées* belonged entirely to the past, that the genre was dead and buried, having completely lost its license of plausibility. But there were loopholes—or mouse-holes—in the wall of disdain with which any would-be writer of such *contes* was faced, which could not only be employed but perhaps even enlarged, if anyone were so inclined. There is not a single story in this volume that can really be described as confident in its inventions. Every one is, to a greater or lesser degree, uneasy, manifestly uncertain of the attitude of readers who might pick it up. Many of them attempt to follow the time-honored principle of real sportsmanship by "getting their retaliation in first," either by laying down a preliminary argument to support the case that what they are doing is not idiotic, or by cheerfully asserting that, although it might be idiotic, its humor will excuse its idiocy. Several of the stories are, however, unrepentantly earnest, a few of them in deadly earnest. Seriousness in the composition of fantastic narratives had always required courage, or at least a conscientious appeal to prestigious precedents, but the nineteenth century required a more determined artifice in attempted seriousness than any of its predecessors, and a more ostentatious calculation. There is an invariable element of defiance and determination in that ostentation, a tacit or explicit insistence that what is being done is not only excusable but worth doing, and there is a bitter seriousness even—and perhaps especially—in the blatant comedies.

At the beginning of the century, in the aftermath of the Revolution and its ironic transfiguration into the Napoleonic Empire, prose fiction tended to pay far more attention to the development of naturalistic narratives than fantastic ones, and where fantastic motifs survived, and even thrived, they did so in a context of enchantment very different from that of *contes de fées*. It was an era of anxious imaginative fiction that was dubbed "Gothic" in England, often replete with what was known in Germany as *sturm und drang* (storm and stress). The French Romantic Movement lagged behind the German Movement, and took a great deal of inspiration from it, its prose fiction taking particular inspiration from the disturbing hallucinatory fantasies of E. T. A. Hoffmann. However, the Romantic Movements also brought about a new interest in the folklore of the past, exemplified in England by Walter Scott's interest in traditional ballads, the Ossianic inventions of James Macpherson and a general renewal of interest in the imaginary history of England invented by Anglo-Norman romance. In Germany, similar fascinations were supported academically by Jakob Grimm's scholarly fantasy proposing that German folklore contained and preserved the essential *volksgeist* of the German-speaking peoples.

Ironically, most of the alleged folktales collected by Grimm and his younger brother were actually of recent origin and not German at all; many of them were derived from identifiable French originals, some of which reflected in their turn a tendency among the salon writers to adapt their own ventures from Italian tales recycled or improvised by Giovanni Straparola and Giambattista Basile. In spite of their imposture—or perhaps because of it—the tales claimed by the Grimm brothers became the new archetypes of what the English language persisted in calling "fairy tales," although the Grimms preferred "*kinder- und hausmärchen*" [children's and household tales]. They provided models for various writers in different countries, most importantly the Dane Hans Christian Andersen, whose original contributions to the reburgeoning and reconfigured genre were sufficiently faithful to their models that at least one was collected by the Grimms in the later years of their activity as a "German folktale." The notion that such tales were good for children—in more than one sense of the word "good"—became the principal license for the new composition of fantastic tales, creating a literary marketplace in which *fées* could make a comeback, tentatively at first and eventually more robustly.

It is perhaps ironic that, although the French writers of the Parisians salons provided so much fuel for fake folklorists like the Grimms, fantastic tales of foreign origin became more popular in early nineteenth-century France than anything produced domestically. In much the same way that antiquity lent such material a certain cachet, so did foreign origin; Macpherson, Scott, Hoffmann and Andersen all became heroes to the French Romantics, while native writers largely went unhonored if they drew from similar sources of inspiration. Nevertheless their number gradually increased in the course of the century, and *fées* made a tentative and gradual return to the substance of their work. They were not the same *fées* that Madame d'Aulnoy and her associates had designed for their own purposes, although the feminist quest adopted by those writers had not made much progress in the interim, and they often bore more resemblance to English "fairies" or to generalized agents of enchantment used for symbolic purposes, but in slowly renewing interest in the label they paved the way for a partial reconstitution of the potent imagery of the 1690s.

Fées made their most evident comeback on the French stage, where a genre of *féeries* [fantasy plays] developed over the decades, in parallel with the genre of vaudevilles and overlapping it to some extent, both genres being essentially light and frivolous. Whereas the precursors of vaudevilles developed verbal wit and physical comedy, however, *féeries* tended to trade far more heavily on pure spectacle; they often made elaborate use of static *tableaux* and ballets, the principal appeal of which was the display of young female bodies, decoratively if somewhat scantily clad. *Féeries* did not necessarily feature *fées*—many preferred an Oriental décor derived from Antoine Galland's alternative context of enchantment, the *Mille-et-une nuits*—but they did provide an opening for them, and took abundant inspiration from folkloristic notions of supernatural beings who gather by night to dance and attempt to tempt mortals, fatally, into joining their farandoles. The rediscovery and repopularization of Madame d'Aulnoy's work in the nineteenth century was assisted by the adaptation of several of her stories into spectacular theatrical versions, which were among the most sophisticated *féeries*.

By the middle of the century, the influence of the theater was becoming manifest in some examples of prose fiction, in combination with the provision made by the proliferation of publication for children. The title-story of the present collection is an interesting example, containing significant reference to a one-act play co-authored by a writer who was to become one of the most prolific writers of vaudevilles, as well as an ambitious writer of Romantic prose fiction, "X. B. Saintine" (Joseph X. Boniface), and one of the most prolific playwrights and librettists of the era, Eugène Scribe. The novelette was published by one of the great pioneers of publishing for a juvenile audience in France, P.-J. Hetzel, in the last volume of his *Nouveau magasin des enfants* to be issued before he fell foul of the fallout of Louis-Napoléon Bonaparte's *coup-d'état* and was exiled from France for several years. A prominent member of the Romantic Movement as well as a radical Republican, Hetzel had persuaded several other leading members of the Movement to contribute to his *Magasin*, including the doyen of Romantic prose, Charles Nodier, as well as younger recruits like Alexandre Dumas and George Sand; the other work featured in the volume containing "Les Fées de la mer" was a long adaptation by Dumas of E. T. A. Hoffmann's most famous *kunstmärchen* [art-folktale], which was adapted for the Parisian stage in the same year (1851) by Jules Barbier and Michel Carré in *Les Contes fantastiques d'Hoffman*. The play in question subsequently became in inspiration for Jacques Offenbach's operatic *Tales of Hoffmann* (1881), which inspired Pyotr Tchaikovsky's ballet *The Nutcracker* (1892) in its turn.

Hetzel was not personally fond of fantastic fiction and his own fiction, written under the pseudonym P.-J. Stahl, is stubbornly naturalistic, but he was prepared to give Nodier, Dumas and George Sand as much imaginative freedom as they cared to take, and they took abundant advantage of that license, while remaining much more circumspect in their work

16

for other publishers—as Alphonse Karr also did. Although Hetzel reprinted the volumes of the *Nouveau magasin* in 1860 when he was allowed to return to Paris, he was careful in his next major venture to plow a more sternly rationalistic furrow, mentoring and guiding the career of his most famous disciple, Jules Verne. George Sand took his philosophy seriously enough to attempt to draft *fées* to the cause of the popularization of scientific ideas, producing her own pseudo-Vernian fantasy in the phantasmagoric *Laura* (1866), and penning the story reproduced in the present collection, which follows a curious precedent set by the opinionated Comtesse de Genlis, who somehow imagined herself to be stubbornly anti-Romantic, although her work certainly does not given that impression.

The influence of the theater was important to another marketplace that opened up for would-be writers of *contes de fées* in the middle part of the century: fashion magazines. Fashion magazines were one of the great successes of popular publishing in the 1840s, often lavishly produced, latterly with color plates, and hence expensive, although their price proved not to be a deterrent, setting an important precedent for what was later to become an entire sector of "slick" magazines, a powerful magnet for advertisers. Although the principal agency of such periodicals was the clothing actually marketed in boutiques, their illustrations routinely went in for gaudy spectacle in exactly the same fashion as the theater, for the sake of color and variety. In much the same way that theater and dance co-opted the imagery of "*fées*," into their "*féeries*," so did the magazines devoted to the popularization of pretentious costume. One of the most successful fashion magazines of the 1840s was titled *La Sylphide*, after the 1832 fantasy ballet created for the star dancer Marie Taglioni, and its print section immediately became hospitable to writers associated with the Romantic Movement, following a path that had been frayed by Emile de Girardin, the great pioneer of the French popular press, whose own fashion magazine, *La Mode*, founded in 1829, was the earliest commercial success of the publishing empire that eventually generated the popular daily *La Presse* in 1836.

Girardin recruited his editors and writers in the literary salons he attended, where all the leading members of the Parisian Romantic Movement came together, and following his marriage in 1831 to Delphine Gay, a precocious star of the movement, her salon became the center of that recruitment. She and her husband were pioneers of publication for children before Hetzel got into the act, and her work was a significant influence on the children's stories written subsequently by George Sand and the Comtesse de Ségur, as well as the editorial policies of her husband's employees Jules Janin and S. Henry Berthoud. The fiction published in the fashion magazines was often anodyne, but the marketplace was important to several of the leading popular writers of the day, including Charles Deslys, one of those who dabbled most frequently in new *contes de fées*, and whose first novels were the Perrault-inspired *La Mère Rainette* (1847) and *Les Bottes vernies de Cendrillon* (1849). The sector also played host to a few works of far greater sophistication, including "La Dernière fée" by Jules Sandeau, the one-time collaborator and lover from whom George Sand borrowed her pseudonym.

Sandeau appropriated his title from *La Dernière fée* (1822; tr. as *The Last Fay*), an early novel by Honoré de Balzac, published under the pseudonym Horace de Saint-Aubin. After breaking with George Sand in the early 1830s Sandeau was hired by Balzac to serve as his secretary, in which employment he supervised a reprint of the 1822 novel, supplemented with a fanciful "biography" of its fictitious author. Balzac's metatextual novel features a protagonist brought up in isolation from society who becomes obsessed with an illustrated edition of the tales of Madame d'Aulnoy and is fascinated by a "*fée*" who seems to have stepped out of one of her tales, but eventually proves to have emerged from the *féerique* social milieu later to be refracted in fashion magazines like *La Mode* and *La Sylphide*. Sandeau's *dernière fée*, by contrast, is a purely symbolic figure, whose particular symbolism is mirrored and echoed in numerous later tales by other hands.

The cachet of respectability given to new *contes de fées* written for children by Delphine de Girardin and George Sand was exploited by other writers, including some who made their reputation outside the Romantic Movement. The writer who became the great propagandist of Naturalism, Émile Zola, produced a volume of children's stories that had no hesitation in following Sandeau's example in producing proto-symbolist parables, but placed them in a didactic frame reminiscent of the work of the Comtesse de Genlis and Delphine de Girardin. The result is undoubtedly awkward, but casually unrepentant in its irony.

It was not until the development of another new marketplace, however, that nineteenth-century *contes de fées* were able to make a decisive leap out of niche markets and into the general current of respectable popular literature marketed for adults. That marketplace was provided by a nascent generation of cheap newspapers, made possible by new technologies of printing and paper manufacture. The economic side-effects of those technological developments resulted in an explosive proliferation of Parisian newspapers from 1880 onwards, whose sheer profusion encouraged experimentation in search of any and all potential methods of attracting and appealing to readers who were spoiled for choice.

The fierce censorship that had been introduced in the 1850s under the Second Empire, which was relentlessly hostile to anything that smacked of satire or political mockery, had put a damper on the development of any fiction whose acceptability had not been pre-demonstrated, and put a severe curb on fantastic and humorous fiction. Although that censorship eased somewhat in the 1860s and relented further in the first decade of the Third Republic, it had had a lingering effect on fashions in fiction, and the aftermath of the Franco-Prussian War had also had a chastening effect on the uses of imagination—as wars always tend to do, flights of fancy seeming irreverent in the wake of tragedy. By 1880, however, relaxation had definitely set in and the bridle had been dropped.

One newspaper whose editor encouraged experiments with fantastic fiction with some enthusiasm was *Gil Blas*, founded at the end of 1879 by the sculptor Augustin-Alexandre Dumont, the scion of a family of artists whose previous generations had played a significant role in the Romantic Movement since its inception. The first feuilleton featured in the newspaper was a humorous fantasy signed "Quatrelles" (the pseudonym of the dramatist and librettist Ernest l'Épine, a prolific author of work in that vein), and toward the end of 1880 Dumont began publishing a series of short stories under the heading *Contes fantastiques* by the prolific Théodore de Banville. Banville had been one of the founders of the neo-Romantic "Parnassian Movement," which had not been completely starved of support by the Second Empire censors in spite of the difficult economic climate they had maintained, and he was a highly respected poet, although he made his living, necessarily, from writing prose, and was immediately attracted to the new marketplace.

Banville reprinted the *contes fantastiques* in book form as *Contes féeriques* (1882), which can be seen in retrospect as a landmark work in the history of French fantastic fiction, but which must have been markedly less successful than his numerous collections of naturalistic comedies, because, always a hard-headed professional, he never did anything like it again, although the stories give every evidence that he was enjoying himself in their flamboyant composition. The tales introduce their fantastic devices forthrightly into the heart of contemporary Paris, and are as unsparing in their extravagance as they are in their sophisticated sarcasm. *Fées* appear regularly therein as agents of enchantment, appearing and disappearing at whim, and demonstrating an ability to work casual miracles at the flick of a wand, but always subject to a relentless authorial irony that forces them to leave the world essentially unchanged by their gifts.

The attitude and methodology of Banville's *contes de fées* was perhaps a little too sophisticated for the readers of the Parisian popular press; following the commercial failure of the book, fiction of that sort was gradually eased out of the pages of *Gil Blas* as well as the pattern of Banville's own work, but while the experiment was still in progress, it had a considerable and lingering influence. Among the other writers who began to supply Dumont with short fiction on a regular basis was Banville's fellow ex-Parnassian and long-time friend Catulle Mendès, who supplied numerous fantasies of his own, including a series headed *Contes du Rouet* [Tales of the Spinning-Wheel), many of which were collected in a book of that title in 1885 (subsequently reprinted, with slightly modified contents, as *Les Oiseaux bleus*, tr. as *Bluebirds*).

Although Mendès did write many humorous fantasies set in contemporary Paris, some featuring *fées*—although he preferred to employ angels and the god Eros as symbolic agents of enchantment in contemporary tales—he had a particular fondness for writing pastiches of traditional tales: "fairy tales" in a mold reminiscent of the Grimm brothers' recyclings and Hans Christian Andersen's pastiches; and also for sarcastic parodies of the miraculous largesse of the saints. Unlike Banville, he did not allow himself to be put off such ventures by lukewarm reader response, and he continued producing them in profusion until the end of the century. He was spared the effects of increasing editorial hostility because he became an editor himself, working for a number of periodicals, in the pages of which he indulged his whims.

For a while, Mendès was the editor of *La Vie populaire*, the literary supplement of the best-selling Parisian daily. *Le Petit Parisien*, whose pages he filled with material by his *Gil Blas* associates, most prominently Banville, Armand Silvestre and Guy de Maupassant—but he did not encourage Banville to write *contes fantastiques* for that publication, and was moderate in his own productions of that sort. In 1889, however, he was hired as the literary editor of *L'Écho de Paris*, where he gathered a stable of writers commissioned to supply him with items of short fiction on a weekly or fortnightly basis. There, het himself off the naturalistic leash much more extravagantly, and permitted other members of the stable to do the same. The extent to which they took advantage of the license varied considerably, but most of them did so to some extent, and the policy was continued in the pages of *Le Journal*, to which most of the members of the *Écho* stable migrated in the mid-1890s. The gradual ebbing away of fantastic material became increasingly obvious as the nineties progressed, but the precedents were still in place after 1900, not just in *Le Journal* but in several of its rivals, including the weekly literary supplement of *Le Figaro* and the thrice-weekly supplement of *La Lanterne*. The slow fade did not reach near-extinction until the outbreak of the Great War, which killed off fantastic fiction much more comprehensively than the briefer interruption of the Franco-Prussian War.

The later stories in the present anthology were not all commissioned by Catulle Mendès, or imitative of his work, but he undoubtedly played a significant role in facilitating their proliferation. The selection demonstrates, however, the extent to which other writers shared similar inspirations when they felt free to take a brief holiday from the relentless demands of convention. Georges de Peyrebrune, who chose the forename of her pseudonym in honor of George Sand, was one of the most popular writers of her generation, but she always maintained a subtle subversive feminism within her sentimental fiction, and her awareness of the thwarted feminism of Madame d'Aulnoy is obvious in her deliberately brutal pastiche of Aulnoy's most oft-recycled motif—a motif used as a template in more than one of the stories included herein.

The newspaper writer who took the greatest inspiration from Mendès, and who tried hard to outdo him in his exercises in emulation, was Jean Lorrain. Although the irony of his work is clearly akin to that of Mendès and Banville in its sarcasm, it lacks the amiable flippancy of those writers, being much more earnest in tone. He eventually assembled many of his fantasies in the volume *Princesses d'ivoire et d'ivresse*

22

(1902), whose contents are distributed in several English-language collections. Other writers, like Mendès' closest associate, Armand Silvestre, developed the more broadly comic aspect of the genre—the brief farce by Henry Gauthier-Villars provides a further example—but Lorrain's work bears more resemblance to that of "antiquarian" writers who developed "authentic" folkloristic materials in a relatively reverent manner, like Paul Arène and Antoine L'Estoille. That *modus operandi* lent itself well to much more extensive narratives, as in L'Estoille's prose epic *La Chanson de l'alouette* (1880; tr. as *The Song of the Skylark*), and inevitably seems to represent the more "literary" arm of the genre. The stories by René Maizeroy and "Jacques Frehel" (Alice Télot) included herein adopt a similar policy, and their reliance on antiquarian sources certainly does not prevent them from maintaining a certain contemporary relevance or accumulating a certain affective force, although their careful narrative distance prevents them from matching the harrowing brutality of such pure symbolist fantasies as those by Paul Margueritte, Lucie Delarue-Mardrus and André Beaunier, some of the few writers who managed to take the reborn genre of *contes de fées* to new extremes in the pages of newspapers at and after the turn of the century.

It is arguable that the stories in the present volume are not really *contes de fées* at all, in the strict sense that the works of Mademoiselle L'Héritier, Mademoiselle de La Force, the Comtesse de Murat and Madame d'Aulnoy were, which have more coherency, as a result of being produced in accordance with an actual manifesto, partly in deliberate competition. The best of the post-1880 stories do, however, retain conscious and conscientious echoes of the original *contes de fées* of the 1690s, and in spite of the interference in the genre's subsequent history by antagonistic ideologies—and partly because of resentful rebellion against that interference—they maintain residues of the same spirit as well as fragments of imagery. Although the imagery in question is routinely distorted, it still remains partly parasitic on the heroic endeavor of the small group of salon writers, and a belated testament to their enterprise and creativity. At any rate, the collection helps to complete the convoluted and fascinating story begun in the earlier volumes of the series.

Brian Stableford

Stéphanie de Genlis: *The Isle of Monsters*

(Les Jeux champêtres des enfant et de l'île des monstres,
1822)

There was once a king and a queen who only had one
daughter, the beautiful Princess Ernelinde, who was brought
up by the ingenious Clairvoyante, the most celebrated fay of
her time. As was customary, the princess was endowed at birth
with the most brilliant and the most lovable qualities; she had
many graces, intelligence, a good memory, a taste and talent
for the arts, and generosity; in sum, almost all the gifts that
render a princess accomplished.

By a strange fatality, however, there has always existed
in courts and governments a forgetfulness of past events,
which renders experience almost useless to kings and their
ministers. For example, at all the births of princesses, they
continually forget to invite one implacable and powerful fay,
and in spite of the fidelity of thousands of historians on this
point, that is what happened at the birth of Ernelinde. One
punctilious and susceptible fay was forgotten, who suddenly
arrived and who said, bitterly: "You have scorned my gifts; I
shall annul all of yours; I give this child secret pride and presumption."

At that fatal oracle, all the courtiers protested that those
two vices of mediocre minds would only be a just sentiment
and consciousness of the extent of her talents and the strength
of her genius; but the fay Clairvoyante lowered her eyes, sighing, and foresaw all the harm that would inevitably be attached
to that kind of malediction.

The princess reached the age of seventeen with a superi-
or mind, delightful talents and an education astonishing for her
age. She was sensitive, generous and benevolent, but the deadly charm acted nevertheless on her character. She was accessi-

ble to all kinds of flattery, and, thinking that she knew everything, she became a stranger to the desire for instruction. Study no longer appeared to be anything but a superfluous effort for her.

In the end, she even neglected reading, thinking that it was impossible for her to find anything new in books. She had a particular liking for natural history, but she no longer occupied herself with it, imagining that the entire universe was represented by specimens in hothouses, museums and the king's palace menagerie. The scholars attached to the court had repeated to her so many times that she had a education infinitely more extensive than all the professors in the realm that she was convinced of it, and did not apply herself to anything. She delivered herself to vain dissipation and frivolous amusements, and gradually forgot what she had learned.

All the representations of the fay were futile; Ernelinde had lost any kind of docility and only had confidence in her own enlightenment. However, as she had always been as celebrated for her brilliant education as she was for her rare beauty, her hand was requested by the greatest princes in Asia, who came to her father's court to dispute her conquest.

The fay Clairvoyante, whom she did not consult, wanted nevertheless to direct her choice in favor of the amiable and virtuous Almanzor. If Ernelinde had only listened to her heart and her reason, she would undoubtedly have preferred that young prince to any other, but he was not a flatterer and his sincerity wounded Ernelinde more than once, so she ended up convincing herself that Almanzor did not have enough intelligence and enlightenment to be able to appreciate her superior merit. One of the prince's rivals, who lavished the most emphatic and the most extravagant praise on the princess, did not win her heart, but he seduced her pride. Nevertheless, she could not resolve to dismiss Almanzor in a positive manner.

As Ernelinde had intelligence and imagination, she became an author; she composed a play in the "romantic" genre—which is to say, neglecting all the rules established by reason and taste, and consecrated by immortal masterpieces.[1] That play, which was a tragedy, was performed at court, and as no one was ignorant of the name of the author, it was applauded excessively. In the midst of that universal adulation, only Almanzor maintained a bleak silence.

That prince, who loved all the arts, had a superior talent for painting. Ernelinde had asked him to paint a picture for her, and three weeks after the aforementioned performance, Almanzor announced to her that the painting she desired was finished. Ernelinde promised herself secretly to criticize it severely.

That was an authorial vengeance that she was only too authorized in taking. Almanzor's painting, although brilliant, had a ridiculous falsity of color and a shocking bizarrerie. It represented a landscape whose skies were a bright pistachio green, against which trees were designed of a beautiful flax-gray with silvered trunks. The princess protested against the ridiculousness of the painting.

"Madame," Almanzor said to her, "I wanted to conform to your taste; you reject everything that is taken from nature; you disdain all plausibilities and routes frayed by great mas-

---

[1] Madame de Genlis (1746-1830), an enthusiastic educationalist who served as a volunteer professor to numerous aristocratic children, eventually became a vocal adversary of the *philosophes*, especially Jean-Jacques Rousseau, whose theories of education she followed in part while opposing in detail. Rousseau had a powerful influence on the French school of Romantic literature, but this characterization of Romanticism is simplistic and misguided. She did not live to see the publication by Charles Nodier, the great pioneer of French Romantic prose and a keen amateur entomologist, of "Sibylle Merian (1833, but probably written considerably earlier) a story that is very similar to "L'Île des monstres," but which substitutes a real entomologist for the imaginary fay as a agent of enlightenment.

ters, and the desire to please and imitate you has made me invent this 'romantic' genre of painting."

The princess, suffocated by anger, withdrew, ordering Almanzor never to appear before her eyes again.

The fay tried in vain to appease Ernelinde. The latter, beside herself, got so carried away that the fay, in spite of the natural docility of her character, finally resolved to punish and confound the arrogance of her presumptuous pupil, and she made her this speech:

"It's time to put an end to your extravagance. You think you know everything; I have repeated to you in vain that there are inexhaustible sources of instruction in nature, and that an infinite number of things exist of which you are ignorant. There are even a large number that are before your eyes, and which you do not know, so inattentive and scantly reflective you are. I am imposing a penitence of twenty-four hours upon you. I shall transport you to the isle of monsters.

"That is not a fantastic land created by my art. It exists and it will make you aware by means of its extraordinary productions that you have very superficial ideas about geography, botany, natural history and many other sciences. In spite of the fear that will grip you, you will have nothing to dread on that marvelous island. I shall give you a sovereign power over all the ferocious monsters that you will encounter there."

With those words, the fay touched Ernelinde with her magic wand. The princess fell into a profound sleep, and when she awoke she experienced an inexpressible astonishment.

She found herself in a wood, all the trees and flowers in which were unknown to her. She was sitting on a monstrous tree devoid of leaves, the top of which was severed. She saw that she was so high above the ground that she dared not descend for fear of killing herself. She fixed her gaze on an extraordinary object placed opposite her; it was a very singular kind of grotto leaning against two or three small rocks; it did not appear to contain anything, and formed a sort of oval niche. Ernelinde could only discover the hollow—which is to say, the interior of the grotto, the ornaments of which she admired, for it was entirely lined with charming flowers that Ernelinde was seeing for the first time. Those flowers, more or less open, had all their leaves, buds and stems, and all the freshness of the most beautiful plants.

The princess, passionately desirous of visiting that pretty grotto, made a slight movement to let herself slide from her tree, and immediately found herself on her feet on sand strewn with large pebbles and enormous shells, which, instead of wounding her, seemed to flatten out under her feet like the lightest dust—a prodigy that she attributed to a particular generosity of the fay.

She was getting ready to go into the grotto when she saw two monsters approaching that caused her to recoil in astonishment and fear. One, the size of a sheep, had a head entirely covered with eyes. That new Argus had a stout, yellow and black hairy body, eight legs and two terrible hands of a sort terminated by claws in the form of pincers. The other monster, brighter and no less strange, as large as an ox, had a pink skin strewn with large pearls; its triangular head was ornamented with fringes; its feet were full of rings and pearls, and its toenails were cut up into festoons.

"Just Heaven!" cried Ernelinde. "If it's true that these animals are not vain phantoms, how far I am, in fact, from knowing all that nature produces of the extraordinary. But they aren't illusions, because the fay is incapable of lying."

As she spoke, the princess hastened to enter into a thicket of flowering bushes that was on the other side of the large felled tree that she had just quit. Suddenly, she heard a small harmonious sound behind her; she turned round and saw a kind of enormous bird with large silver filigree wings stuck to the bark of the tree, which was singing a little tune as varied as it as melodious..

The princess had stopped to listen to it, but a new monster that was heading toward her, making prodigious leaps, forced her to flee. That animal, larger and more agile than a cat, had six legs bristling with spines and hooks; its back was scaly and its broad belly furrowed and hairy; its mouth as armed with a long, sharp trunk, still dripping the blood on which it nourished itself. Seized by horror, Ernelinde, seeing that it was about to reach her, tried—but without hope—to repel it with her feeble hand. Immediately, the animal leapt backwards and disappeared into the undergrowth.

Reassured by that success, Ernelinde continued walking, but she fell back into terror on finding herself suddenly surrounded by a multitude of animals that were equally frightening and miraculous. The one nearest to her, as long as her arm and flattened in form, was covered with a scaly and tiled skin; two horns were mounted on its head; it had fourteen legs and a long forked tail. Another, even larger, was bright green, with feet of a beautiful lemon yellow, and terrible sledgehammers on its head. Another bore charming ornaments on its head, which were two magnificent tufts of beautiful feathers arranged in bouquets that would have sat very well on the head of a pretty woman; furthermore, that animal, which was neither a bird nor a quadruped, had a similar panache placed on the posterior of its body.

One of the nastiest of those animals had a round and flat face, brown in color, which was exhaling a fetid odor. Among all those monsters, however, the princess distinguished two that struck her by virtue of the splendor and richness of their adornment. One, the color of seaweed, was ornamented with superb turquoises; the other bore a magnificent royal mantle sewn with fleurs-de-lys.

The princess, entirely hardened against those monsters by the idea that she had an absolute empire over them, decided to continue walking, although they barred her way, forming a great circle around her; she advanced, and saw with an extreme surprise that, although walking very lightly, she crushed and killed a rather large number of them.

Unable to doubt then the supernatural power that she had over them, she was about to continue her route when she touched one of the monsters in passing, which immediately made a noise similar to that of a firearm, followed by a thick sky-blue smoke that formed a transparent cloud around the animal; it did not stop there, for it unleashed a further twenty shots; that artillery caused the princess a considerable fright. However, seeing that no harm came to her, she gathered her courage and started running, in order to leave all those monsters behind.

She was suddenly stopped in her course by finding herself on the rim of a sort of gulf, but as pretty as a gulf can be. It was bordered and lined internally by a superb drapery the color of fire; a monster defended the entrance to it. That yellow, black and hairy monster appeared to be armed with a shiny lance; it seemed to be holding a triangular palette and bore four large brushes between its legs.

After having examined that new marvel, Ernelinde drew away in order to go in search of others. A few paces further on she thought she saw a large pile of dead leaves; she drew closer and, to her great surprise, she saw that the apparent heap was an animal which flew into the air, lifting its head toward the sky.

The princess perceived a quantity of birds of immense dimensions. She saw others less gigantic, of a dazzling beauty; some had heads covered with precious stones, other bore wings of silver gauze ornamented with golden and nacreous scales, and their bodies were multicolored.

"What variety and richness there is in nature!" Ernelinde exclaimed. "How were so many phenomena and treasures able to escape my knowledge?"

The princess saw many other miraculous things, but, fatigued by a journey that had lasted for four or five hours, she invoked the fay in order to ask her to produce by means of her art a spring or stream that could offer her a means of slaking her ardent thirst. Scarcely had she formulated that wish than she saw before her a mass of water contained in a crystal carved into facets, in the form of a cup, but gigantic, for the princess estimated that it was three or four feet in height. As the water came up to the rim, the princes advanced to drink from it, but in casting her gaze upon the water she saw that it was full of frightful snakes that were agitating in all direction below the surface. Her fear was brought to a peak on perceiving among those reptiles an infinite number of death's-heads, all of which were moving!

Ernelinde recoiled, shuddering, and as she turned her eyes to the right a new prodigy came to distract her from her thirst; she perceive a long avenue of trees, so tall that their summits seemed to plunge into the clouds. The princess, who had a poetic turn of mind, compared them to columns made and placed there to sustain the majestic vault of the heavens. She launched herself into the avenue and soon discovered in the distance a palace in proportion to the immense height of the trees. As she was admiring its structure she saw a giant emerge from the pompous edifice, the sight of whom made her tremble, for in general, human monsters are the most frightful of all.

The giant, compared to whom the famous Goliath would only have been a dwarf, was holding a bow and carrying a quiver over his shoulder; he advanced toward the princess. At that moment, a new monster, more frightful and a thousand times more extraordinary than all the previous ones, suddenly appeared fifty paces away from the princess. She judged that it was twice or three times as big as an elephant; it offered no distinct form, and resembled an enormous balloon. It stopped in front of the princess and became motionless, staring at her intently and opening a terrible mouth.

For her part, Ernelinde could not help attaching her gaze to the formidable creature; she fell into a horrible state of stupor and soon experienced the most inexplicable sensation. She felt the effect of an incomprehensible attraction caused by the invisible supernatural power of ferocity over terror. The monster was attracting her; she could only resist with extreme difficulty the invincible force that was drawing her toward it: a redoubtable emblem of the infernal power that, in spite of our enlightenment, so often pushes us and precipitates us into profound abysms.

The horrified Ernelinde was finally about to launch herself into the hideous and menacing maw, which was opening to engulf her, when the giant, who was watching over her, took a sharp arrow from his quiver and launched it at the monster, which immediately rolled in the dust and fell dead. Disengaged from the frightful weight that was oppressing her, Ernelinde breathed in, blessing her liberator.

At the same moment a sonorous voice became audible; it was that of the fay, who pronounced these words distinctly: "Ernelinde has been cured of her presumption; she will know henceforth that the more one is instructed, and the more things one has seen, the more aware one becomes that an infinity of prodigies exists that feeble human reason cannot explain, and that the longest and most assiduous research and study are required for us to discover and know a multitude of curious facts that we have continually before our eyes, without our perceiving and suspecting them.

"In sum," the voice continued. "Ernelinde ought to know now that one only ought to seek the extraordinary and the marvelous in nature, because everything can be found there, and that our imagination alone, without that necessary and sublime guide, can only ever produce extravagances. So, Almanzor, appear under your true features; there is no more need now, in order to please my pupil, to adopt false colors and gigantic forms."

With those words, the enchantment ended. Ernelinde, who for several hours had only been seeing objects with microscopic eyes, recovered her ordinary sight; nature reappeared to her eyes in its everyday aspect; that which it hides from our gaze was veiled, as usual, and what it permits us to discern showed itself in its veritable dimensions.

Ernelinde realized that the terrain she had just traveled was only a large meadow devoid of trees, all of whose little plants, grass and moss had had offered her the appearance of a vast forest and an immense nursery composed of unknown trees. She found herself once again in the beautiful avenue of elms that led to her father's palace and realized with pleasure that the apparent giant who had caused her so much alarm was

Prince Almanzor, who threw himself at her feet to await anxiously the first words to emerge from her mouth.

The fay appeared, and Ernelinde threw herself into her arms, saying to her: "You have returned me to reason."

At those words, the prince secretly recovered a little hope. They returned to the palace; the fay gave her pupil a little notebook written in her own hand, containing explanatory notes on all that she had seen in the course of that memorable day. Ernelinde recovered all the modesty appropriate to youth, and all the deference and regard due to those who surpass us in experience. Finally, she acquired the fortunate mistrust of oneself that preserves one from grave faults and great ridicule.

Having become a veritably accomplished princess, Ernelinde married the amiable Almanzor; that union was happy, as those formed by reason and virtue always are.

Ernelinde obtained from the fay the gift of the marvelous wand that gives eyes the property of a microscope; subsequently, she often made use of it to correct those who combined presumption with ignorance or superficial knowledge; almost all the courtiers made the voyage to the Isle of Monsters. The princess engaged them easily not to boast on their return; the secrets of humiliated self-esteem are always well-guarded. People were astonished, however, that all the lords of the court had suddenly become good naturalists.

However, as everything is discovered in the end, that mystery was generally known after a few years, and gave rise to a proverb that was in vogue at the court for a long time; when one encountered a proud and loquacious ignoramus, one said: "It's necessary to send him to the Isle of Monsters." That proverb was good for Asia, but did not catch on in France, for, inundated with new enlightenment as we have been for seventy years, one sees so many wise, modest, enlightened, eloquent and profoundly educated people—so many great men that they can be compared to the stars in the firmament—that no one can count them.

Notes[2]

Everything that Ernelinde saw is veritable, but the fay cast a charm on her eyes that gave them the property of magnifying objects, as the largest and best of all microscopes can; at the same time, in order that she should be completely deceived by hat illusion, the fay determined that the charm would not extend over her own person, and that the princess, in looking at her hands, feet, garments, etc., would see things in their ordinary aspect; but that everything else she saw would be so prodigiously magnified that she would discover a multitude of details of which she was unaware, and that she would not even recognize things that she saw very frequently.

When she was sitting on a tree-trunk she could only see a few square inches of ground. The apparent grotto was only half of a melon, the whole interior of which was moldy. Mold, seen through a microscope, presents a multitude of foliage and flowers such as has just been described. (See the article on mold in Bomare.[3]) Then she walked over ordinary sand, the

---

[2] These notes are grouped and placed in the original text as they are here, but they are divided up there by numbers corresponding to numbers placed in the text at strategic points; the judgment that the refinement can be reckoned superfluous might be reckoned dubious, but its retention would have made it awkward to include my own footnotes.

[3] Jacques-Christophe Valmont de Bomare (1731-1807) published a six-volume encyclopedia of natural history in the 1760s, *Le Dictionnaire raisonné universel d'histoire naturelle*, which was expanded in later editions. It is Genlis' primary reference, although it was somewhat outdated when the story—which might have been written considerably earlier—was published. Some of the Latin names Genlis quotes from Bomare subsequently fell into disuse, and some of the "facts" cited therein have proved to be mistaken, sometimes ludicrously so.

little stones and shells of which produced in her eyes the illusion that abused them.

There was a domestic spider as seen through a microscope; it has eight eyes placed in an oval on its head. In addition to the eight legs that the spider uses to walk it had two other limbs close to the head that do not reach the ground, the arms and hands of which it uses to manipulate prey that it seizes in its claws or pincers, which are in front of its mouth. The infinite divisibility of matter, although demonstrated, always frightens the imagination; if one considers the delicacy of spider-silk one can scarcely conceive that it is composed of six thousand threads.

There is a Brazilian toad named *aquaqua* whose skin is bright red and granulated, which makes it appear to be covered in pearls. Its head is almost triangular, like a priest's bonnet, ornamented with pointed fringe, quite similar to a bishop's miter. Its eyes are full of fire; its feet are pearly and its nails crenellated. Such is the description of the toad given by Bomare.

There is a kind of grasshopper or locust found on the king's island near the Mergui coast,[4] which sings, as has just been described. Always stuck to the trunk of a tree, when they have commenced their little tune they cannot be prevented from finishing it by killing themselves. The little song, which is very varied and charming, resembles that of a canary. Bomare does not mention that species of grasshopper in his dictionary, but the fact is exactly true; we have that detail from voyagers and mariners most worthy of faith. Our grasshoppers also have a kind of little song; only the males sing, the females being mute. The cicada, or "singer" in Latin, belongs to a different genus; one of those insects is equipped with a saw; the males are provided on the underside with little drums destined to sing their amour and summon their females; their song is shrill and makes itself heard in the mornings and in the heat of

---

[4] The Mergui Archipelago is in southern Myanmar (formerly Burma).

the day. The mechanism of the little drums is demonstrated by tugging the muscles that form then; one can make a dead cicada sing, provided that the parts are still fresh. A little paper scroll rubbed gently on the drum makes it resonate. Peasants claim that, as soon as the animals sing, there are no more cold days to fear.

Then there was a flea as seen under a microscope, and a woodlouse, named *asellus* in Latin. Woodlice are used in medicine; it is said that they purify the blood, that they are beneficial against asthma of every sort and against dropsy, scrofula, scirrhus, cancers, etc. It is sad that by crushing them and applying them to the throat in cataplasms they can cure exhaustion.

There was then a *cerocome*, an insect that resembles the cantharis beetle but is smaller; it can be found in the environs of Paris. It is particularly unusual by virtue of its antennae, composed of eleven rings, the first ten of which are very short, while the last, thicker that the others, forms a third of the length of the antenna on its own and gives it the form of a sledgehammer. The definitions of these various genera of insects and the parts that characterize them are given in the notes to *Veillées du Château*.[5]

The spiny caterpillar was the monster covered with darts, and the animal with the bouquet of feathers was the feathery caterpillar. "From the first ring after its head," Bomare writes, "little feathers emerge, which are not simple hairs but beautiful plumes arranged in bunches. A similar feather is located in the posterior part. These species of caterpillars are found on plum trees" [The nine-volume edition of the *Dictionnaire d'histoire naturelle*; article *Chenille*.] Caterpillars offer the most singular phenomena, among others that the famous observer Lionet (according to the savant author of Monsieur

---

[5] Madame de Genlis' *Veillées du château* was published in 1764; its citation here might be thought to add weight to the suspicion that the present story might have been composed before the Revolution if it were not for the following citation.

Delille's poem of the three kingdoms[6]) has counted more than four thousand muscles discernible in the willow caterpillar.

After a bug came the tubercular caterpillar, which is pale green, strewn with tubercules or protuberances that resemble beautiful turquoises; it is sometimes as long as three inches, and is encountered on pear trees. It produces the beautiful butterfly known as the large peacock. (Bomare.)

Another caterpillar known as the royal cloak caterpillar is, according to Bomare, "the emblem of temporary grandeur" because its apparent lily flowers only last five or six days in the insect and then disappear.

Everyone kills insects while walking that they do not even perceive.

The bombardier or cannoneer beetle is a species of insect thus named because as soon as it is touched it makes an explosion with its anus similar to a gunshot, which is followed by bright blue smoke. Monsieur Solander,[7] by tickling one of these insects on the back with a pin, made it fire as many as twenty shots in succession. (Bomare.)

There was a little hole formed by the tapestry bee, which digs a nest in the ground in which it will deposit its egg; it lifts up a poppy petal, which it then cuts up in order to line the interior of the nest, leaving a little fold all around that forms a pretty border the color of fire around the hole. The description of the monster is that of the bee. (See Bomare for the description of this insect.) There was also an insect that resembles exactly a pile of dead leaves. (Bomare.)

The princess saw, without recognizing them, birds, butterflies and beetles. Winged insects whose wings are enclosed in cases known as elytra are called beetles; flies have no elytra.

---

[6] Jacques Delille (1738-1813). His long poem *Trois règnes de la nature* was written in 1794 but does not appear to have been published until 1808. The "famous observer" cited is elusive, although other secondary references to him can be found.

[7] The Danish naturalist Daniel Solander (1733-1782)

The gigantic crystal vase was an ordinary glass full of water, and the snakes were animalcules that escape the naked eye, and which are found everywhere, especially in water and other liquids. They have been discovered since the invention of microscopes, which have revealed to us an entire world of the infinitely small. Leeuwenhoek estimates that the thousands of millions of new moving bodies that one discovers in a common drop of water are not as large, put together, as an ordinary grain of sand. Monsieur de Malezieu[8] has seen in a microscope animals twenty-seven million times smaller than a mite. If you takes a drop of liquid from an oyster or from plants that lived in the water and examine it by means of a strong magnifying glass or a microscope, you will see a large number of creatures that sometimes move and swim in all direction and sometimes make rapid movement while at rest, without that being determined by a foreign impulsion. Those animalcules can swim, and avoid obstacles that oppose their path in the water drop, which is an ocean for them. (Bomare.)

The little insects Ernelinde saw in the crystal vase that resemble death's-heads do exist, and form in water in which anemones have rotted; Bomare does not mention them, but new experiments have made these strange animalcules known.

When the princess was in the avenue at the end of which her father's palace was located, the gigantic aspect of the trees and the architecture prevented her from recognizing it. The final monster was a snake from the Indies called a boa; it is said that it is so big that it can swallow an ox whole. Lemeri[9] says that some of them can be found in Calabria, and that one

[8] Nicolas de Malezieu (1650-1727), a member of the famous salon hosted by the Duchesse de Maine at Sceaux.

[9] Possibly the physician Louis Lémery (1677-1743) rather than his more famous father, the chemist Nicolas Lémery (1645-1715), although the cited allegation sounds as if it comes from the latter's *Nouveau recueil de secrets et curiositez, les plus rares & admirables de tous les effets que l'art & la nature sont capables de produire* (1697).

was killed during the reign of the emperor Claudius in the belly of which a child it had swallowed was found. Numerous mariners and many modern voyagers whose evidence cannot be suspected agree in saying that the horrible animal, by staring fixedly at an animal in front of it, attracts it gradually and forces it to throw itself into the mouth that it always keeps open in such an instance.

Jules Sandeau: *The Last Fay*

(La Mode, 5 April 1844, falsely represented as a translation from a German poet and reprinted numerous times before and after the end of the century.)

I

I was sixteen years old when she appeared to me for the first time. It was, I remember, a beautiful evening in May. I had emerged from the city on my own; I was going aimlessly over fields, thoughtful and anxious without knowing why. I had been that way for some time, and I had an appetite for solitude.

I saw the sun sinking in a sea of purple and gold; shadows were descending from the hills into the plain, the stars lighting up one by one in the blue of the sky. Frogs were singing on the edges of ponds, the trills of a nightingale burst forth at long intervals. I could also hear the stirred foliage quivering and the long grass curbed by the breeze with a sad and soft murmur. The moon, which had risen ruddily on the horizon like a red hot disk emerging from a furnace, was asleep, white and radiant, over the nacre of a bank of cloud, from which its rays fell in streams of silver over the shoulders of the night. The warm atmosphere was charged with intoxicating scents, and I listened, along the hedges in flower, to the calls of little birds caressing one another in their nests.

I was going along, opening my heart to all those rumors and perfumes, when I perceived a group of young women holding hands, returning to the city. They were singing in chorus about spring and amour; their youthful voices vibrated in the silence of the dormant fields like the distant voice of a cascade. I hid behind a hawthorn bush and I saw them pass by like a swarm of those white shadows that assemble by night

41

around lakes to form light dances and which vanish in the first light of dawn. By the light of the stars I distinguished their blonde and brunette heads; I heard the rustle of their dresses; I inhaled in long draughts the mysterious emanations that they left in their passage, which seemed to me more intoxicating than the embalmed scents of the evening.

When they had disappeared, I was seized by an unfamiliar trouble, and having sat down on a mound on the edge of a meadow that extended at my feet like an ocean of verdure, I hid my head in my hands and remained plunged in a profound reverie, listening and trying to understand the confused sounds and the tremors that were occurring within me.

What I was experiencing I cannot say. My heart felt as if it were oppressed and about to burst. It was as if there were a hidden spring within it that was seeking an exit, like a captive wave trying to spread out. I cried; I wept; I found in my tears I know not what sensuality.

How long did I remain thus? When I got up I saw, a few paces in front of me, a celestial creature who was looking at me, smiling. A tunic whiter than lilies fell in gracious pleats along her tall, slim body, allowing the sight in the grass, which they scarcely brushed, of two naked feet as white as Paros marble. Her blonde hair was floating freely around her neck; her cheeks had the freshness and brightness of the flowers that crowned her head; in the rose-tinted alabaster of her face her eyes were shining like two periwinkles blooming in the snow at the first kisses of April. Her arms were bare; one of her hands reposed on her breast while the other appeared to be beckoning to me with a benevolent gesture.

I remained mute and motionless for a few moments, contemplating her. Undoubtedly she came from Heaven, for her beauty had nothing of the daughters of earth, and I saw a radiant atmosphere around her that enveloped her like a luminous vestment.

"Who are you, then?" I exclaimed, eventually, extending my bewildered arms toward her.

"Friend," she replied, in a voice softer than the nocturnal wind, "I am the fay that the King of the Genii put to sleep in your bosom at the moment of your birth. This morning, I was still asleep; I have just woken up, at the first disturbance of your heart. My life is made of your life; I am your sister and I will be your companion until the day when, detached from you like a flower withered on its stem, I shall abandon you in the middle of the road whose first half we have traveled together. That day is not far off, young friend! The rose that only lives for a single morning is the image of my destiny. In order to love me, do not wait until you have lost me, for neither your tears nor your regrets will be able to reanimate me when I am gone. Hasten! My hand is not armed with a magic branch or an enchanted wand, and I have no other adornment than the flowers mingled with my hair, but I shall heap you with more treasures than any benevolent and prodigal fay ever lavished on a royal cradle. I shall put a crown on your head that many kings would estimate themselves fortunate to purchase at the cost of their own; I shall compose you a cortege such as palaces and courts rarely see. Invisible and present I shall follow you wherever you go; you shall feel my fecund influence everywhere; I shall embellish the places through which you will pass; by night I shall embalm your couch; I shall give my soul to all of nature in order to smile every morning at your awakening.

"Oh, we shall have fine feasts! Only, child, learn to appreciate the goods that I bring you; seize them before they escape you; learn how to touch them without withering them and to enjoy them without exhausting them; make a provision of them for the other half of the road, which you must complete without me. I have told you, friend, that I only have a short time to live, but it depends on you to prolong my frail and precious existence. I am like the rare plants for which it is necessary to husband the sunlight and the rain. My feet are delicate, do not exhaust them in following you. The brightness of my cheeks is frailer than the freshness of the convolvulus of the hedgerows; if you do not want to see it tarnish one day, do not expose me to excessive ardors and only draw me along under thick shade. Be careful, finally, that no remorse poison the regrets, already too bitter, that my loss will leave you. Let my memory be good, so that I can still cheer your heart with mild reflection for a long time after I have ceased to illuminate and warm your life."

With those words, she leaned her blonde head toward me, like a guardian angel inclining over a cradle, and I felt her lips over my forehead, fresher and more perfumed than the mint that grows on the edges of springs. I opened my arms to seize her but the white apparition had already vanished like a dream, and I only embraced the nocturnal wind.

Was it not a dream, in fact? I continued to go through the countryside, sometimes running like a madman, and sometimes throwing myself down on the grass, which I moistened with my hot tears; sometimes, I pressed the slender stem of a birch tree against my breast, which I believed I felt quivering and palpitating under my mad embraces; sometimes, I extended my arms toward the stars and spoke to them amorously. I talked to the flowers, to the trees, to the bushes; I felt a torrent of sap within me that overflowed everywhere and spread out over nature entire. The dike had broken; the spring had pierced the rock. I laughed, I wept; I was swimming in a boundless sea of inalterable joys and nameless felicities.

When the orient began to pale, it seemed to me that I was witnessing the reawakening of creation for the first time. My heart swelled; I inhaled the air with pride and I believed for a moment that my soul was about to detach itself from my body in order to fly away, light and free, through space, mingled with the soft vapors that the rising sun was detaching from the hills. From the top of the mountain, which I had reached, I measured the horizon with a conquering gaze; one might have thought, on seeing me, that the earth had just been created for me and that I was the master of the world.

II

I was not thirty[10] when she appeared to me for the second time. It was, I remember, an evening in October. I had emerged from the city on my own. I was going through fields, somber and depressed, without knowing why. I had been thus for a long time, and without having an appetite for it, I was in search of solitude.

The sky was low and veiled; a chilly wind was stripping the last leaves from the trees with a sinister sound. The hedges only had their berries for adornment. Only the lugubrious barking that was coming from a distant farm and a thread of blue smoke that was rising through the branches revealed life in the desolate countryside. However, a few frightened birds were fluttering from branch to branch here and there, and black crows were dotting the plain; battalions of cranes were filing slowly through the gray evening air.

I went on, mingling my soul with the mourning of nature. For a long time I had been seized, like her, with the cold melancholy that accompanies the end of fine days. Having sat down at the foot of a leafless bush, I saw passing before me two old women who were walking slowly, each bent down under a thorny bundle, winter provisions that they were bringing under the thatch.

Strange memory! Bizarre comparison! In that same spot, long before, on a May evening, I had seen a group of young women holding hands passing by, returning home singing. I had been sixteen then, and the bush was in flower!

I hid my head between my hands, and, passing through my mind the days that had gone by between that evening in

---

[10] Jules Sandeau (1811-1883) was thirty-three when this story was published. His relationship with George Sand (Aurore Dupin, 1804-1876, then Madame Dudevant) begun in 1831, had not lasted long, although it produced a sentimental novel, signed "J. Sand," and had left him severely disenchanted.

May and that evening in October, I soon sank into a bleak and profound ennui.

When I got up, I saw, a few paces in front of me, a white and pale figure that was looking at me sadly. She was so changed that I hesitated to recognize her. She was no longer surrounded by the luminous atmosphere that had enveloped her on her first appearance. A tattered tunic exposed her beautiful bruised breast. Her feet were bleeding; her arms dangled lifelessly along her thin sides. The azure of her eyes was marbled with black; tears had hollowed out furrows in her livid cheeks. The unfortunate woman could hardly stand up, and like a lily withered in its broken stem, she seemed to be inclined toward the ground.

"What do you want with me?" I asked her.

"Friend, the hour has come when we must separate, but before quitting you forever, I wanted to bid you an eternal adieu," she murmured, in a plaintive voice, sadder than the winter wind.

"Go away, oh, go away!" I cried. "Deceptive fay, what have you done for me? Where are they, the goods that you announced to me? I've sought them in vain on my route. Where are the treasures that you were to strew under my feet? I have only found poverty. What has become of the diadem that you were to place on my forehead? My head has only borne a crown of thorns. Where has the brilliant cortege gone that you promised to compose for me? I have had nothing for an escort but despair and solitude. You talk about separating, but unless you are the genius of dolor, what has there ever been in common between us? Oh, if it is true that you have followed me everywhere, and that I have been subject to your influence everywhere, go away and be accursed, for you must be the Evil Spirit!"

"I am neither the Evil Spirit not the genius of dolor," she replied, in a melancholy fashion, "but it is the destiny of men only to know me after they have lost me, and to know the price of my benefits when there is no longer time to enjoy them. Friend, you were ingrate, like the rest of your brethren.

You are accusing me, and I feel sorry for you. In a moment, you will know me, and you will want then, at the price of the tears that God still has in reserve for you, to see me for only a single day as you saw me for the first time.

"You ask, bitterly, where the goods are that I promised you? I have kept all my promises; but you, cruel man, have disdained the treasures that I poured out for you untiringly, with a prodigal hand. For a diadem, I set on your forehead the freshness, brightness and serenity of a spring morning. For a cortege, I gave you amour and faith, hope and illusion. Your poverty I made so cheerful and so beautiful that many power-ful and rich men would gladly have exchanged their palaces and their opulence for it. Your solitude I have populated with enchanted dreams. Your despair I have enabled you to love, and I have been able to intoxicate you with your tears, to the point that your greatest misfortune henceforth will be no long-er to be able to shed them. When you walked, I awoke around you sympathy and benevolence; you only encountered amica-ble gazes and fraternal hands; Heaven smiled on you, and even the earth flowered under your footsteps.

"In your turn, respond: what have you done with my mu-nificence? What have you retained of my largesse? What re-mains to you of so many felicities that I have sown along your path? If you have retained nothing, is it me that you ought to blame for that? If you have not been able to enjoy anything, is it me that it is necessary to accuse?"

At those words, a belated glimmer illuminated by being. I sensed that a veil was falling from my eyes and I was struck by terror on seeing my own heart clearly.

"Stay, oh, stay! Don't go!" I cried, in a suppliant voice. "Render me those goods, which I misunderstood; my eyes have opened to the true light. Render me amour and illusion, render me faith and hope. Enable me to love for a single day, enable me to believe for a single hour, and. whoever you are, I will bless you as I die."

"Alas," she said, "it is me who is going to die. Can you not see that? Look at me; I have suffered greatly; I am only the shadow of my former self. For a long time, an unknown malady has been consuming me; a devouring breath has desiccated my bones and dried up the spring of life in my breast. The blood no longer reaches my heart; touch my hands and you will feel the icy humidity of death.

"If you had wished, though, I would still have had long days ahead of me. It is you, cruel man, who have killed me prematurely; I have used up my strength and bruised my feet in following you. In vain I begged for mercy; you cried 'March!' to me and I went on. I went, exhausted, breathless, tearing my robe on the brambles of the path, my forehead burning in the ardors of midday. You did not give me the time to renew my girdle and replace the flowers detached from my paling crown. Truly, if we encountered some embalmed refuge, some mysterious oasis, in the hollow of a valley, I said to you: 'It's there that happiness resides; friend, it's there that it's necessary to pitch out tent!' You continued your dogged course and you dragged me pitilessly through the arid steppes.

"Is there an outrage that you have spared me, a storm from which you have preserved my head? How many times have I set down on the edge of a ditch, weary and discouraged, and decided to abandon you! But I loved you, ingrate, and when, astonished no longer to feel me close to you, you turned round in order to summon me with a gesture and your voice, I got up and flew after you. Today, it is finished; friend, I can do no more! My blood is congealed, my gaze is troubled, and my legs are folding up beneath me. Open your arms; clasp me to your bosom; it is in your heart that I received life, it is on your heart that I want to die."

"You shall not die!" I cried, opening my arms to receive her. "But speak, strange creature! Who are you, then?"

"I no longer know," she said. "I was your youth."

At those words, I tried to seize her, but she had already disappeared, and I perceived nothing in her place but a few withered flowers fallen from her hair; I picked them all up, but I did not find a single one that had retained any perfume.

Delphine de Girardin: *The Fay Grignote*

(Contes d'une vieille fille à ses neveux, 1832)[11]

I. The Accusation

The fay Grignote was a little mouse, the prettiest little mouse that ever nibbled on the earth. She was madly cheerful; she had little wide-awake eyes that bulged from her head and gave her a very pleasant and capricious physiognomy; she was always trotting, jumping and playing, unable to remain tranquil for a single moment except to meditate a few niches.

Her great pleasure was tickling the feet of schoolchildren, running between their legs at any moment and making them laugh without any reason while they were having their lessons, which caused them to be scolded by their master, who always thought that they were making fun of him.

Have no fear that she made them laugh during recreation! No, truly, that was a permitted pleasure and Mademoiselle scarcely cared about what was permitted. What she liked was trouble and scandal; she did not go to tickle children in their parents' home, nor at a play or a dance—nowhere, in short, where people were amusing themselves; on the contrary, she left them there to get bored entirely at their ease. On

---

[11] This collection, the stories in which were written before Delphine Gay became Delphine de Girardin (1804-1855)—hence the misleading subtitle—but not published until afterwards, was issued a quarter of a century in advance of the Comtesse de Ségur's *Nouveaux contes de fées pour les petits enfants* (1857) and surely provided the model for it. Madame de Ségur's collection includes "La petite souris grise" (tr. as "The Little Gray Mouse"), which might well have been partially inspired by the present story.

the other hand, as soon as they were in class, or at mass during the sermon, which was even worse, she arrived, all sprightly and malign, and there were no extravagances that she did not invent in order to make the poor children burst out laughing.

If one of them fell to the ground she would suddenly tickle the others, and they laughed at him. Then the master called them heartless, and they all seemed malevolent.

The children, who did not know that it was the fay Grignote, did not understand their gaiety themselves.

"Why are you laughing?" one said to his comrade.

"Me? I'm laughing because I saw you laugh. What about you?"

"Me? I'm laughing at that great simpleton Mélibert, who is laughing like a madman over there. Look how he's holding his sides!"

And they all recommenced laughing more loudly, for the fay Grignote was scuttling under the table and amusing herself tickling them without them knowing it.

Meanwhile, the masters complained loudly about the stupidity of pupils; punishments and lines rained down over the entire class like hailstones. The entire class could be put in detention at once but they continued laughing nevertheless, and the strangest thing was that they were unable to explain why they were laughing so much.

The parents became indignant at not being able to take their children out on Sunday, when they had taken the trouble to come and fetch them. They got annoyed and scolded their sons, threatening not to love them any longer, and went home furious. The children wept a little on seeing them leave, but once they returned to class the wicked fay came again to scuttle between their legs, and the laughter recommenced, They were always laughing, while eating, while running, even while weeping—yes, while weeping—and while doing penance, with the dunce's cap on their heads. It's true that the punishment in question, now out of fashion, is well-designed to amuse.

Two Sundays had passed, and for two Sundays all the pupils had been put in detention—all except one, that is, who was always so sad and so sulky that there was no means of punishing him for gaiety. That pupil, older than the others, was named Louis, but his comrades called him Loony, to make fun of his ill humor.

On Sunday morning, therefore, Louis was the only one of the pupils who obtained permission to go out. His comrades watched him leave enviously, and in the evening, when he came back, he was bombarded with abuse; he was called hypocrite, old Loony, dirty philosopher and other insults of that sort.

"What do you do, then, hypocritical dog, to remain serious when everybody is laughing, and never get put in detention?"

"I work," Louis replied.

"A fine answer! We work too, but there are moments when we can't help laughing. Why don't you ever laugh?"

"Because I have nails in my shoes."

That reason seemed so stupid to the schoolboys that they looked at one another and believed for a moment that their comrade was mocking them.

"What are you talking about, with your shoes?" said a handsome youth named Richemont. "What can your shoes do for you?"

"Give such forceful kicks to the fay Grignote that she no longer comes trotting in their vicinity/"

"Grignote!" repeated all the children. "What is the fay Grignote?"

"She's a malevolent mouse," said Louis, "who is the cause of all your chagrins."

"A mouse!" said Richemont. Oh yes, Grignote! That's the name of a mouse. And you claim that it' her who gets us scolded. How?"

"She scuttles under the table, between your legs, during lessons; she tickles you and makes you laugh."

"Well then, we'll do as you do and put nails in our shoes."

"You'd do better to set a mouse-trap."

"A mousetrap in my shoe!" cried an ingenuous little boy.

"No, imbecile, a mousetrap under the table, with some pork fat inside."

"Pork fat!" said Richemont, astonished. "Can one catch a fay with pork fat?"

"Certainly—exactly like any other mouse, when the fay is a mouse," said Loony. "Try, anyway; you'll see that when Grignote is caught, the master will no longer scold you."

Several children refused to believe in the existence of the fay Grignote, and those who accepted that explanation of their laughter could not admit that a marine fay would ever allow herself to be trapped, above all to be trapped by pork fat.

II. The Master's Back

In the meantime, the master came in; he had just been inspecting a building that he was having constructed in the garden, and without perceiving it he had leaned on a newly-finished wall, with the result that he was daubed with plaster; his back was all white. That did not prevent him, however, from being as grave and severe as on any other day.

The pupils had no sooner perceived him with his white back, which he exhibited in all the classes, than the fay Grignote came to tickle their legs, and they started to laugh like maniacs.

The youngest were the first to burst out; the bigger boys bit their lips, making a semblance of coughing or picking up their pen—which they had not dropped—in sum, inventing all kinds of contortions to hide their desire to laugh. There was one in particular who was twisting his mouth in horrible grimaces, through which a malign smile betrayed him in spite of his efforts. The master was not duped by that hypocrisy.

"What's the matter with you, Monsieur?" he said, severely. "Why are you laughing?"

"I'm not laughing, Monsieur," replied the insolent liar. "I have a toothache this morning, which is tugging my mouth to either side, which always gives me the appearance of smiling, although I have no desire to do so."

At that unworthy lie, the schoolboys could not maintain their seriousness, and the fay Grignote recommenced her scuttling. This time, the laughter was sudden and general. Even Loony sensed that the nails in his shoes were insufficient to defend him. He started to laugh, and his gaiety was all the greater because it was rare. It was great Germanic laughter, a leaden joy that fell back upon the master like an insult.

"You too, Monsieur, you're joining in with the laughter!" cried the master, in a fury impossible to describe. In becoming so annoyed, he marched back and forth, exposing his broad white back, the cause of all the trouble, at every turn. The more agitated he became, the more the children laughed, and the more the fay Grignote tickled their legs.

Finally, no longer able to stand it, the master resolved to make a violent decision. "Messieurs," he said, "Such insubordination merits an exemplary punishment; the entire class is put in detention for a third time. Not one of you will go out on Sunday—not one, you hear!"

With those words, the indignant master left; but as the fay Grignote, frightened by his loud voice, had returned to her hole, the children were no longer thinking of laughing; the white back that was drawing away no longer excited their gaiety.

There was consternation among the pupils; they had not gone out for two Sundays already, and had not seen their parents, and they foresaw how discontented the parents would be if they were refused permission to see their children for a third time.

Then the smallest began to weep, because they were the most innocent; the bigger ones, on the contrary, entered into an extreme fury, because they were the most culpable. When one is in the wrong, one is very glad to take it out on someone, and those pupils who had denied the existence of the fay

Grignote most ardently were the first not to doubt any longer, as soon as they had such a fine opportunity to accuse her.

Scarcely had the master left the class than the wrath exploded.

"Grignote," they cried, "wicked Grignote! You're the cause of all our misfortunes!"

Those words were the signal for the revolt.

"Yes," said Richemont, one of the hotheads of the school, "it's Grignote, I'm certain of it; I felt something pushing my legs while the master was speaking"

"That was me," said the naïve little boy, who did not understand that it is necessary to lie in order to accuse someone, and who already felt a certain sympathy for Grignote.

"Oh, it was you?" said Richemont, impatient at being contradicted in his lie. "Well, this will teach you to push my legs!" And the malevolent child, as he spoke, punched the ingenuous small boy hard. Then, transported by anger, he climbed up on a table and cried: "Vengeance!"

And all his companions repeated: "Vengeance!"

There was a concert of imprecations against the unfortunate Grignote; each one, in accordance with his character, pronounced an insult, and as there were at least thirty in the class, there was a frightful racket. Nothing could be heard but *Grignote*...always Grignote.

"Accursed Grignote!"

"Infamous Grignote!"

"Abominable Grignote!"

"Perfidious Grignote!"

"Miserable Grignote!"

"Infernal Grignote!"

"Thieving Grignote!"

"Hypocritical Grignote!"

"Rascally Grignote!"

"Evil Grignote!"

"Grignote the *grignote!*"[12]

"Scheming Grignote!"

"Grignote the spy!"

"Grignote the coquette!" said one sixteen-year-old, finally, for whom that word was an insult.[13]

When the imprecations were exhausted, the regrets commenced. Everyone recalled the pleasure that had been promised to him for that third and fatal Sunday, which they were condemned once again to spend in school.

"Sunday!" cried one. "There's a fair at Saint-Cloud; Maman was going to take me."

"Sunday!" exclaimed another. "It's also my aunt's birthday; we were going to have tea with her."

"And Papa was going to take me to Franconi's!

"And I was going to the Jardin des Plantes!"

"And I was going to the king's mass!"

"And my uncle was going to give me a rifle!"

"And my brother was going to buy me a pony!"

"And Grandpapa was going to give me a watch!"

"And my Maman is ill!"

"And my sister is getting married!"

"And my guardian is in London!" It was the sixteen-year-old again who said that; the naughty boy was only happy when his guardian was away.

But I would never end if I were to enumerate all the regrets to which the punishment inflicted on the pupils gave birth in their hearts; I shall limit myself to telling you about their vengeance.

---

[12] Literally, the verb *grignoter* means to nibble, but it can also mean to wear down; this insult can be construed as "Grignote the tease!"

[13] Delphine Gay, who had the reputation of being a terrible coquette, naturally refused to consider the term insulting.

III. The Prisoner

The best talker in the class declared that there was not a moment to lose, and that it was necessary at all costs to trap Grignote, because they were have no rest until Grignote was caught, and only the capture of Grignote could appease the master's anger.

"The master is too just," he proclaimed, hoping that the latter might hear him, "to punish us for the crime of another. I have no doubt that as soon as he knows that Grignote alone is guilty, he'll let us off, and all his anger will fall upon her alone."

At that speech, the pupils clapped their hands, and the orator took advantage of the general enthusiasm to ask for funds—which is to say, the money necessary to purchase a little pork fat and a mouse-trap. Every pupil made a contribution of ten centimes, and they soon gathered a sum large enough to procure the wherewithal to trap all the mice in the neighborhood, and a few rats into the bargain.

It was Thursday and they still had two whole days to devote to the numerous steps that ought to return their good Sunday to the schoolboys. The ruses made good progress: the mouse-trap was purchased; the pork fat was already grilled; in order to attract their persecutor the pupils scattered breadcrumbs in all the college rooms. It was a shame to see so many enemies and so much anger accumulated against such a little mouse.

The mischievous Grignote knew nothing about the plot. Since the day of the master's great wrath she had fled, and was hiding in a girls' school, where she provoked many follies, for little girls are even more prone to laughter than boys.

However, seeing that calm had returned to the boys' school, she returned on Friday evening to sleep in her usual hole, far from suspecting the treason that awaited her there.

When she came in there was no one in the classroom; all the pupils were in the dormitories. The mouse wandered around under the benches, and she was agreeably surprised to find so many breadcrumbs on the floor; as she ate them without any danger she did not suspect any ruse. From crumb to crumb she arrived at the perfidious pork fat—which, alas, the imprudent fay did not suspect.

Scarcely had she tasted the deceptive dish than she heard a terrible noise, that of the trap-door falling back; the mouse-trap closed and the mouse was caught.

At that moment, the poor fay was as unhappy as a veritable mouse would have been who had fallen into a similar trap; anyway, she was a fay of the second order, a quasi-fay devoid of any power. Her role on earth was to make people laugh, and nothing is more scorned that that.

She immediately sensed the full extent of her misfortune, and she spent the night moaning desolately.

The next morning, when the schoolboys saw her in the mouse-trap, they experienced a delirious and ferocious joy, the joy of the culpable who have triumphed.

"To the cat!" they cried, immediately, to frighten her. "To the cat! To the cat!"—for there is an instinct of cruelty that bears us to proclaim before our victim the name of her enemy: in fact, that is the cruelest of insults.

The mouse-trap was placed on the table, and the schoolboys, having sat down on their benches, prepared to judge Grignote.

First they exposed their grievances, and there were a great many; the poor fay was trembling all over. Several malevolent pupils threatened her with their fists, others stared at her; the former heaped a thousand insults on her and the latter, cheerfully cruel, gave her ironic compliments.

"See how pretty she is," they said. "Poor prisoner, I feel sorry for her."

The ingenuous child, believing in good faith in their interest, unaware as yet what irony is, took them at their word in their benevolence, and added his sincere pity to their perfidious compassion.

"She is pretty, isn't she? She resembles a baby rabbit."

Poor child! That eulogy earned him a punch.

However, the master was soon due to return; it was necessary to hurry in order to force the mouse to confess her crime.

"We're going to deliver you to the master," said Loony to the unfortunate fay. "His wife has a cat that will do justice to you."

"To the cat! To the cat!" they all cried again, including the poor innocent, who as afraid of being beaten if he did not shout.

"Messieurs," said the fay, "deign to hear me. I confess that I've been very culpable in attracting such dire punishments to you; I won't seek to excuse myself. Alas, I know only too well that it isn't those who suffer from our actions who can find excuses for them. I recognize mine, Messeigneurs, so it isn't to your clemency that I address myself, it's to your reason. It's in the name of your interest that I speak. If you accuse me to your master, he won't believe you. Your cruelty would be futile, whereas your pity might be profitable to you."

"Well, all right," said one of the judges, whom that reasoning had softened. "We'll leave you your life, but swear to us never to make us laugh again, or else..."

"Alas, how can I make a promise that it would be impossible for me to keep? Trust me: I can't swear no longer to make you laugh, but I'll undertake not to have you scolded again. Isn't that sufficient for you?"

"I'll accept gladly," said one of the pupils, "for what annoys me isn't laughing, it's being put in detention."

"Leave it to me," added the fay, "Not only won't you be scolded in future, but your faults will be pardoned, and I promise you that you'll obtain permission to go out on Sunday."

"We'll go out on Sunday?" they all cried at the same time.

"I'll see to it, on my word of a mouse and a fay."

The children, overwhelmed by joy, immediately changed their hatred into enthusiasm; they carried the fay in triumph in her mouse-trap, and then set her free.

Then, delivering themselves to hope with the same vivacity with which they had previously delivered themselves to their regrets, they recommenced their acclamations.

"We're going out on Sunday! Sunday! Sunday!"

"I'm going to the fair to Saint-Cloud!"

"And I'm going to my aunt's birthday party!"

"And I'm going to Franconi's with Papa!"

"And I'm going to the Jardin des Plantes!"

"And I'm going to the king's mass!"

"And I'll have my rifle!"

"And I'll gallop on my pony!"

"And I'll go to the Tuileries with my watch!"

"And I'll be at my sister's wedding-feast!"

"And I'll be able to see Maman!"

"And I'll be able to go out on my own, without my guardian!"

IV. Ingenious Means

Soon, however, the great hope dissipated. The eve of Sunday had arrived, and the children had not obtained their mercy. They were beginning to mistrust Grignote and to repent of their clemency.

The little fay had no time to lose in carrying out her projects; she meditated them in silence, on the lookout for a favorable opportunity. Although very young, and a mouse, she knew that the success of *coups d'état* depends on good timing, and she waited with the patience of a man of genius for the moment to act to arrive.

All the pupils had met up in the refectory; it was supper time. That day they had been served a large plate of haricot beans, which did not look too good. The sauce was so light and so abundant that I believe an entire spring had passed through it. It was as if the sad beans were submerged in it.

Richemont, who, as we have already said, was a practical joker, after having pursued a haricot fruitlessly in the depths of that ocean---which is to say, his plate inundated with sauce— suddenly took off his jacket. The unaccustomed action attracted the attention of the master.

What are you doing there, Monsieur?" he said, angrily. "Why have you taken off your jacket?"

"In order to go in search of my beans by swimming," replied Richemont, brazenly.

The master was about to get annoyed, but at the same moment Grignote ran between his legs and, far from getting angry, he smiled.

Encouraged by that success, Grignote recommenced her scuttling, and the master ended up on entirely good terms with his pupils.

His wife, who was very mild, took advantage of his good humor to ask him for mercy for the poor schoolboys.

"Do you want to punish these children because they laughed, when you, who are a serious man, the father of a family, aren't able to remain serious? That would be unjust."

He master allowed himself to be softened, and mercy was granted to the children. Then there was a general delight, and they cried with a common accord:

"Hurrah for our good master!"

"Hurrah for Grignote!"

"Hurrah for the fay Grignote!"

"The immortal Grignote!"

"The adorable Grignote!"

"The beautiful Grignote!"

"The charming Grignote!"

"The loving Grignote!"

"The dainty Grignote!"

"The favorite Grignote!"

"The beloved Grignote!"

And since that time, Grignote has become the friend of small children.

Alphonse Karr: *The Fays of the Sea*
(Nouveau magasin des enfants vol. IV, 1851)[14]

A young man was sitting in the corner of a room in an inn, and before him was an excellent supper that he had not touched, he was so preoccupied.

Another man, sitting in another corner, would gladly have given all his attention to a good meal, but the innkeeper did not bring him anything. Suddenly, he looked at the young man who was supping, appeared to recognize him, stood up and exchanged a few words with him—which did not excite the attention of the other customers until the moment when the young man who had something to eat but was not hungry said to the man who was hungry but had nothing to eat: "Alas. my dear monsieur, everyone has his chagrins; if, like me, you had had your lover turned into a goldfish..."

But that story might seem obscure, and I shall take it up again later...

There was once a poor hut with a thatched roof on the edge of the sea in Normandy. That hut belonged to a fisher-man, who lived there with his wife and son. The accommoda-tion was not sumptuous; the beds were made of ferns torn up on the edge of the woods. Père Laurent, the fisherman, was skilled in his craft, no one was better at making and repaired

---

[14] The one-time schoolmaster Alphonse Karr (1808-1890) had one child, born in 1834, of a marriage that had ended before 1840. Although at the heart of the Romantic Movement and a rather waspish satirist in his early journalism, his quasi-autobiographical fiction evaded censorship; he was not for-mally exiled after the 1851 *coup d'état*, but he left Paris never-theless in 1855 and settled in Nice.

nets; no one was better at anticipating, when the sun set, what the weather would be like the following day. Unfortunately, he was no longer young, and fatigue and poverty had weakened him. His son André was strong and courageous, and had an excellent heart; for his poor parents he was the hope and security of their old age.

One morning, André, who had gone to search for lobsters under the rocks, came back with a little girl whom he had found lying asleep on a pile of seaweed. She was s so small that she could not speak yet. Marthe, André's mother, tried for a long time to discover who the poor abandoned child might belong to. She had it reported throughout the land that a child had been found, but no one came to claim her. Marthe said: "It's God who has sent her to me," and from that day on the little girl became the child of the house. They called her Marie, a good and charming name made with the letters of the word *aimer*. She grew up with them, calling André her brother and Père Laurent and his wife her father and mother.

The days and the years succeeded one another. They were not very rich in the thatched hut, and sometimes had great difficulty earning the necessary bread, but they all loved one another and were united. André helped his father and promised to be a good fisherman one day. They were happy.

One day, when the fishing had been poor and André and his father were returning to land without having caught a single fish, they perceived a seagull that resembled a dove floating on the sea, which was trying in vain to take flight and flee their approach. They steered their boat toward it and picked it up easily; it had been wounded by a hunter.

"Upon my faith," said Père Laurent, "it's Heaven that has sent us supper," and he enclosed it in a basket.

When they arrived on land, Laurent charged his son with hauling the boat on to the shore and bringing the little seagull that had appeared so conveniently to the house. He went inside. Marthe was in a very bad mood when she learned that they had not caught a single fish.

"Fortunately," said Laurent, "we found a seagull that will provide us with supper."

"A seagull!" said Marthe. "That's not very good. It's tough meat."

"You can cook it for longer, with onions and a little butter; we can have an excellent soup."

"A soup, you say? It isn't a soup that I want to cook; I want to make a stew, and if you let me do it my way, it won't be bad."

"It would be better to make soup."

Marthe insisted on the stew, Laurent on the soup, and they ended up quarreling. They fell into accord, however, because it was provisionally necessary to pluck the seagull, and Marie was sent to ask André for it.

She found André sitting on the edge of the sea, plunged in a profound reverie.

"André," she said to him, "give me the seagull so that I can take it to the house.

"The seagull?" said André. "It's flown away."

"Oh my God! How you're going to be scolded! Maman has already peeled the onions in order to cook it."

"Oh," said André, "if you knew what had happened to me!"

"Tell me."

"This is it: I was about to return to the house, and I was holding the poor bird, which was trembling, in my hands. I looked at its white neck. Its wings were such a soft gray, its little red feet and its black eyes were so bright. I felt a great pity in thinking that it was going to be plucked and eaten. 'Poor little thing,' I said, 'If you weren't wounded, I'd let you go.'

"As I said that, I opened my hands; the gull shook its feathers, flapped its wings, and...doubtless it had only been stunned by its injury, for it flew away and was lost in the clouds."

"You did well," said Marie, "but what are we going to say so that Maman won't scold you and Papa won't beat you?"

"That's not all; you don't know everything yet. As I set off again for our hut I heard a tiny voice calling my name: 'André! André!' I looked around in vain, thought I had been mistaken, and continued ion my way. But the voice called my name again, and I perceived a seagull that was fluttering around my head. 'André! André!' it said."

"What! The seagull could talk?"

"Yes, it talked quite well. 'André,' it said, 'Wait a little so I can thank you. You've saved me from a horrible death in an ignominious saucepan, and I want to make you a little present, but it's necessary for you to wait here while I go and fetch it.' With those words, it plunged into the sea, as the other gulls do in order to catch fish, but it soon came back, carrying this little bell.

"'Listen carefully,' it said, when it had perched on my shoulder and I had relieved it of its burden. 'This little bell is gold; the clapper is a precious pearl. It's the pearl...' Then it said something of which I can remember the words, but I don't understand the meaning very well: 'It's the pearl that Cleopatra thought she had dissolved in order to drink it,[15] but it was stolen by a genie who could not tolerate the destruction of such a perfect pearl, and thrown into the depths of the sea.

"'When you shake this little bell and you ask for something, what you ask for will be granted immediately—but remember this: after the third wish is granted, the pearl will disappear and fall back into the gulf, where the guardians of the sea's treasures will seal it again in the nacreous oyster in which it was born, and which serves it as a jewel-case. Think carefully, therefore, about what you ask of it.'

---

[15] The highly unlikely story that Cleopatra once dissolved a pearl in vinegar, in order that she might drink it, can be found in Pliny's *Natural History*, and Macrobius' *Saturnalia*, but has been cited many times since.

"With those words, the seagull disappeared, and I remained, stunned and amazed, at the spot where you found me."

The two young folk looked at the little bell. It was the size of a thimble, and the pearl as large as a pea, but so round and uniform that it charmed the eyes.

"Now," said André, "it's a matter of knowing whether the seagull was making fun of me; I'm going to try out the bell."

"What are you going to ask for?"

"Something for you."

"No, for you."

André put an end to the argument by agitating the little bell, which produced a sweet and limpid sound; then he said: "I want a gold chain for Marie."

At that moment, the sun, which had just set, had left a rich orange tint on the horizon. A black dot stood out against the orange, which grew and approached, and they did not take long to recognize a jet black cormorant skimming the sea.

When it arrived close to Andre and Marie it passed over their heads and dropped a delicate gold chain, so slender that it could have passed through the eye of a needle, and so long that when André put it around Marie's neck it went around six times.

Then a menacing voice shouted to André—that of Père Laurent.

The onions to be cooked with the seagull had already been in the butter for some time, and Marthe was beginning to say that her stew would be spoiled and worthless.

"Let's see that bird," said Laurent.

"It's flown away," said André.

The furious Laurent seized André by one ear and dragged him to the house, in spite of Marie's tears and supplications; it was not until they arrived at the hut that he was able to explain himself and relate what had happened. At first, they refused to believe him, but the sight of the little bell and Marie's chain shook their incredulity slightly. Perhaps they were not gold, though, and perhaps André had found them. Perhaps...

"Wretch!" shouted Père Laurent. "If you've stolen them...I'll kill you!"

"Listen," said André, "it's very easy to convince you and to repair the wrong I've done you by letting the gull escape. I'll agitate the bell and ask for a good supper."

"Well," said Père Laurent, "let's see what there is that might be good to eat."

They thought about it for some time; but supper time had already passed, and they fell into agreement that a sumptuous supper, the best that it was given to rich people to make, was incontestably composed of cabbages and lard.

André rang his little bell and said: "I want cabbages and lard."

Then he looked out of the door to see whether the cormorant would bring the cabbages and lard, but he could not see the cormorant.

"You can see," said Père Laurent, "that you've lied, and that your seagull was making fun of you!"

However, an odor spread through the house.

"That's singular," said Marthe, "How good that smells!"

"In truth, it's the smell of cabbages," said Laurent.

"It's coming from the fireplace," said Marie.

"There's nothing before the fire," said Marthe, "except the big covered pot in which I wanted to cook the seagull; but the odor's coming from there, that's certain."

She uncovered the pot in front of the fire, and I leave you to imagine how surprised she was when she found it full of cabbages and lard, all fuming. They hastened to sit down at the table, and had a supper such as Laurent's family had never had in their lives.

Marie was the first to think that, of the three wishes André had, only one remained. They agreed that it was necessary to reserve it for some unforeseen necessity, and they did not take long to resume their old habits of labor and poverty.

Some time after that, one day when Père Laurent had departed on his own to go fishing, because Andre had nets to repair in the house, and for her part, Marie had gone to look for shrimp on the sea shore, Marthe said to her son: "Look how bad the weather is getting; I wish your father had come back."

"That's true," said André. "Clouds are rising in the wind; we're going to have a storm."

And he went out of the house in order to go to the shore.

The sea was growling dully, and becoming black. The wind was blowing in gusts and lifting waves, which did not take long to become frightening.

"Oh my God," said André, "What weather we're going to have! There's a big ship out there, which is furling all its sails; the wind must be terrible where it is. If my father doesn't get back soon, he's doomed. Ah! It's doubtless him that I can see coming toward the shore—but the sea is furious now; he won't be able to land."

At every moment the tempest was becoming more terrible; at moments the little boat that Père Laurent was manning could be seen on the crest of a wave, but then it disappeared and one could believe that it had been swallowed up and lost.

Marthe and her son, their hearts constricted and their hands joined, interrogated the horizon with their gaze.

"Ah! There it is again; but it's near the coast that the sea is most furious!"

At that moment they were distracted from their terror by another and greater fear. Marie, surprised by the sea, had taken refuge on a rock, which the water had not take long to surround; the waves that were breaking and roaring against the rock, and covering the unfortunate child with foam, were about to engulf her at any moment. André threw himself into the water in order to go to her aid, but the angry sea rolled him and threw him back several times, bruised by the rocks.

Marie, who was on her knees, raising her arms to the heavens, called for help, but André could not reach her.

"André," cried the mother, "your father is about to be lost!"

"And Marie, poor Marie," cried André, weeping.

"André," said the mother, "use your bell!"

"That's true, my bell!" And he took it precipitately from his bosom, where he had hidden it. "But Mother, I only have one wish left to formulate, and I can only save one of the two. Can my father not save himself by swimming?"

"Alas, no; his limbs are too stiff now, and you can see very well that you can't triumph over the waves. Hurry to save your father, or he's doomed."

"André," cried Marie, "help me!"

"Will you leave your father to perish?" said Marthe.

André agitated his bell, crying: "I want to save my father!"

At the same moment, the pearl that formed the bell's clapper disappeared, and André threw the bell away. Immediately, a powerful wave lifted up Père Laurent's boat and came to place it gently on the sand of the shore. But the same wave had covered the rock that served as Marie's shelter and had carried the unfortunate girl away.

André had thrown himself into the sea in the hope of reaching Marie, but he was thrown back again, bruised all over, on to the shore. Then he said nothing; he did not weep—but when night fell and the sea calmed down he went to the rock on which he had seen Marie for the last time. He knelt down and said a brief prayer; then, with his arms folded over his breast, he said: "I've saved my father, but I'm going to die with Marie."

Then he let himself fall and disappeared under the waves.

In one of the deepest gulfs of the sea there is an immense cavern entirely composed on nacreous shells, corals and madrepores of every kind. All the magnificences of the sea are assembled there with remarkable care; seaweed, wrack and marine plants of a hundred species carpet the depths; in the surroundings is *the treasure of the sea*, composed not only of the most marvelous things it produces, and which it is not permitted to the avidity of commerce or the avidity of science to know, such as pearls as big as pumpkins, but also of everything that shipwrecks have taken from humans, everything that the Ocean has swallowed. In no matter what region, under what sky, each shipwreck has occurred, everything has been transported faithfully into this place, compared with which the greatest depths are mere fords; for the sea is twenty-five leagues deep there.

One would not believe all the riches that the sea has devoured since men began to tempt fortune on its waters. In the midst of the treasures of which we speak there are two mountains, each nine leagues in height; both are composed of coins, one of silver and the other of gold. It is into that treasure that Cleopatra's pearl was brought by the genies of the sea when it escaped from André's bell. It was also there that the inanimate body of André was brought after he had thrown himself into the sea in order not to survive Marie, whom he had not been able to save.

In fact, all the drowned are there, lying on beds of marine herbs, surrounded by horrible crabs that want to devour them but cannot, because the soul, still captive within the prison of the flesh, obliges them to respect the body.

On land, however, those who loved the dead, those who have prayed for a long time for their fortunate return, those whose joy died with them, pray for the deliverance of their souls, and as an ardent prayer emerges from the heart of a daughter, a wife, a lover or a sister, a radiant soul launches forth, and rises from the abysms of the Ocean with the rapidity of thought into the profundities of the sky, where it is received by the angels.

But André was not dead, and he soon recovered consciousness, extended on a magnificent bed formed of the finest seagull down, that which they tear out themselves in order to make their nests and warm their offspring. The bed was placed in a grotto of nacre, pearls and coral, but it was not until later that he saw all that magnificence; his gaze was initially occupied by two beautiful young women, who had been watching over him while he slept. They were clad in long green robes, and their hair was attached with strings of fine pearls.

"Where am I?" he cried. "Am I dead, then, and is this the Other World? In that case, why do I not find Marie here? I only wanted to come in order to rejoin her."

"André," said the older of the two beautiful women, who might have been about twenty years of age, "you are not dead, and the place where you are, although it is a world very different from the one that you inhabit, is nevertheless not the one that humans call the Other World. You are in the empire of the sea; the depths of water that it has been necessary for you to traverse in order to come here are our sky. You have performed actions up there that give you a right to the gratitude of all the fays of the sea. But the fay Smaragdine, before whom you will soon appear, can answer your questions better than I can. If you care to come with us, we will take you to the foot of her throne."

André got up and made a sign that he was ready. Then the younger of the two fays took a pink shell that was attached to her belt, and by blowing into it made three sounds of a delightful sweetness heard. At that signal, a hippopotamus came running, a magnificent marine horse with a green mane,[16] which offered its back to André; he wanted, politely, to allow the two young woman to mount up before him, but they told him that they had no need to do so. In fact, they started swimming, and escorted him playfully.

It was not long before André saw his hippopotamus stop in front of a cavern a hundred times more magnificent than the

---

[16] The illustrator of the original edition of the story construed the term "hippopotamus" in the narrow sense of its Latin meaning (water horse) and depicted the creature in question as a sturdy horse, rather than the African mammal to which the name is usually attached. Although not explicit, the text seems to endorse that supposition.

one in which he had awakened. The young fay drew two sounds from her pink shell, and the two of them preceded André, ordering him to follow them.

The grotto was formed of the rarest shells and the most extraordinary madrepores; red and white coral, nacre and pearls were distributed there with an infinite artistry; but what dazzled André's eyes most of all was a woman of such great beauty that for a moment, he thought her more beautiful than Marie. Like his companions she had a green robe, and her blonde tresses were constellated with black pearls, which brought out their suave color.

André bowed before her, but she took him by the hand, and after having pressed it to her heart she made him sit down beside her.

"I cannot help, my dear André," she said, "testifying all my tenderness to you. before even telling you the cause of it. I must tell you, before anything else, that Marie is not dead, but that only your love and your courage can save her, and that she is running the greatest dangers."

"Oh, Madame," cried André, "tell me what those dangers are!"

"I don't know yet myself; only Proteus, the old god so well-known by means of college texts and exercises, can inform us of Marie's fate. It's true that he is now stuffed, but he still sometimes renders oracles, and today is one of his days. While you go to take a modest meal, I shall tell you all that you need to know; then we shall go to the museum of the sea, where a great many ancient things are conserved that were once living and feared but are mere curiosities today."

"What need have I to eat, Madame?" said André, vehemently.

"André," said the fay severely, "have you, then, been reading bad books, those books of tales in which knights do not eat, drink or sleep? You will perhaps have need of all the strength of your soul and all that of your body in order to save Marie."

"I will obey you, Madame," André replied. "You inspire respect in me, similar to that which I have for my mother, with a mixture of the tenderness I have for Marie—and dare I say, Madame, that it seems to me that you resemble Marie a little. I will obey you in everything you care to order me to do."

Then the young fays served André a meal composed of fish and shellfish, but which tasted so exquisite and so different those he had eaten before that he could not help manifesting his astonishment.

"There are certain fish," said Smaragdine, smiling, "that we do not permit to expose themselves to the hooks and nets of fishermen, and which we reserve for ourselves. None of us would wish to eat the insipid fish of which men make their most delicate feasts; but I shall tell you why you are sharing our privileges, including that of breathing underwater, and why you can command here as I do myself.

"Although very extensive, our power has limits; for example, once a year, in the form that it pleases us to choose, we must spend a month exposed to all the good and evil fortunes of the creature whose form we have chosen.

"Being very young, I was curious to see what was happening on land, and with a young fay, one of my companions, we put on human form and visited the court of Prince Gulfiah. He was the handsomest and the most virtuous man that the land had ever possessed. He proved to be sensible to my feeble attractions, and I married him. That was a mistake, and I paid very dearly for it. To begin with, the fay Langouste, my companion, who had neglected nothing in order to attract Prince Gulfiah, conceived an immortal hatred against me, to which the superior council of fays left me exposed, in order to punish my imprudence.

"In fact, such alliances with the inhabitants of the land are the cause of an eternally unfortunate race; the children that result from them have a superiority over other humans for which the latter never pardon them, and which renders them exposed throughout life to a jealousy to which they always end up succumbing.

"Furthermore, I could not be unaware that I would be forced to quit my husband after a few days and that I would leave him delivered to despair. I tried in vain to avert what was going to happen, and to convince him that I would spend one month of every year with him. He thought I was mad, and when I had to plunge into the sea again on the fatal day he thought that I had simply drowned, gave me a magnificent funeral, and killed himself on my empty tomb, alas!

"If he had only thought of throwing himself into the sea, I would have been able to save him, like you.

"Marie was the fruit of that sad union, and she was born here, where we are."

André stood up abruptly, threw himself at Smaragdine's knees, and covered her hands with kisses. The fay ordered him by means of a sign to get up and to listen to the continuation of her story.

"I knew that all the hatred of the barbaric Langouste would be turned against the innocent creature that I had just brought into the world, and that Marie would only be shielded from her perfidies if she attained the age of fifteen years without Langouste being able to take possession of her. Our conduct during the month that Langouste had spent at the court of Prince Gulfiah had been judged light by our elders, and we had been forbidden to encounter one another in future among humans in our real form. I imagined having Marie taken to the land immediately after her birth by the two young fays that brought you here, preferring to deliver her to the dubious compassion of humans rather than the hatred of my rival, who, unable any more than myself to reappear on land with her form and her power, would not be able to pursue a poor little girl there.

"It was you who found Marie; you took her to your parents and you took care of her in a touching fashion during her childhood. When the moment came when I had to change appearance, I took the form of a seabird; that form exposes us to much greater risks, but it permitted me to see my little Marie. Once, a hunter fired a rifle shot at me that broke a wing, which was my arm, and I came back here dying, after having hidden in a cleft in a rock until daylight, which permitted me to return to the sea. Langouste was hiding in a hole nearby; in the form of a cormorant she had tried to blind Marie."

"Ah, I remember!" said André. "I remember that malevolent cormorant, which I struck fortunately with a stone I threw."

"The greatest danger that I ran," the fay continued, "was when your father picked me out of the sea; the onions were already peeled and my sauce was made, when you rendered me liberty and life. Under the pretext of thanking you, I gave you a talisman that, I was sure, would enable you to protect Marie. Heaven ordered otherwise. Langouste took possession of Marie, whom you believed to be drowned and did not want to survive.

"Judge now how I must love you, and what place you occupy in my heart, along with my dear child. Let us combine our efforts, our courage and our love, and Marie will be returned to us. I have only given her life, alas; it is you who have protected her. Marie belongs to both of us equally."

On the order of Smaragdine, the hippopotamus was brought back, on the back of which she took her place with André. The horse did not take long to carry them to the museum where they would find Proteus, who only rendered oracles at rare intervals since he had been stuffed.

While traversing the long galleries of the museum, the fay pointed out to André the principal curiosities that had been assembled there.

"This," she said, "is the whale that swallowed Jonah; this is the red lobster that a modern writer saw in the sea;[17] this is a stuffed siren and a triton preserved in alcohol; this is the great sea serpent that the newspapers encounter once a year; here is

---

[17] Possibly a reference to an oft-quoted reference to a recommendation in an 1829 manual of painting by Jacques de Montabert to avoid gross errors like painting uncooked lobsters red.

a nereid and a dolphin; the latter died of fear—that was the one with which, one day, a young and immense pianist wanted to renew the miracle of Arion,[18] who attracted fish; this is the fish that was lacking, and caused the death of the celebrated cook Vatel, who could not survive his dishonor on seeing that it was necessary to serve a dinner without fish; this is the brother of the fish that a tyrant threw into the sea in order to expiate a good fortune whose duration caused a just fear, and the father of the turbot whose sauce the Roman senate disputed—the white sauce was decided by a majority of forty-six votes; this is the famous cachalot that the Paris newspapers saw within the jetties of the port of Cherbourg. But silence...here's Proteus; he's already responded to several people. Let's move closer.

"Proteus, from whom the heavens have no secret, tell an unhappy mother what has become of her daughter; tell an unhappy lover what he must do to recover the one he loves."

Proteus responded in a faint voice, as befits a stuffed god:

"Your daughter, O Smaragdine, is in the power of the fay Langouste, your former companion in coquetry at the court of the unfortunate Prince Gulfiah. Langouste has changed her into a goldfish, and she was fished up this very morning at the mouth of the Seine; she has not been fried, as you might fear, but she is in continual danger of being.

"As for you, André, try to recognize your fiancée among the goldfish that you might encounter, but to render her to her original form it is necessary that you recover possession of the little golden bell and Cleopatra's pearl. Your name means 'man of courage'; continue to show yourself worthy of your name."

After those words, Proteus fell back into torpor.

Smaragdine surrendered to the most profound despair. "O my daughter," she said, "perhaps at this moment you are

---

[18] The reference is to an anecdote told about Frédéric Chopin.

bring put over the fire of the stove where you are to be fried. O barbaric Langouste! O too cruel destiny!"

"Forgive me for interrupting you, dear Mother," said André, "but I believe the most urgent thing is for me to set out in search of Marie. Help me to recover my dear bell and send me back to land, since Marie was fished up this morning."

"As long as it has been thrown in the water," cried the fay. "You're right, André; the bell is in my pocket; it was brought back to me at the moment you threw it away. But the pearl belongs to the treasure of the sea, and it has been returned to the oyster that serves it as a casket, which is defended by a formidable guard of marine monsters. If you triumph over the monsters and can penetrate the vicinity of the treasure, you'll recognize the oyster easily; it's covered with nacre without as well as within.

"Unfortunately, I cannot help you in the combat you are going to deliver. Only your courage and your love can protect you. The hippopotamus will take you as far as the treasure where the oyster in guarded, but there it will be obliged to abandon you. If you succumb in your enterprise, deprived of everything I have loved, I shall rid myself of a sad immortality; at the first opportunity, when I have to choose a form, I shall become a fish, and I shall seek a net with the same care that other fish put into avoiding them. If you are victorious, the hippopotamus will take you back to land. Then, if you find Marie, throw the bell into the sea and it will be returned to me. Until then, we shall not see one another again."

Smaragdine embraced André, and reminded him that the golden bell would only obey him three times. She gave him a coral ring that would turn white every time it touched a person or an object that, by virtue of a enchantment, did not have its natural form, and a dagger with two blades whose handle was in the middle. Then she watched him set forth, carried away by the hippopotamus, and returned to shut herself away in her grotto.

André allowed himself to be carried by the hippopotamus. After an hour, the marine horse slowed down. André thought at first that it was tired, but he soon perceived that it was trembling, and it refused to go any further; he realized that they had arrived. Her got down from the horse, gripped the dagger, and advanced resolutely in the direction in which the hippopotamus had been heading until then. Soon he saw the two mountains of gold and silver; he took a few more steps and found himself facing an enormous shark, which, having seen him, was already diving to swallow him.

André pronounced Marie's name, marched straight ahead, and lifted the arm equipped with the dagger. The shark gnashed its triple row of teeth, opened its immense mouth, and closed it again in order to sever the arm of the insensate challenger, but as its two jaws, in coming together, were pierced by the two blades of the dagger, it opened its mouth again and fled, spreading around thick black blood.

The shark was succeeded by the most hideous inhabitants of the sea, enormous crabs, lampreys, squid spreading clouds of ink, and jellyfish with venomous stings. André triumphed over disgust as he had triumphed over horror. He opened a path with his dagger and headed for the place that the animals appeared to be defending most fiercely. In fact, he did not take long to perceive an enormous and shiny oyster.

The squid troubled the limpidity of the water in vain; he seized the oyster, and in spite of its two valves closing convulsively, he opened them with the blade of his dagger and took the pearl that was hidden therein. Approached to the bell, it adapted itself to it of its own accord, and André, after having thanked God, returned to the place where he had left his horse, which he found still trembling.

He put himself back in the saddle, and the horse began a rapid gallop, traversing mountains and passing over rocks.

Soon André, seeing the sky through the clear water, thought that the sea was less deep; then his head emerged from the water and then the hippopotamus deposited him on the beach at Trouville, which was covered with bathers. He was welcomed by cries of horror, because the hippopotamus had put him down on the part of the beach reserved for women. He hastened to go inland and sit down on the sand in order to warm himself in the sunlight and think about what to do next.

It was true that the golden bell of which he had become the possessor ought to be a great help to him, but he thought that it would only be submissive three times, that it would be necessary to make use of it to return Marie to her true form, that he might make a mistake, and that, prudently, he only ought to make use of the power of the bell once for himself.

He reflected for some time, for he did not want to act as he had the first time he had had the precious talisman in his hands.

He thought at first that he would doubtless have to travel a great deal, and had a desire to ask for a good horse; but that horse would become fatigued, and it would be necessary to feed it. Then, he would need clothes himself. He did not know anyone in the world except his parents and Marie. He almost asked for a friend to aid him in his search, in order to make the nights seem less cold, the route less long, and a lack of success less discouraging. I don't know what good influence woke him up from that dream, for his own reflections would surely not have done him any good. He was at the fortunate age when one believes in friendship; he could not know yet that at the end of life, it is only those who have really done you harm that you have loved a great deal, and that in proportion to the affection you have had for them.

He decided to ask for a purse with five gold coins that would be renewed every time he spent them. Scarcely had he pronounced that wish, while agitating the bell, than he felt the purse in one of his pockets.

Meanwhile, a few people who had seen him emerge from the sea fully dressed, had approached in order to look at him. A young man came up to him and asked him where he had come from.

"I've come from far away," André replied.

"What do you do?"

"I'm a fisherman."

"Where are you going?"

"I don't know."

"Are you making fun of me?"

"Certainly not. I'm looking for goldfish, and I'm going everywhere that I think I might find one. IF you know of any, you'd give me pleasure by indicating them to me."

"I only know the famous pacha Sha-ha-ba-am who has goldfish," replied the young man.[19]

The people surrounding André and his interlocutor began to laugh, because they knew about *The Bear and the Pacha*, a play once performed at the Varietés by Potier, Vernet and Odry, in which the pacha Sha-ha-ba-am is said to have watched goldfish for two hours in succession. But André, who did not know very much, asked where Monsieur Sha-ha-ba-am lived.

The young man who had made fun of André thought he was being mocked in his turn by the fisherman's sang-froid, and turned his back without responding. As for André, he was hungry; he went into an inn and ordered dinner. He found himself beside a traveling salesman, of whom he asked: "Is it true, Monsieur, that the pacha Sha-ha-ba-am has goldfish?"

The traveling salesman looked at him with astonishment; then, pulling himself together and darting a knowing glance around the table at the other guests, he said: "Where have you come from, then, that you don't know the pacha Sha-ha-ba-am, his goldfish and his two bears?"

---

[19] The pacha or Sultan Sha-ha-ba-am, or Shahabaham, was cited frequently in humorous periodicals in the first half of the century; the oft-reprinted vaudeville to which subsequent reference is made, and in which he might have originated, was first performed in February 1820 and was credited to Eugène Scribe and "Xavier" (Joseph Xavier Boniface, who subsequently signed himself X. B. Saintine). The actors cited appeared in a version staged by Brunet in 1833.

"I don't care about the bears," André replied, "but if he really has goldfish, I'd like to know where he lives."

"Doubtless in Turkey, in his quality as a pacha; I don't know the street or the number, but when you're in Turkey you only have ask the first commissionaire; everyone knows him."

"And you're sure that he has goldfish?"

"I can't say precisely that I've seen them, but I've heard it said twenty times that he spends two hours a day watching his goldfish circle in a bowl."

"Is it far from here to Turkey?"

"That depends how much money you have."

"I have as much as I want."

The traveling salesman thought in his turn that André was definitely mad, and he got up from the table.

André said nothing further about goldfish, but he told the innkeeper that he wanted to go to Turkey. As André paid without haggling, the innkeeper could see that he had a lot of money. One respects the folly of people who have lot of money; that is known as "amiable eccentricity." The innkeeper told him that it was necessary to go to Le Havre, where a steamship would take him to Russia, and from there he would easily be able to complete his journey.

André did as he was told, but when he arrived in Le Havre he learned that the ship was not leaving for a week.

One evening, while he was at a play, he was slightly surprised to hear the name of the great Sha-ha-ba-am pronounced; he pricked up his ears and looked around. Soon he heard he illustrious Marecot say: "His Highness is busy gazing at his goldfish; he'll be at it for a couple of hours."

André understood then that people had been making fun of him and that the pacha Sha-ha-ba-am was only a character in a comedy.

But, he thought, *immediately, what does that matter to me? Since Sha-ha-ba-am looks at goldfish, it doesn't matter that the pacha is an actor; I don't care about that. It isn't necessary to go to Turkey; I'll go to see the goldfish.*

He emerged from the theater and asked how to get on to the stage. The stage entrance was shown to him; he presented himself and the porter said to him: "You can't go in."

André, who had only had money for a few days, but was already beginning to understand its power, replied coldly: "You're mistaken, for here's twenty francs."

The porter recognized that he was, indeed, mistaken, put the twenty francs in his pocket and let André go up to the theater.

André asked to speak to the actor who was playing the role of Sha-ha-ba-am.

"That's me, Monsieur," said a passing Turk.

"Would you be good enough to let me see your goldfish?"

"My goldfish?" said the Turk. "I haven't seen any here; perhaps they're reserved for supper."

"Are you going to eat them?" asked André.

"Why not," replied the Turk.

"I forbid you to do it," cried André, leaping at his throat.

The Turk cried out; the stage-hands seized André and threw him out.

It chanced that, in the evening, when he was eating supper sadly in a corner, he was recognized by Sha-ha-ba-am, who was sitting in another corner, not eating. Sha-ha-ba-am approached him and said to him: "Monsieur, I am really sorry to have had you thrown out of the theater, but you had made me miss my entrance and the public was already somewhat discontented. After that, not caring very much, I decided to break my engagement and to return to Paris; I'm too unfortunate in this accursed city.

"Alas, my dear Monsieur," said André, "everyone has his chagrins, and if, like me, you had had the woman you love changed into a goldfish..."

"That's undoubtedly a great misfortune," said the actor.

This was where we were when I thought it appropriate to resume my story later.

"That's undoubtedly a great misfortune," said the actor, "but for the moment it's impossible for me to imagine one greater than that of having no supper."

"Is that to say that you're asking me to share supper with you?"

"Undoubtedly; at the same stroke it would give you a supper and me an appetite.

The actor sat down at the table opposite his Amphitryon and did not take long to do honor to the dishes and the wine. He even began to find life in general something sweet and cheerful, and La Havre a particularly agreeable city.

"You said just now," said André, "that you were going to go to Paris."

"To Paris or somewhere else," replied Sha-ha-ba-am, "unless I stay here. For the true sage, life can be as charming in one place as another."

"Are there many goldfish in Paris?" asked André.

"In Paris," replied the actor, "there's a great deal, and even too much, of everything, and I know there are a lot of goldfish there. There are goldfish in the ponds of the Tuileries and the ponds of the Luxembourg; there are some in all the pork-butchers' shops and almost all the pastry-makers' shops. It's rare to see them in other shops, except those that sell them. No one knows why that affinity exists between the pastry-makers, the pork-butchers and the goldfish. Shoemakers have magpies and porters have canaries. A few bourgeois have goldfish too, but it's ten to one they've previously been pork-butchers or pastry-makers."

"Would you like me to go to Paris with you?" asked André. "You can help me in my research. I have money, plenty of money; you seem to have more intelligence than me, or perhaps more experience. You're cheerful…when you've eaten… You can direct me and stop me falling into discouragement. We can live together comfortably, while searching for my poor Marie, and if the barbaric Langouste falls under our hand…"

"I'll confess to you," said the actor, "that I don't share your opinion on the langouste, and I've never had anything against it. It's sometimes reproached for causing indigestion, but this is the first time I've heard it called barbaric."[20]

"I shall always seem to be saying puzzling things," replied André, "as long as I haven't told you my story."

"I'll listen to it gladly while smoking a cigar and drinking a glass of punch."

André ordered the punch and the cigars, and told Sha-ha-ba-am the story that we already know. The story interested the actor keenly, who swore not to quit André until he had recovered Marie.

A diligence passed during the night, and the two new friends climbed into it; they arrived in Paris the following morning.

In Paris André never stopped thinking about Marie, in spite of his friend Sha-ha-ba-am, who announced goldfish to him everywhere he thought that he would find a few pleasures, and tried by all means to distract him from his dolor. André had gone into the shops of all the pottery merchants who sold goldfish, and those of all the pork-butchers, and almost all the pastry-makers.

The coral ring had remained the most beautiful red. None of the fish he had seen had been anything else.

The comedian tried in vain to make him develop a taste for pleasures. André only wanted Marie.

One day, when the two friends were dining together, André confessed that he was beginning to despair.

"I know!" said Sha-ha-ba-am. "There's one goldfish I know that we haven't visited; it belongs to one of my friends, a woman of letters. If you wish, I'll introduce you to her this evening. That goldfish has never appeared to me to be an ordinary fish; it's the object of too much care."

_____

[20] The trivial noun *langouste* is the French term for the rock lobster, sometimes also applied to crayfish.

André wanted to go right away. "I don't have the courage to have good dinners," he said, "when I think that, for such a long time, Marie has been eating nothing but breadcrumbs."

So the matter was agreed; the comedian took André to the home of the woman of letters; but there was no longer anything on the mantelpiece except this epitaph, which a gallant friend had stuck to the bowl:

Everything must perish
Within your purview,
Even your pet goldfish
Has died of love for you.

"Alas," cried André, "as long as it wasn't Marie!"

After numerous explanations, however, it was evident that the woman of letters' goldfish had belonged to her a long time before the metamorphosis of the unfortunate Marie, and consequently could not have been her.

The actor had been keeping André company faithfully for a month when he suddenly disappeared. André searched for him everywhere without obtaining any news of him. One thing astonished him even more in the midst of that astonishment, which was that in a waistcoat left behind by Sha-ha-ba-am he found a coral ring similar to his own. He put it on the finger where he already had one, and the second ring turned white.

"What!" he said. "Has the second ring the same virtue as mine, then? And does mine only have that form by virtue of an enchantment?

By virtue of a chain of reasoning be came to be so curious to penetrate that mystery that, seizing his little bell, he wished that the ring would resume its previous form. Then he saw two rings on his finger, one of coral, which had turned red again, while the other was formed from a wisp of straw.

André was sorry that he had been unable to repress his curiosity. He only had one wish to formulate now, and he remembered that he had already lost Marie once in that way. He threw the straw ring in the fire and had a suspicion that Sha-ha-ba-am had stolen the veritable coral ring from him and put another in its place? But with what intention? He could not think of a single reason that was not absurd.

A few days later, as André was at some theater or other, he suddenly cried: "Oh my God!" His neighbors turned round and imposed silence on him with multiple *Ssshes*. André had just recognized Sha-ha-ba-am on the stage. He waited for the intermission and had himself taken to the dressing room where the actor was changing his costume.

"My dear friend," he said, when he went in, "it seems to me that you ought to have quit me a little more politely, and at least bid me adieu."

"Pardon me, Monsieur..."

"You have no need of my pardon. I know that people of your profession always regret the theater and end up by returning to the stage sooner or later, but at least you could have spared me anxiety and told me you were going."

"But Monsieur," said the actor, "there has been some mistake. I don't recall ever have had the honor of seeing you before...although.... Oh, yes...it's you...it was you who tried to strangle me in the wings of the theater in Le Havre."

"Yes, and it's me who invited you to supper the same evening after the performance, told you my story and brought you to Paris, where, without reproach, I believe I have procured you a rather agreeable existence for a month."

"I assure you, Monsieur, that since the day you tried to strange me with regard to some fish or other..."

"A goldfish."

"Yes, a goldfish...well, since that time I've never encountered you, and I won't hide it from you that our first relations didn't inspire me with the desire to do so."

"Come on, my dear friend; if you didn't want to see me anymore, you were free to do so, but stop mocking me or I'll get annoyed..."

"What! Are you going to strangle me again, Monsieur?"

"No, but I ought not to expect a similar action on your part."

The actor summoned a few of his comrades, who all affirmed to André that he had only been in Paris for three days. They showed André the timetable of the diligence he had taken.

"Well, Messieurs," said André, "if you would like, after the performance, to give me the pleasure of all coming to supper with me, you'll see that I'm not as mad as you seem to suppose, and in order for you not to think that I've given orders to the people at my inn, I'll only go back with you."

André's invitation was accepted with all the more enthusiasm by the actors because they were counting on amusing themselves at André's expense, but it was their turn to be astonished. In fact, as soon as the innkeeper perceived the actor, he said: "Ah, you've been found, Monsieur Runaway. You've given us a great deal of anxiety. Personally, I thought you'd gone forever, for you left almost intact a bottle of the Beaune that you love so much."

"Truly, my friend," said the actor, "you recognize me?"

"Do I recognize you? In the week since you've been gone, you haven't changed enough for me not to recognize you."

All the inn servants recognized Sha-ha-ba-am; the waiter who served at table put before him an opened bottle of Beaune and a napkin rolled up in a metal ring. André, who no longer knew what to think, nevertheless had the bottle changed, and especially the napkin.

After supper, the actor tried on the forgotten waistcoat; it fitted him so perfectly that he forgot to take it off and kept it. It was necessary to end up attributing the thing to one of those extraordinary resemblances, or one of the powers of transformation that certain actors possess—such as Garrick, for example, who once posed for a portrait of one of his friends, which was very accurate.

We can, however, explain to our readers what seemed, with reason, so inexplicable to André and his friends.

The Sha-ha-ba-am with whom André had supped and come to Paris was none other than the fay Langouste, who, profiting from the month that she had to spend in another form than her own, had assumed that of the actor in order to link herself with André and disrupt his plans. In fact, under that form and giving the appearance of directing him in his journeys and his plans, Langouste, who knew perfectly well where Marie was, had always led him as far away from her as possible; furthermore, she had stolen the coral ring that was to serve him to recognize metamorphoses and had replaced it with the straw ring that she had enchanted. While André had had his ring in his possession Langouste had avoided giving him her hand, in spite of the familiarity that existed between them, because the ring would have turned white and would have warned André that Sha-ha-ba-am was not what he appeared to be. She had attempted by all means to lead André to her own desires, which could only be satisfied by means of the little bell, but André had always resisted.

When the month had expired, however, Langouste had been obliged to return to the empire of the seas and to resume her natural form. She had done that so precipitately that she had forgotten in a waistcoat the ring without which André's research would be futile. But what she had not forgotten was to steal his purse, the famous purse in which gold coins were always reborn as they were taken out.

It took André some time to perceive that misfortune because, precisely in fear of losing the purse, he did not carry it on his person, and because, since the departure of the actor, occasions for expenditure had diminished considerably; the five louis that he had had in his pocket on the eve of Sha-ha-ba-am's disappearance had sufficed for his unexpected expenses for a fortnight. After further unfruitful attempts, however, he decided to return to his parents and ask the innkeeper for his bill. It was only then that he found that he no longer had the purse.

The furious innkeeper wanted to take the golden bell from him, but André sold all his garments and only kept an extremely simple costume. He only had to shake the bell to have millions, but that was the sole means of rendering Marie her charming form if he were ever fortunate enough to find her.

André was strong and courageous, but he did not know any other métier than that of a fisherman; he obtained work as a furniture porter. In the beginning he went to bed without supper more than once, but it did not come to mind once to have recourse to his bell.

André had to suffer all ordeals; he fell ill. A water-carrier as poor as he was, who lodged in the same building, cared for him, with the aid of his wife, and saved him from death. André was without work for some time; the water-carrier and his wife shared the little they had with him, and he recovered fairly rapidly; but the water-carrier had a fall and was confined to bed in his turn. André took over his barrel and dragged it through the streets, going into the houses in order not to lose the water-carrier's customers.

Before having his own barrel, the water-carrier had only possessed two buckets, which it was necessary to return to the fountain to fill up every time the contents had been emptied. It was only after several years of labor that he had amassed sufficient savings for half the price of a barrel; he had borrowed money for the remainder. He had hoped to finish paying for the barrel after a year, and then he hoped to save enough to buy a donkey. It was only in the distant future, and after a good supper, that he glimpsed the possibility of one day having a bigger barrel and a horse.

In spite of André's aid. Pierre's illness had harmed his receipts; payment of the debt was about to fall due; Pierre could not pay. He was put in prison. This time, André picked up the bell momentarily, but he paused on thinking about the sad fate of Marie, the despair of Smaragdine, and also a little of himself, who had no other happiness than the hope of one day recovering his dear sister.

He set about working all day and half the night. On the produce of his labor he nourished Pierre's wife and child, and took him a little money so that he could obtain a few favors in prison. Every week he set aside what he had been able to save.

After six months, that sum had already accumulated considerably. André was exhausted, but he thought that in another two or three months he would have rendered liberty to the man who had saved his life.

One evening, however, when he wanted to add a silver coin to the little treasure, he asked Pierre's wife to bring it to him. A few moments later, she uttered a great scream and came back very pale; with haggard eyes she told him that the money was no longer there, that it had been stolen. André was unable to speak for some time; then, yielding to discouragement, he began to weep.

They were supposed to visit Pierre in the prison the next day; the wife told him that she would never dare tell him about the further misfortune, and André assumed the responsibility of telling him.

"Is it soon, then," Pierre asked, "that I shall be getting out of here? You've talked to me about two months, which is a long time, but if that were to be prolonged further I'd kill myself. I've had as much of prison as I can bear."

André went away without daring to tell him that everything had to be recommenced and that it would doubtless be necessary for Pierre to remain locked up for eight or ten months. He returned home and said to the wife: "I didn't dare; let's keep working, Pierre will be patient for another two months, between now and then the good God will doubtless take pity on us."

But those two months passed without anything new happening, except that he began to accumulate a little money again. Pierre counted the hours with so much impatience and so much joy that André could no longer stand it, and he returned to the house one day with a thousand francs.

"It's necessary not to say anything to Pierre," he recommended to the wife.

"But where did you get this money?" she asked.

"You'll know later."

The next day, Pierre was free. How beautiful everything seemed to him in his poor house! How good it was to sit on his chair! Two days later they went back to work. Sunday arrived; Pierre's wife put the cooking-pot on the fire; they wanted to celebrate Pierre's deliverance. But André, who had appeared sadder every day, was surprised by the wife with tears in his eyes.

"What's the matter, André?" she said. "You've contributed so much to our happiness, can't you share it with us?"

"Yes, of course," said André, "but I won't be having supper with you this evening."

"Would you like to shut up? I've bought two bottles of wine."

"All right... listen; I'll tell you the truth...but it's necessary that Pierre doesn't know. I'm a soldier; I've received my call-up papers. I have to be in Saint-Denis tomorrow, in order to be sent to my company."

"But how did you become a soldier, André?"

"I sold myself, my good Marguerite."

"Oh! I understand. Oh, my poor André! That, then, is the origin of the thousand francs. I have to tell Pierre."

"What would be the point? Pierre couldn't do anything about it anymore than you can; it would torment him; his head is a little weak since his imprisonment. It's better to say nothing. I'm young; seven years will soon pass; besides which, I have no detestation for the military profession—only I would have preferred not to sell myself; I'm afraid that my comrades won't esteem me."

"Tell them about your good deed, Andre, and they'll honor you."

"Listen Marguerite; in order that Pierre doesn't suspect anything, I'll sup with you this evening, and I'll leave tonight without saying anything. I'll arrive in Saint-Denis in time. Tomorrow, tell him that I've received a letter from my poor parents, and that I'll return soon. Later, he'll no longer think about it."

"Oh, no; later I'll tell him everything; isn't it necessary that he prays for you as well in the danger, and isn't it a happiness to have reasons for loving one's friends? I don't want to deprive him of that."

"Shh, Marguerite, here comes Pierre; it's necessary that we finish our day as usual."

Shortly afterwards, André and Pierre were dragging the barrel through the streets, shouting: "Water! Water!"

Sometimes André forgot to shout, for he was sad in spite of himself, and Pierre said to him, laughing: "You're saving your voice, André; you must have a fine song to sing to us this evening."

As they were passing along one street, a porter called out: "Hey, water-carriers, one of you take a pail up to the fifth floor, at the end of the corridor."

"I'll go," said André, who feared that Pierre might divine his preoccupation. He filled his two buckets and climbed the five flights of stairs.

There is certainly no canton in Switzerland that has as many inhabitants entitled to call themselves montagnards as Paris has; every house is, in fact a small mountain for those who live at the summit.

The summit of this particular mountain was occupied by two chalets—or apartments. One of them belonged to Émile Mennot; he was a poor devil of a musician, who did not know himself yet whether he had any talent, but he already made plenty of noise on his piano. He had not yet encountered the circumstance or the protection through which that noise had to pass in order to become music. No newspaper had yet called him an "immense pianist." He gave a few poor lessons for which he was paid poorly.

In winter be played a piece of his own composition in a few houses, which was applauded on condition that he played square dances for the rest of the night. He was not paid for that; people did not even seem to honor him for it, but apart from the fact that he only snapped up a few pieces of cake and glasses of punch here and there, which the servants allowed him to take after vigorous resistance, such opportunities were lacking during Lent. Then he put on a concert, a soirée, or a musical matinee, depending on the number of tickets he hoped to sell. The matinées economized on lighting. He sent twenty-five ten-franc tickets to the mistress of a house in which he had played dance music during the winter, begging them by means of an obsequious letter to accept one of the tickets and place the others for him. The mistress of the house sometimes took a dozen for the men of her society, saying that the musi-cian was a young man of great talent, in whom she was inter-ested, and who would not take long to be counted among the foremost masters of his art. That phrase was her entire contri-bution; she sent back the unsold tickets, with the result that everyone had paid for the music at her balls except her, and people had danced for free. The return of the concert consisted of the fact that he sometimes recruited one or two pupils to replace those he had lost. Then he could renew the black coat that he had only made to last through the winter with difficul-ty.

At the moment we find him he was furious; for two years he had given lessons to two children of the owner of the house in which he lived; those lessons paid the rent—the inexorable rent—and he was invited to his landlord's soirées. That day there was a big dinner; the preparations had occupied the en-tire house since the day before. He had perceived that while giving his lesson and waited for his invitation, which would be all the more welcome because his purse was completely empty for the moment, but he waited in vain; the lesson dragged on but the invitation did not come. He went out thinking that the proprietor, who lived directly below him, would come up in the morning in order to put more politeness into it, but the morning passed and nothing happened.

At four o'clock he went to ask whether he might have forgotten his wallet; he was told that no one had seen his wallet, but there was not a word about the dinner. He went back to his apartment, from which he could hear all the preparation and smell all the odors. The pastry-maker, who was bringing a fish torte and small hot pâtés, mistook the floor and knocked on his door. For a moment he had a desire to intercept them, but he thought that it might be necessary to pay for them. He heard all the guests ringing, one by one.

It's hard, he thought, *to have, in the fumes of that feast, the worst dinner I've ever had in my life, a hunk of bread and a little butter. But why the devil haven't I been invited? The skinflints! I presume that there won't be dancing and that some tragedy will be read. They're wrong...I listen to tragedies admirably. That accursed odor of truffled turkey is coming up through the fireplace. All the same, I have go set my table too.*

He took a hunk of bread, a knife and a little butter and began to eat at the window, in order to escape the provocative fumes. On the window-sill of the proprietor's apartment below there were two pots of flowers and a bowl containing four goldfish. Without really thinking about what he was doing, Émile Mennot made little pellets of breadcrumbs and tried to throw them into the bowl. One pellet ended up falling into it and was instantly swallowed by one of the fish.

I'm very good, he thought. *I'm feeding the fish of that frightful miser. All in all, I prefer giving my breadcrumbs to the sparrows. It seems that he doesn't feed his fish very well; they seem to be famished.* "Oh," he exclaimed, suddenly, "what's more, we're going to laugh at dinner. I have butter, I have a stove, look out!"

He put the butter back on the plate, assembled a few of the embers scattered in the hearth, set them on a poor earthenware stove, struck a match, ignited them by blowing on them, and then put his butter in the pan.

We'll put them on the fire later, he thought.

He opened a cupboard, took out a little pin-cushion that contained a needle and thread. He attached a bent pin to the end of the thread, the other end of which he attached to his cane. He hid the pin in a bread pellet and lowered the improvised fishing line into the proprietor's bowl.

The musician was not possessed by joy; his heat was scarcely beating. *It'll bite, it'll bite.* And, in fact, one of the fish had just seized the bread pellet, and, at the same time, the pin, which held it captive by the chin. Mennot pulled it out of the bowl and hoisted it all the way up to his room.

Stamping his feet with pleasure, he unhooked it and put it on a plate, where the fish did its best to dance a jig.

That's one, thought Mennot. He baited his hook again and recommenced fishing. A second fish followed the first, and a third followed the second.

I believe it's time to put my fry-up over the fire, the fisherman said to himself. In fact, he put his frying-pan over the fire and the butter in the frying-pan, and as the butter began to sing he thought: *Now the fourth, and the fry-up will be complete.*

At that moment, someone knocked on his door.

Oh my God, he thought. *Perhaps they've found that they're thirteen at table and have come to fetch me in order to ward off the ominous presage...*

But that hope was of short duration; it was André, who had brought up two pails of water in response to the porter's invitation.

"Come in!" shouted Mennot

"Monsieur," said André, "it's the water-carrier."

"What do I want with a water-carrier?"

"The porter told me to bring a pail up to the fifth floor."

"I didn't ask him for any; it must have been my neighbor, at the end of the corridor."

"I knocked and there was no reply."

"That's because she's gone out."

"So I have to take my water all the way downstairs again, then?"

"That wouldn't be amusing. Look to see if there's room in my bucket."

And as André was about to lift the lid of the bucket, Mennot gestured to him with his hand. "Shh! Don't move, It's biting."

"What's biting?"

As he asked that question, André approached, and saw with a frightful constriction of the heat three fish arranged on a plate; only one as still moving. He touched it with his ring, but the ring remained red.

"Ah!" said Mennot, in a triumphant tone. "Here it is!" And he tugged his line, from which the fourth fish was dangling; but it was struggling so much

That Mennot, who could not put his hand on it, shouted: "Hey, water-carrier, you grab it!"

André took the fish in his hand, but he went pale, and shoved Mennot away as he came to take it off him. He unhooked the fish delicately, and threw it into one of his pails, where it resumed swimming.

"Come on," said Mennot, "no playing around—my fry-up is going to burn."

But André, breathless with shock, could not speak, and contented himself with pushing the musician away when he tried to recapture the fish. After a few moments, however, he recovered his self-possession and, taking out his little golden bell, he shook it, saying: "I want Marie to resume the form in which I knew and loved her."

At that moment the pail was tipped over and a charming young woman appeared in the middle of the room. It was her; it was Marie! Mennot had gone as pale as André.

André was at Marie's knees, kissing her hands. As if she were emerging from a long sleep, Marie looked around; then she recognized André, uttered a loud cry and threw herself into his arms.

At that moment, someone knocked on the door. It was Pierre, who, anxious at not having seen André return, for whom he had been waiting in the street for a quarter of an hour, had eventually come upstairs. He remained in the doorway, stupefied.

André wiped away a little blood from the wound that the hook had inflicted on Marie's lip; he was laughing and weeping.

Suddenly, he cried: "Oh! The mother! The mother!" He took the bell, the clapper of which had disappeared, and threw it out of the window, saying: "To Smaragdine!"

"Say, André," said Pierre. "I beg this lady and this monsieur to excuse us, but it's getting late and we're expected for supper."

At that moment a beautiful white and gray bird flew in through the musician's window, which was still open; it was a seagull, and André exclaimed: "Smaragdine!"

She was holding in her beak the purse that Langouste had stolen from André; she deposited it in his hands, and then perched on Marie, to whom she gave a thousand caresses.

"Marie," said Andre, "look after that beautiful bird carefully; you shall soon know how dear it ought to be to you; only know that it's to her that you owe no longer being a goldfish—or rather, not being on monsieur's stove."

"Oh my God," said Mennot. "What about my fry-up? It's ruined!"

"And our supper," said Pierre.

"Leave your fry-up and your supper," said André. "I'll take charge of supper. I've become rich and happy again," he added, looking at Marie. "Let's go find your wife and child. We're going to have a terrific supper. You, Monsieur Musician, are a worthy fellow; you can buy a pail of water from me so that I don't have to take it downstairs again. But what shall we do with my other pail of water?"

"What shall we do with it?" said the musician. "We'll water my landlord's two geraniums, and he can throw the buckets out of the window below."

They went down to the street and hailed a passing cab. A water-carrier was also going past with two buckets.

"Hey, friend," said André, "would you like a small barrel? This one is yours." And he gave him the stupefied Pierre's barrel, to whom he said: "Didn't I tell you that I'm rich. Do you want to humiliate me by remaining a water-carrier? Did you want to deprive me of the joy of sharing with you in my turn?"

They went to fetch Madame Pierre, and then had a terrific supper, as André had announced. André then told his story; then he drew from his five-louis purse for a quarter of an hour and gave the musician what he took out of it—which is to say, nearly a hundred thousand francs.

Then he said to Pierre and his wife: "Would you like some money?"

"No," said Pierre, "since you have some."

"That's true. Would you like to come with me?"

"Where are you going?"

"It's the seagull that will guide us."

They sat adieu to the musician, and then departed in a carriage harnessed to five horses. The postillions, paid a louis per rein, went like the wind. Marie held the seagull in her arms, against her bosom. The seagull pecked Marie incessantly. When they approached the house of André's parents, the gull escaped, plunged into the sea and disappeared.

André learned then that his parents had left the country two days before.

A richly-flagged boat was floating on the sea; the seagull was flapping its wings at the top of the mast. André had his companions climb into it. The gull then took flight, but gently, in order to indicate the route.

André, who had not forgotten his old métier, steered the boat skillfully; it went much faster than his old boat had ever gone.

Eventually, it landed on the most cheerful island that can be imagined; it was covered with citrus trees in flower; the most beautiful birds made delightful songs heard there. Two old people were waiting on the beach for the new arrivals; they were André's father and mother. I need not tell you how joyful they were to see André and Marie. When they knew what Pierre, his wife and child had done for André, they became old friends from the very start.

The island was an enchanting abode. Smaragdine, who had obtained permission from the council of fays to show herself in her natural form again, appeared, resplendent with beauty; she announced that the island was Marie's dowry, and a day was fixed for the wedding.

The desired day finally arrived. There was no one at the dinner but the parents, the couple, Pierre, his wife and child, but nothing was lacking at the feast—not even Langouste, who figured therein as a main dish and was eaten with mayonnaise.

In the bosom of their families and amid their friends, André and Marie lived happily for a long time, and did not have too many children.

Charles Deslys[21]: *The Fays' Place*

(La Sylphide, 10 February 1853)

In one of the densest parts of the great woods of Meaux
there is a round clearing carpeted elegantly by the green velvet
of wild moss, which is covered, even at midday, by the silent
shadow of the branches of gigantic oak trees. It is the favorite
rendezvous of all the surrounding threads of floating spider-
silk. Either by a caprice of nature or the will of the nocturnal
breezes, all those frail cotton-reels that spring takes pleasure in
spreading over the meadows, all those floating webs that April
suspends and balances from the stems of flowering furze, all
those light tangles that the sunlight catches in the evening,
flutter momentarily in the darkening air, assembling like swal-
lows in autumn, navigate toward the forest like a fleet of white
sails returning to port, engage melancholically in long pathways already pitch-dark, and finally come together in the fresh
oasis of verdure that we have just described, and there go gently to hook on to the branches, like thousands of frail ham-
mocks suspended in order to rock pale rays of moonlight silently.

Once, the mysterious retreat was known throughout the
region as the Rabbits' Place. This is why:

On the sandy border of the vast basket of foliage, a quantity of little yellow mouths gape. It is an archipelago of bur-
rows, a camp of long-ears, a hive of white-tails.

What is more, by virtue of a particularity that seems prodigious, that entire congregation of rabbits is reputed, for ten

---

[21] Charles Deslys (1821-1885) worked in the theater as an
actor and singer before turning to the writing of popular fiction and plays in the late 1840s.

leagues around, to be invulnerable, both to the hunter's lead and to the poacher's snares.

In the surrounding area, game-bags can be filled freely, but once within the protective boundary, the munchers of wild thyme appear to have reached the magical threshold of a kind of sanctuary, where their tribute enjoys the privilege of immortality. It is in vain that the Nimrods of the region burn their gunpowder and in vain that the filthy poachers spread their brass wire around; not a single rabbit will fall and not a single rabbit will be caught. People go as far as to claim that they have sometimes been seen sniggering; a few even affirm that they have seen them squatting brazenly on their hindquarters and permitting themselves, with their forepaws, the mocking flicks of the nose at which the gamins of the Parisian faubourgs excel.

Thus, throughout the edge of the forest, the unbreakable opinion of village savants has no hesitation in guaranteeing that the Rabbits' Place is inhabited by four-footed farfadets, or even fays lurking under grey skins.

Those fays and farfadets resume their veritable forms at midnight and deliver themselves to strange frolics in the moonlight, under the great oaks. That, at least is what was said in the Gibelotte Couronnée tavern on the night of the fête of Germiny-l'Evêque.

"You're making fun of everyone!" cried Jean Gaillard, the most famous poacher of Armentières, suddenly, as he popped the cork of his third bottle of fine sparkling wine.

"Go and see, if you're so clever!" replied the fiddler, who was slaking his thirst between two square dances at the next table.

"It would be necessary to challenge me! said Jean Gaillard, wiping his lips with the back of his hand.

"You'd dare to do it?" said the whole population if the tavern, incredulously.

"Do you want to bet?" proposed the poached, boldly.
"What?"

"That tomorrow, at eight o'clock, I'll bring back here a dozen rabbits from the Place of the Fays."

"Get away!"

"Half of them alive and seized by the neck, the other half killed by this rifle."

"Impossible!"

"Well, then, let's bet a dozen bottles, one per rabbit. Do you want to?"

"Right! It's on!"

With that Jean Gaillard, finished off his fourth bottle in a single draught, filled his brandy-bottle, borrowed snares from the innkeeper, passed his game-bag over his left shoulder, put his rifle over his right shoulder, bid adieu to the drinkers, left the village in fête, and took the path to the forest ostentatiously.

The month of April was about to end and the earth was amorous. The perfumed breath of spring flowers was rising like a cloud of incense toward the sky, from which the dew was descending like diamond snow through the night. A thousand harmonious crepitations were running through the grass, a thousand crazy murmurs fluttering in the air, The moon was inundating the horizon with its palest light, and all along the long silver ribbon that the Marne unrolled through the meadows nothing could be hear but the soft plaint of the blue waves and the sprightly song of reeds disturbed by the breeze.

The poacher soon quit the river, strode across the plain and lost himself in the forest, where everything was silent except for the echoes half-awakened by the distant fanfare of the band at the fête.

A few minutes more, and he reached the Rabbits' Place.

Then Jean Gaillard lay face down and crawled slowly through the undergrowth as far as the aforementioned great nest of moss.

It was something admirable at that moment; myriads of threads of spider-silk intersected and enlaced, balanced atop one another, forming an immense net of white cashmere, between the mesh of which appeared, like a marvelous illumination, the incessant fireworks rained down by the moon through the black foliage.

Far from looking up, however, the hunter gazed, at ground level, at a spectacle far more attractive to him than the fêtes of nature.

The entire tribe of privileged rabbits was outside, frolicking in the moss: grazing, trotting, leaping, gamboling and skipping. Some of them were sitting, standing, lying on their backs or curled up, in all possible melancholy attitudes and all clownish postures. There were rides, battles, gallantries, capers, tussles, concerts and conversations to render Decamps infidel to monkeys:[22] in sum, a true recreation of long-ears, a bewildering ballet of white-tails.

"What luck!" murmured Jean Gaillard, avidly. "I could have wagered for a hundred. But let's not lose our head by wanting to hurry the miraculous catch too much. Let's lay the snares first…afterwards, the rifle!

What was said was done—and briskly, I can assure you. The poacher extended his traps with so little noise that the entire band continued its frolics in the dew, and not a single rabbit suspected the peril, except for the occasional experienced bald-ear who reared up here or there, or an old doe with a tailed whiter than the others, who suddenly shook herself like an alarm bell.

Satisfied with his work, therefore, Jean Gaillard retreated a few paces and extended himself nonchalantly under a bush, thinking: "Let's wait!"

In the meantime, he emptied the brandy bottle, sip by sip.

Then, something extraordinary began to happen within him. His limbs grew heavy, his ideas became confused; he

---

[22] The painter Alexander-Gabriel Decamps (1803-1860) was the founder of an "orientalist school" of French painting; he was very fond of painting monkeys, and his most famous canvas, *The Connoisseur Monkeys*, satirized the jurors of the Académie who had refused his works for the annual Salon.

saw everything in the surroundings change and spin as in the fantastic dream of a bad night.

And it was even worse a moment later.

Suddenly, a noisy fanfare of joyous voices resounded in the forest, and the branches parted in all directions around the Rabbits' Place, which immediately disappeared as if by enchantment—or rather, its residents were transformed into as many young women crowned with flowers, white nocturnal fays, who, laughing madly, started to run, dance and play in that spring palace, neither more nor less than their gray-robed predecessors.

Some leaned over to pick up little balls of coral and little amethyst bells from the moss; others lunched themselves into the branches and seemed to balance on the threads of spider-silk; sometimes they all joined hands in order to perform a rapid farandole, in which floating girdles and loosened tresses whirled simultaneously.

Jean Gaillard kept quiet, scarcely daring to breathe. At one moment, he thought that the fays had perceived him and were fluttering toward his bush with grimaces and bursts of laughter. Then he felt himself tremble all the way to the roots of his hair, and he swiftly lowered his eyelids.

However, curiosity is almost as powerful as fear, and the poacher soon reopened one eye.

The fays were flying away, throwing handful of spring flowers at one another.

A few seconds later, the sound of their hectic course was lost in the wood, and then the dying fanfare of their bursts of laughter and the distant murmur of their joyful sings—and that was all.

As they drew away, long ears seemed to emerge from the earth again, and then white tails; and finally, messieurs the rabbits recovered possession of their green empire.

At the same time, the black foliage turned red, and little birds chirruped the reveille in the scarcely-finished nests of their new amours.

"Look out!" Jean Gaillard said to himself, "Look out! Here comes the daylight!"

And he tried to get up.

But he slipped on the moss and found himself trapped by an unfamiliar multitude of little light creepers. They were the threads of spider-silk that, miraculously, had all gathered around his body to envelop him from head to foot.

"Damn!" he said, amazed. "Madame la Vierge is trying to catch me in her nets!"[23]

Already, though, a few rabbits had already regained their subterranean villas, and the poacher raised his rifle.

He pulled the trigger twice. Nothing! He tried for a second time. Nothing again! He tried to fire the weapon for a third time. Still nothing!

Of course, not a single rabbit still remained outside the warren.

The furious poacher tried incontinently to discover the cause of such a fatal event, and raised the hammer of his rifle again. The pan was full of a kind of scarlet jam.

Stupefied by such a primer, he let the butt of the gun fall on to the ground and dug his finger into the barrel. The barrel was full of the same marmalade, all the way to the mouth.

He tasted his finger and immediately cried: "What a charge! Who has taken it into his head to stuff my rifle with strawberries?"

He could not help laughing, for he had not yet lost his last hope. Fortunately, he thought, after a moment, he still had the snares, and it would truly be too much bad luck if he did not find his the rabbits therein.

All the snares had been tightened.

"Good!"

And in each of them he found...a little bunch of violets!

---

[23] The popular French term for floating threads of spider-silk is *fils de Vierge* [Virgin's hair].

That was too much, and Master Gaillard came back with his head down and his game-bag empty, through the dew empearled by the rising sun.

He was obliged to pay for the dozen bottles, and to confess that the old folk of Germigny-l'Évêque might have been right about the fays and the rabbits,

Even so, there are now young skeptics in the villages, and one of them claimed that the freshness of the night, especially combined with the warmth of the brandy, might well have finished rendering the poacher intoxicated, and that one has strange dreams when drunk.

Then, the next day, it was learned that the young women of Armentieres had traversed the forest when returning from the fête, and in their joyful flight they had picked strawberries and violets. One of them, in fact—the daintiest and most mischievous, Jean Gaillard's own fiancée—whispered in his ear a few days later: "That's what happens to ungallant fellows who stay in the tavern all night during an April ball."

In sum, you can believe it or not, as you wish. All that I can affirm personally is that the peasants in the vicinity of Meaux scrupulously avoid passing through the forest at midnight, and that, from Armentières to Germigny and from Varedde to Fublaine, the Rabbits' Place is now known as the Fays' Place,

Émile Zola: *The Fay Amoureuse*

(Contes à Ninon, 1864)[24]

Can you hear the December rain beating our windows, Ninon? The wind is moaning in the long corridor. It's a wretched evening, one of those evenings when the poor shiver at the doors of the rich, whom balls draw into their dances under gilded chandeliers. Leave your satin shoes there and come and sit on my knee, next to the blazing hearth, Leave your rich adornment there; this evening I want to tell you a tale, a beautiful tale of enchantment.

You should know, Ninon, that there was once a somber and lugubrious castle on the top of a mountain. It was nothing but towers, ramparts and drawbridges laden with chains; men clad in iron watched over the battlements night and day, and only soldiers found a good welcome with Comte Enguerrand, the lord of the manor.

If you had seen him, the old warrior, walking in the long galleries, if you had heard the outbursts of his curt and menac-

---

[24] The *Contes à Ninon* were written by Émile Zola (1840-1902) in his youth; they were not, in fact, written for an actual child but with a view to publication by his first employer, the bookseller Louis Hachette, who had taken responsibility for the reprinting of the *Nouveau magasin des enfants* when Hetzel returned from exile and had issued the Comtesse de Ségur's *Nouveaux contes de fées* (1857), whose subsequent works proved so popular that he founded the long-enduring Bibliothèque rose in 1860 to issue them. The *Nouveaux contes à Ninon* that Zola published in 1874 follow a markedly different narrative strategy, moving away from the *fantastique*—in which he was following the example of the Comtesse de Ségur.

ing voice, you would have trembled in fear, exactly as his niece Odette, a pious and pretty demoiselle, trembled. Have you ever noticed, in the morning, a daisy opening to the first kisses of the sun amid nettles and brambles? Thus blossomed the young woman among the rude knights. As a child, in the middle of her games, when she had perceived her uncle, she stopped and her eyes swelled with tears. Now, grown up and beautiful, her bosom filled with vague sighs, and a fear that was even more bitter seized her every time that Seigneur Enguerrand appeared.

She lived in a remote tower, occupied in embroidering beautiful banners, setting down that work when praying to God, and contemplating from her window the emerald countryside and the azure sky. Often, at night, getting up from her bed, she had come to gaze at the stars, and there, many a time, her sixteen-year-old heart had launched forth toward celestial space, asking those radiant sisters what could be agitating her thus. After those sleepless nights and those amorous impulses, she had a desire to suspend herself around the neck of the old knight, but a rude word or a cold gaze stopped her, and she picked up her needle, trembling. You should feel sorry for the poor girl, Ninon; she was like a fresh and scented flower whose brightness and perfume are disdained.

One day, the desolate Odette was dreaming as her eyes followed two turtle-doves that were flying away, when she heard a soft voice at the foot of the castle. She leaned over and saw a handsome young man, who was asking for hospitality, with a song on his lips. She listened; she did not understand the words, but the sweet voice oppressed her heart; tears ran slowly down her cheeks, moistening a sprig of marjoram that she was holding in her hand.

The castle remained closed; a man-at-arms shouted from the walls: "Go away; only warriors are at home here."

Odette was still watching. She dropped the marjoram stem, warm with tears, which fell at the singer's feet. Raising his eyes, the latter saw the blonde head, kissed the branch and drew away, turning around repeatedly.

When he had disappeared, Odette knelt down on her prie-dieu and she said a long prayer. She thanked Heaven, without knowing why; she felt happy, while remaining ignorant of the subject of her joy.

That night, she had a beautiful dream. She seemed to see the sprig of marjoram that she had thrown away. Slowly, from the bosom of the quivering leaves, a fay emerged—such a dainty fay, with wings of flame, a crown of forget-me-nots and a long green robe, the color of hope.

"Odette," she said, harmoniously, "I am the fay Amoureuse. It was me who sent Lois, the young man with the sweet voice, to you this morning; seeing your tears, I wanted to dry them up. I travel the world gleaning hearts and bringing those who sigh closer together. I visit cottages as well as manors, it pleases me more frequently to unite the crooks of shepherds than the scepters of kings. I sow flowers beneath the feet of my protégés, I enchain them with threads so brilliant and so precious that their hearts quiver with joy. I live in the plants of pathways, the sparkling logs of winter fires and the curtains of marital beds; and everywhere that my feet are placed, kisses and tender conversation are born. Weep no more, Odette; I am Amoureuse, the good fay, and I have come to dry your tears."

And she went back into her flower, which folded up its foliage and became a bud again.

You know very well, Ninon, that the fay Amoureuse exists. Look at her dancing in our hearth, and pity the poor folk who don't believe in my beautiful fay.

When Odette woke up, a ray of sunlight was illuminating her room, birdsong was rising outside, and the morning breeze caressed her blonde tresses, perfumed by the first kiss that it had just given the flowers. She got up joyfully and spent the day singing, hopeful because of what the good fay had said to her. At intervals she looked at the countryside, smiling at each bird that passed by, sensing surges of enthusiasm within herself that made her jump and clap her little hands.

Evening came and she went down into the great hall of the castle. Next to Comte Enguerrand was a knight who was listening to the old man's stories. She took her distaff, sat down beside the hearth, where a cricket was singing, and the ivory spindle turned rapidly between her fingers.

While hard at work, having cast her eyes upon the knight, she saw the sprig of marjoram in his hand, and she recognized Lois of the sweet voice. A cry of joy almost escaped her. To hide her blush she leaned toward the ashes, stirring the logs with a long iron rod. The fire crackled, the flames were alarmed, noisy sparks sprang forth and suddenly, in their midst, Amoureuse emerged, smiling and urgent. She shook from her green robe the fiery particles that were running over the silk, like golden spangles; she leapt into the room, invisible to the comte, and came to place herself behind the young couple. There, while the old knight related a terrible battle against the Infidels, she said to them softly:

"Love one another, my children. Leave memories to austere old age, leave long stories next to the ardent firebrands. Let the crackling of the flames mingle with the noise of your kisses. There will be time later to soften your chagrins by recalling these pleasant hours. When one loves at sixteen the voice is unnecessary; a single glance says more than a long speech. Love one another, my children; let old age talk."

Then she covered them with her wings, so well that the comte, who was explaining how the giant Buch Tête-de-fer was slain with a terrible thrust by Giralda of the heavy sword, did not see Lois depositing his first kiss on the forehead of the quivering Odette.

It's necessary, Ninon, that I talk to you about the beautiful wings of the fay Amoureuse. They were as transparent as glass and as delicate as a fly's wing; but when the two lovers found themselves in danger of being seen, they grew and grew, and became so dark and so thick that they stopped gazes and stifled the sound of kisses. So the old man continued his prodigious story for a long time, and for a long time Lois caressed the blonde Odette, unknown to the malevolent suzerain.

My God, what beautiful wings they were! Young girls, I'm told, sometimes rediscover them; more than one knows

109

how to hide herself thus from the eyes of old parents. Is that true, Ninon?

When the comte had finished his long story, the fay Amoureuse disappeared into the flame and Lois left, thanking his host and blowing one last kiss to Odette. The young girl slept so happily that night that she dreamed about flowery mountains illuminated by thousands of stars, each one a thousand times brighter than the sun.

The next day, she went down into the garden, seeking dark alleyways. She encountered a warrior, saluted him, and was about to draw away when she saw in his hand the sprig of marjoram bathed with tears. Again she recognized Lois of the sweet voice, who was about to enter the castle again in his new disguise. He sat her down on a grassy bank next to a spring. They gazed at one another, delighted to see one another in broad daylight. Warblers were singing, and one sensed in the air that the good fay was prowling around. I will not tell you everything that the discreet old oaks heard; it was a pleasure to see the lovers chatting for such a long time—so long that a warbler that was in a nearby bush had time to build a nest.

Suddenly, the heavy footsteps of Comte Enguerrand became audible in the pathway. The two poor lovers trembled; but the water of the spring sang more softly, and the fay Amoureuse emerged, laughing and urgent, from the clear water. She surrounded the lovers with her wings, and then glided lightly with them, going past the comte, who was astonished to have heard voices without seeing anyone.

She cradled her protégés as she went, repeating in a whisper:

"I am the one who protects amours, the one who closes the eyes and ears of people who no longer love. Have no fear, beautiful lovers, love one another in the bright daylight, in the pathways, near the water of springs, wherever you are. God has put me down here in order that men, those mockers of all sanctity, never come to trouble your pure emotions. He has given me my beautiful wings and said to me: 'Go, and may young hearts rejoice.' Love one another; I am here and I am watching over you."

And she went away, plundering the dew that was her only nourishment and drawing Odette and Lois, who were holding hands, into a joyful round.

You might ask me what she did with the two lovers. Truly, my friend, I dare not tell you. I'm afraid that you would refuse to believe me, or that, jealous of their good fortune, you would no longer return my kisses. But you're very curious, naughty girl, and I can see that it's necessary to satisfy you.

Now, learn that the fay prowled around all night. When she wanted to separate the lovers she saw that they were so sorry to quit one another that she began whispering to them. It appears that she said something very beautiful to them, for their faces became radiant and their eyes widened with joy. And when she had spoken and they had consented, she touched their foreheads with her wand.

Suddenly... Oh, Ninon, how your eyes are widened by astonishment! How you'd stamp your foot if didn't finish!

Suddenly, Lois and Odette were changed into sprigs of marjoram, but marjoram so beautiful that only a fay could make one similar. They found themselves placed side by side, so close to one another that their leaves mingled. They were marvelous flowers that were to remain in bloom, eternally exchanging their perfume and their dew.

As for Comte Enguerrand, he consoled himself, it's said, by relating every evening how the giant Buch Tête-de-fer was slain by a terrible thrust of Giralda's heavy sword.

And now, Ninon, when we go into the country, we'll search for enchanted marjorams in order to ask them in which flower the fay Amoureuse can be found, Perhaps, my friend, a moral is hidden in this tale, but I have only told it to you, with our feet before the fire, in order to make you forget the December rain that is battering our windows, and to inspire in you this evening, a little more love for the young storyteller.

George Sand: *The Dust Fay*

(Contes d'une grand'mère, vol, 2, 1875)

Once, a long time ago,[25] my dear children, I was young
and I often heard people complaining about a little old lady
who came in through the windows when she had been expelled through the doors. She was so delicate and thin that one
might have thought that she floated instead of walking, and
my parents compared her to a little fay. The domestics detested her, and sent her away with thrusts of a feather duster, but
she was no sooner dislodged from one place than she reappeared in another.

She always wore a wretched, trailing gray dress and a
sort of pale veil that the slightest wind caused to fly around
her head, tousled with yellow wisps of hair.

By virtue of being persecuted, she made me feel sorry for
her, and I let her repose in my garden, even though she did a
great deal of damage to my flowers. I talked to her, but without being able to get a word of common sense out of her. She
wanted to touch everything, saying that she never did anything
but good. I was reproached for tolerating her, and when I had
let her near me, I was sent to wash and change, by threatening
me with the name that she bore.

---

[25] George Sand (1804-1876) was, indeed, a grandmother when
she began to write stories for children for Hetzel in 1851, rep-
resenting it as an apologetic endeavor motivated by the fact
that she had been such a terrible mother. Although critics
sometimes link the present story with Charles Nodier's hallucinatory fantasy *La Fée aux miettes* (1832; tr. as "The Crumb
Fairy") it probably owed more to John Ruskin's didactic account of *The Ethics of the Dust* (1866).

It was a vile name that I feared greatly. She was so dirty that people claimed that she slept in the sweepings of houses and the streets, and because of that they called her the dust fay.

"Why are you so dusty, then?" I asked her, one day when she tried to embrace me.

"You're silly to fear me," she replied then, in a mocking tone. "You belong to me, and you resemble me more than you think. But you're a child, a slave of ignorance, and I'd be wasting my time demonstrating it to you."

"Come on," I said, "you seem to be talking reasonably for the first time. Explain what you mean."

"I can't talk here," she replied. "I have too much to tell you, and as soon as I'm installed somewhere in your home, I'm swept away scornfully. But if you want to know who I am, call me three times tonight, as soon as you go to sleep."

With that, she went away, utterly a loud burst of laughter, and I seemed to see her dissolve and rise up in a great golden trail, reddened by the setting sun.

That same evening, I was in bed and I began to think about her as I began to doze off.

"I've dreamed all that," I said to myself, "or else that little old lady is a true madwoman. How is it possible for me to call her in my sleep?"

I went to sleep, and immediately I dreamed that I called her. I'm not even sure that I didn't shout aloud three times: "Dust fay! Dust fay! Dust fay!"

At the same moment I was transported into an immense garden, in the middle of which stood an enchanted palace, and on the threshold of that marvelous dwelling, a lady resplendent with youth and beauty was waiting for me, in magnificent festival clothes.

I ran to her, and she embraced me, saying: "Well, do you recognize the dust fay now?"

"No, not at all, Madame," I replied, "and I think you're making fun of me."

"I don't make fun," she said, "but as you can't understand what I say, I'll enable you to see a spectacle that will seem strange to you, and which I'll also render as brief as possible. Follow me."

She took me into the most beautiful part of her residence. It was a small limpid lake that resembled a green diamond mounted in a ring of flowers, where fish of all the shades of orange and cornelian were playing, and Chinese carp the color of amber, black and white swans, exotic teal clad in gems, and, in the depths of the water there were nacreous and crimson shells, and brightly colored salamanders with jagged crests—in sum, an entire world of living marvels gliding and diving over a bed of silver sand, where fine plants grew, each prettier and more flowery than the next. Around that vast basin ran several rows of a colonnade of porphyry with capitals of alabaster. The entablature, made of the most precious minerals, almost disappeared beneath clematis, jasmine, wisteria, bryony and honeysuckle, in which a thousand birds made their nests. Bushes of roses of all colors and all perfumes were reflected in the water, as well as the shafts of columns and beautiful statues of Paros marble placed under the arcades. In the middle of the basin rose the diamonds and pearls of a jet of water that fell back into colossal nacre bowls.

The back of the architectural amphitheater opened over flower-beds shaded by giant trees crowned with flowers and fruits, the interlaced clustered branches of which formed, beyond the porphyry colonnade, a colonnade of verdure and flowers.

The fay made me sit down with her on the threshold of a grotto from which a melodious cascade sprang forth, which coated the beautiful ribbons of hart's-tongue and the velvet of fresh mosses with glittering drops of water.

"Everything you see here," she told me, "is my work. "All of this is made of dust; it's by shaking my dress in the clouds that I furnish all the materials of this paradise. My friend fire had launched them into the air, recaptured them to reheat, crystallize or agglomerate them after my servant the wind had taken them for a walk in the humidity and the electricity of the clouds, and dropped them on the earth; that great solidified plateau is dressed then with my fecund substance, and the rain is made of sand and fertilizer, after having been made of granite porphyry, marble, metals and rocks of every sort."

I listened without comprehending and thought that the fay was continuing to mystify me. What she had been able to do on the ground with the dust, I could accept, but that she had made it with marble, granite and other minerals, and had made it fall from the sky by shaking herself, I didn't believe. I dared not call her a liar but I turned toward her involuntarily to see whether she was saying such an absurd thing seriously.

Imagine my surprise no longer to find her behind me! But I could hear her voice, which was coming from underground and calling to me. At the same time, I plunged under the ground too, without being able to help it, and found myself in a terrible place where everything was fire and flame. People had talked to me about Hell; I thought that was it. Red, blue, green, white and violet gleams, sometimes livid and sometimes dazzling, replaced the daylight, and if the sunlight penetrated that place, the vapors exhaled from the furnace rendered it completely invisible.

Loud noises, shrill whistles, explosions and thunderclaps filed the cavern of black clouds where I felt imprisoned.

In the midst of all that, I perceived the little dust fay, who had resumed her earthy face and her sordid colorless garment. She came and went, toiling, pushing, heaping, brewing and pouring I know not what acids, delivering herself, in brief, to incomprehensible operations.

"Don't be afraid," she shouted to me, in a voice that dominated the deafening sounds of that Tartarus. "You're in my laboratory here. Don't you know chemistry?"

"I don't know a single word of it," I shouted, "and I have no desire to learn one in such a place."

"You wanted to know; it's necessary to resign yourself to looking. It's very comfortable to live on the surface of the earth, to live with the flowers, the birds and the domesticated animals, to bathe in tranquil waters, to eat flavorsome fruits and walk on carpets of grass and daisies. You imagined that human life had always subsisted thus, in benign conditions. It's time to tell you about the commencement of things and the power of the dust fay, your ancestor, your mother and your nurse."

As she said that, the little old woman made me fall with her into the utmost depths of the abyss, through devouring flames, frightful explosions, acrid black smoke, molten metals, and lava, the hideous vomit of all the terrors of volcanic eruption.

"These are my furnaces," she told me, "the subsoil in which my provisions are elaborated. You can see that it's pleasant here for a spirit rid of that carapace known as a body. You've left yours in your bed, and your spirit alone is with me. So, you can touch and embrace my primal matter. You don't know chemistry, you don't know yet what matter is made of, nor by what mysterious operation what appears here under the aspect of solid substances originated from a gaseous substance that was like a nebula in space, and later shone like a sun. You're a child, I can't initiate you into the great secrets of creation, and some time will pass yet before the professors know themselves, but I can show you the products of my culinary art. Everything here is a little confusing for you. Let's go back a step. Take the ladder and follow me."

A ladder, of which I could not perceive either the bottom or the top, did indeed appear before us. I followed the fay and found myself with her in the darkness, but I perceived then that she was luminous and as radiant as a torch. I was, therefore, able to see enormous deposits of a rosy paste, blocks of white crystal and immense sheets of a vitreous and shiny black substance, which the fay set about crushing between her fingers; then she pulverized the crystal into little pieces and mixed the whole with the pink paste, which she carried over what she was pleased to call a gentle fire.

"What dish are you making there?" I asked her.

"A dish very necessary to poor petty existence," she replied. "I'm making granite—which is to say that, with dust, I'm making the hardest and most resistant of stones. That's necessary to contain the Cocytus and the Phlegeton. I'm also making variant mixtures of the same element. This is one that has been manifest under barbaric names: gneiss, quartzite, talcschist, micaschist, etc. Out of all that, which comes from my dust, I shall later make other dusts with new elements, and they will then be slate, sand and sandstone. I'm skillful and patient; I pulverize incessantly in order to reagglomerate. Isn't flour the basis of every cake? For the present, I'm enclosing my ovens, while fitting them all with the ventilation shafts necessary so that they don't all explode. We'll go to see what's happening higher up. If you're tired you can have a nap, for this work takes me some time.

I lost the notion of time, and when the fay woke me up she said: "You've slept for a fair number of centuries!"

"How many, then, Madame Fay?"

"You can ask the professors that," she sniggered. "Let's take the ladder again."

She made me climb up several stages of various deposits, where I saw her manipulating metallic rusts, of which she made chalk, marl, clay, slate and jasper. I asked her about the origin of metals.

"You want to know a great deal," she said. "Your seekers can explain many phenomena by means of water and fire, but can they know what happened between earth and sky when all my pozzolanes launched by the wind of the abyss formed solid clouds, which the clouds of water rolled in their turbulent storms, when lightning penetrated their mysterious magnets and the superior winds sent them back to the surface in torrential rain? That's the origin of the first deposits. You're going to witness their marvelous transformations."

We climbed higher and we saw chalks, marbles and banks of calcareous stone, enough to build a city as big as the entire globe, and as I marveled at what could be produced by sifting, agglomeration, metamorphoses and cooking, she said:

"All this is nothing, and you'll see many other things. You're going to see life hatching in the midst of these stones."

She approached a basin as large as a sea and, plunging her arm into it, she first pulled out strange plants; then animals even stranger, which were still half-plant; then free individuals, separate from one another, living mollusks, and eventually fish, which she made to jump, saying: "That's what Dame Dust can produce when she deposits herself on the bed of the waters. But there's better—turn around and look at the shore."

I turned round; the chalk and all of its composites, mingled with silica and clay, had formed on their surface a fine brown greasy dust, in which singular hairy plants were growing.

"This is vegetal earth," said the fay. "Wait a little, and you'll see trees growing."

In fact, I saw an arborescent vegetation rise up rapidly and become populated by reptiles and insects, while unknown beings agitated on the shore that caused me a veritable terror.

"Those animals won't terrify you in the earth of the future," said the fay. "They're destined to fertilize it with their remains; there aren't any humans here yet to fear them."

"Wait!" I cried. "Here's a luxury of monsters that scandalizes me! Here's your earth, belonging to these voracious creatures that live on one another. Did you need all these massacres and all these stupidities to make us a compost heap? I understand that they weren't good for anything else, but I don't understand such an exuberant creation of animal forms, in order to do nothing and leave nothing worthwhile."

"Fertilizer is something, if it's not everything," the fay replied. "The conditions that will be created here will be appropriate to the different beings that will succeed them."

"And which will disappear in their turn, I know that. I know that creation will be improved all the way to humans—at least, that's what I've been told, and I believe it But I hadn't yet represented this prodigality of life and destruction, which frightens and repels me. These hideous forms, these gigantic amphibians, these monstrous crocodiles and all these crawling or swimming beasts only seem to live in order to make use of their teeth and devour one another."

My indignation amused the dust fay enormously.

"Matter is matter," she replied. "It is always logical in its operations. The human mind isn't, and you're proof of that, you who nourish charming birds and a host of creatures more beautiful and more intelligent than these. Is it for me to teach you that no production is possible without permanent destruction, and that you want to overturn the order of nature?"

"Yes, I'd like that, I'd like everything to have been good, from the first day,. If Nature is a great fay, she could well do without all these abominable trials and make a world in which we would be angels, living as spirits in the midst of an immutable and always beautiful creation."

"The great fay Nature has higher aims," replied Dame Dust. "She doesn't intend to stop at the things you know. She works and invents perpetually. For her, who knows no suspension of life, repose would be death. If things didn't change, the work of the king of the genii would be terminated, and that king, who is incessant and supreme activity, would finish along with his work. The world that you see and to which you will soon return when the vision of the past dissipates—that world of humans, which you believe to be better than that of the ancient animals, the world with which you are perhaps not satisfied, since you want to live eternally in the condition of a pure spirit—that poor planet, still in its infancy, is destined to be transformed indefinitely. The future will make of all of you, feeble human creatures, into fays and genii who possess science, reason and goodness. See what I am enabling you to see, and know that these first sketches of life, summarized in instinct, are closer to you than you are to what will one day be: the reign of the spirit over the earth that you inhabit. The occupants of that future world will then have the right to be as profoundly scornful of you as you are scornful today of the world of the great saurians."

"Good," I replied. "If everything I see of the past ought to make me love the future, let's continue to see new things."

"And above all," said the fay, "don't despise it too much, this past, in order not to commit the ingratitude of despising the present. When the great spirit of life makes use of the materials with which I furnish it, it makes marvels from the outset. Look at the eyes of that pretended monster your scientists have named ichthyosaurus."

"They're larger than my head, and they scare me."

"They're much superior to yours; they become myopic and presbyopic at will. They see prey at considerable distances, as if with a telescope, and when it is very close, by a simple change of function, they see perfectly at a veritable distance without any need for spectacles. At this moment of creation, Nature has but one goal: to make a thinking animal. It gives it s organs marvelous apparatus appropriate to its needs. That's a nice beginning; are you not impressed? It will be thus, and better and better, with all the beings that succeed this one. Those that appear to you to be poor, ugly or paltry are still prodigies of adaptation to the environments in which they need to be manifest."

"And like this one, they'll only think about nourishing themselves?"

"What do you want them to think about? The earth doesn't experience the need to be adored. The sky will subsist today and forever without the aspirations and prayers of creatures adding anything to its splendor and the majesty of its laws. The fay of this little planet knows the great cause, have no doubt of that, but if she is charged with making a being that senses or divines that cause, it is submissive to the law of time, that thing of which you cannot take account, because you live too briefly to appreciate its operations. You believe them to be slow, but they are of lightning rapidity. I shall free your mind from its infirmity and cause to pass before you the results of innumerable centuries. Look, and don't quibble any longer. Take advantage of my complaisance for you."

I sensed that the fay was right and I looked, with all my attention, at the succession of the aspects of the earth. I saw vegetables and animals live and die, more and more ingenious by instinct and more and more agreeable or imposing in form. And the soil was embellished with productions more closely resembling those of our days, the inhabitants of the great garden, which great accidents transformed incessantly, appeared to me to be less avid for themselves and more careful of their progeniture. I saw them construct dwellings for the use of their offspring and show attachment for their locale, to such an extent that, from one moment to the next, I saw one world vanishing and a new world surging forth, like the actions of an enchantment.

"Rest," the fay said to me, "for you've just traveled many thousands of centuries would suspecting it, and Monsieur Human is about to be born in his turn, when the reign of Monsieur Ape comes to an end."

I went back to sleep, overwhelmed by fatigue, and when I woke up, I found myself in the middle of a large ball in the fay's palace. She had become young, beautiful and adorned again.

"You see all these beautiful things and all this beautiful society," she said to me. "Well, my child, all that is dust. These walls of porphyry and marble are the dust of molecules kneaded and cooked to perfection. These chandeliers and crystals are fine sand cooked by human hands in imitation of the work of nature. All that porcelain and faience is the dust of feldspar and kaolin, of which the Chinese have allowed us to discover the employment. Those diamonds decorating the dancers are crystallized carbon dust. Those pearls are calcium phosphate that an oyster sweats in its shell. Gold and all other metals have no other origin than the assemblage, well-heaped, well-manipulated, well-melted, well-heated and well-cooled, of infinitesimal molecules. Those beautiful vegetables, those flesh-colored roses, spotted lilies and gardenias that embalm the atmosphere, are born of the dust that I prepared for them, and those people dancing and smiling at the sound of instruments, those living beings *par excellence* that are called persons, meaning no offense, are also born of me and will return to me.

As she said that, the fay and the palace disappeared.

Then I found myself with the fay in a field where wheat was growing. She bent down and picked up a stone, in which a shell was incrusted.

"There," she said to me, "in the fossil state, is a being that I showed you alive in the first ages of life. What is it now? Calcium phosphate. People reduce it to dust and make fertilizer for land that is too silicious. You see, humans are beginning to advise themselves of one thing, which is that the only matter of study is nature."

She crushed the fossil between her fingers and sowed the dust over the cultivated ground, saying: "This is returning to my kitchen. I sow destruction in order to make seeds grow. It is thus with all dusts, whether they have been plant, animal or human. They have died after being alive, and there is nothing sad about that, since they always recommence, thanks to me, being alive after having been dead. Adieu. I want you to keep a souvenir of me. You've admired my ball gown greatly; here is a little fragment of it, which you can examine at your leisure."

Everything disappeared, and when I opened my eyes, I found myself in my bed again. The sun had risen and was sending me a beautiful radiance. I looked at the fragment of cloth that the fay had put into my hand. It was nothing but a little heap of fine dust, but my mind was still under the charm of the dream and it communicated to my senses the ability to distinguish the smallest atoms of that dust.

I was wonderstruck. Everything was there: air, water, sunlight, gold, diamonds, ash, flower pollen, shells, pearls, the dust of a butterfly's wing, thread, wax, iron, wood, and many microscopic cadavers; but in the midst of that mixture of imperceptible debris, I saw fermenting I know not what life of ungraspable beings, which appeared to be seeking to settle somewhere in order to hatch or to transform themselves, and which melted into a golden cloud in the roseate radiance of the rising sun.

Théodore de Banville[26]: *The Rag-Picker*

(Gil Blas, 24 December 1880)

In quest of bizarre impressions and landscapes, the poet Etienne Silvant was strolling after dinner in the Rue Brise-Miche, amusing himself by taking inventory of that strange street, which would have seemed to belong to the most distant province if the great movement of an ever-dense and compact crowd, circulating between the Rue Saint-Merri and the Rue Maubuée had not simultaneously given it a very Parisian character.

In the vague gleams cast into the street by the insufficient lighting of the shops, he never wearied of admiring the vast rustic workshop of the cooper, where he saw barrels being assembled and circled, the laundry, where young women with bare shoulders and arms were soaping, the carpenter's premises, where only one little apprentice remained, planning by candlelight, the narrow lumber-rooms of second-hand dealers, encumbered by dusty and vague objects, and the grandiose grocery, whose large square bay, open in the parquet near the display-window, permitted the sight of the grocer himself, like a pale Valois, in his cellar illuminated by a gas-jet, doubtless meditating some commercial coup.

He was enjoying that spectacle, animated by the play of shadows and violent thrusts of light, when he was suddenly extracted from his idle contemplation by a frightful, heart-rending scream, as if emerging from a broken breast.

A cart laden with blocks of stone, which took up the whole width of the street, had dispersed the crowd, but a poor old rag-picker who had lost her footing had fallen under the hooves of the restive horses, and was about to be run over,

---

[26] Théodore de Banville (1823-1891).

infallibly. Unfortunately, there were no longer any workmen nearby; only two layabouts in silk caps saw the unfortunate woman in that terrible situation, who drew away without helping her, and one of them murmured, sniggering: "Done for, the old woman!" But Etienne Silvant had also seen her, thin, pale and clad in rags, crushed by the weight of her basket, which had fallen over on top of her; and in the gloom he glimpsed her convulsed face, over which long wisps of her white hair hung down tragically. He launched himself under the horses, seized the rag-picker forcefully, lifted her in his arms, and only just had time to prop himself up with her against the wall of the cooper's establishment.

The horses, vigorously whipped by the carter, finally advanced. The heavy cart passed by, and Etienne was able then to set his chilly and dying companion down. But when she stood up again, without him having ceased to hold her thin hand in one of his, while he surrounded the slender body with the other, the poet was agreeably surprised to see the rag-picker transformed into a beautiful young woman with a svelte figure, whose blonde hair was resplendent under the gaslight, with ripples of golden light. Coiffed in a plush bonnet, ornamented on one side by a little bouquet of plumes, she displayed on her noble visage, still slightly pale, the most charming smile; and her green cashmere dress, with plush trimmings, was irreproachably elegant.

In front of them there was a bright blue coupé harnessed to two black horses, and a correct footman opened the door. The beautiful lady climbed into the carriage, invited the poet to sit next to her with an amicable gesture, and the horses set off, striking sheaves of sparks with their delicate shoes, which struck the stupefied old pavement of the Rue Brise-Miche as they fled.

Then, turning graciously toward Etienne, the lady broke the silence. "I am the fay Eyrx," she told him, "one of those who have the mission of informing Parisiennes of enchantments, irresistible graces and the secrets of communicating life to inert fabrics. But I have to think of those who suffer as well as those who triumph. Giving bits of cloth to charming souls isn't everything; it's necessary subsequently for someone to pick them up from the mud! That's why, every Saturday, I become a simple woman, subject to infirmities, old age and death—and I would, in fact, be dead if you hadn't courageously saved me at the risk of your own life. I have nothing to give you that is truly worthy of you, for the love of fays can only be fatal to men, In any case, I know that you are loved as you merit being loved, and faithfully; not for anything in the world would I want to step on the toes of the charming Madame Estelle Chezely. However," she added, taking a long, thin case from her pocket, made in blue snakeskin, "you'll at least permit me to offer you a good cigar?"

"Madame," said Etienne Silvant, "Except for that of which there can be no question between us, you certainly could not have made me a present more agreeable than this one. And," he went on, opening the case, which was quite visible at that moment because the coupé was rolling along a brightly-lit boulevard, "this is what no Rothschild can procure—which is to say, a cigar of an admirable blond color, which neither crumbles not breaks in the fingers, and which already, without being lit, exhales the most delicious perfume. It will surely give me a smoke full of caresses, mysterious undulations and dreams."

"Yes," said the fay, "it's a good cigar, and no king on earth is rich enough to smoke one like it; but it also has other merits into the bargain. Remark, Monsieur Poet, that it is circled along its length by four little pale stripes, such as one sometimes sees on the finest Havana leaves. When you have lit it and are smoking it, you will only have to make a wish, however unusual, titanic or ambitious it might be, and it will immediately be granted, on one sole condition, which is that you take care to extinguish your cigar before the fire has reached the nearest stripe. You will therefore have four wishes to formulate, which have no limit. So, you can construct at your whim the gardens of Semiramis, find the original edition of Shakespeare with a well-conserved contemporary binding, hang in your bedroom an authentic painting by Zeuxis or Apelles..."

"But can I employ that prodigious power," Silvant interjected, "to relieve the sufferings of everyone, by suppressing unmerited misfortunes and repairing the abominable injustices of fate?"

"Alas," said the fay, "in conformity with supreme designs that we do not have the right to scrutinize, and whose goal and logic escapes us, Poverty is the queen of the world. She places her hideous foot on breasts, snatches the bread from famished mouths, shows to the desperate vengeance and the bloody knife, and, lowering her burned eyes, which no longer have any tears, offers her empty and dried-up teat to wan little children. Perhaps, one day, the human species, that intrepid hero, will topple and stifle the monster, but that hour of deliverance and ineffable joy has not yet come. For the moment, do good with all the ardor, all the bravery and all the obstinacy of your charity, but as for the talisman that I am giving you, it can only serve for your personal happiness."

"Alas!" said the poet.

"So," the fay Eryx continued, "wish for luxury, treasure and domination as much as you pleas, and your wishes will be granted immediately, provided that, after having smoked, you have taken care to extinguish your cigar without the fire having arrived at one of the little pale stripes. But, as it is necessary to anticipate everything, if, on the contrary, it seems to you to be so agreeable to smoke that you do not have the courage to extinguish it, well, then you will remain nothing more than the savant and skillful artist that you are, and your wish will not be realized—but, on the other hand, you will have acquired wisdom."

As the fay Eryx finished speaking, the poet saw that the carriage had just arrived in the Rue de Lille, at the door of the house where he lived. The fay added: "Often, without you being aware of it, I shall give myself the pleasure of fluttering close to you in a ray of sunlight, invisible but present, for I shall always remember that I owe you my life. And if you have need of my help, you can summon me by appealing to me with some of your well-rhymed verses, which will not be difficult for you."

Then she extended to Etienne an admirably gloved hand, and at the same moment as he set foot on his doorstep, the fay, the carriage, the horses and the lackeys disappeared like a dream—which did not cause the poet any astonishment, because the nature of his intelligence bore him not to be astonished by anything, except that which is not supernatural.

Was Etienne Silvant's eccentric valet, Conrad, on one of his honest days, by chance, or was the influence of the fay Eryx already manifest? At any rate, when the poet went into his bedroom, he sensed an atmosphere of gaiety, repose and mysterious and tranquil joy. The antique damask curtains were carefully closed. A big fire of embers and flames, in red and pink sheets, was burning in the fireplace. The lamps were lit, as well as the candles in the candelabra, and posed on the carpet of rich fabric, in that dwelling almost exempt from furniture, the vases were filled with freshly-cut flowers with scarlet corollas.

After having put on his garments of white brushed wool, Etienne lay down on a bed in the Louis XVI style, terminated at the head and foot by unequal panels circumscribed by a molding with a gently curved line. Placed next to him, on a little Turkish tortoiseshell and nacre table, were his Rabelais and a volume of Ronsard's odes; the teapot was being kept warm in front of the fireplace.

After having savored for a moment the immense satisfaction not being at the theater, or in society, or elsewhere, the poet poured tea into a small Japanese cup ornamented with light flowers, and finally lit the fay Eryx's cigar.

Oh, the beautiful smoke, bright, light, serious and celestial, divinely blue, which escaped then from his lips in graciously flying waves! As for the taste of that velvety smoke, simultaneously firm and subtle, caressing all his papillae with an amorous and tender delicacy, it was so perfectly exquisite, so softly suave, that it communicated instantly to the ecstatic smoker the idea and the absolute sentiment of happiness.

Then, while launching the puffs of bright transparent smoke, Etienne Silvant, professional rhymer, remembered that he was the master of the world, more powerful than Nimrod and Alexander, or Bacchus conquering the lands of India, and that, if he wished, he could put in the place where the ruins of the Tuileries groaned, a colossal palace sculpted from a single diamond; or buy the Boulevard des Italiens and have it demolished, along with the neighboring streets, and in place of the houses that populate those rich quarters he could have trees planted in a vast park of green grass, in which he could offer his comrades lion an wild boar hunts, after which he could offer his mistress a *fête galante* copied exactly from the *Fête chez Thérèse* that Victor Hugo has invented so magnificently in his *Contemplations*.[27] That was very simple; in order to realize that prodigy, or again, organize an army of two hundred thousand men composed of clowns wilier than thugs and more agile than the Hanlons,[28] the poet had only to extinguish

---

[27] *Les Contemplations* were published in 1856. The poem is accompanied by an illustration in the original edition, which is an imitation of a Watteau painting of a *fête galante*. Later painters produced other representations in color, notably one by Emile-Antoine Bayard, circa 1886, which Banville might have in mind.

[28] The reference is to the Hanlons (later the Hanlon-Lees, the original three Hanlon brothers being managed and supervised by an older acrobat named John Lees) a troupe of itinerant performers at the first peak of their fame in the 1840s and 1850s, who were experts in humorous gymnastics and contortions, important pioneers of slapstick comedy. They impressed Émile Zola and Joris-Karl Huysmans, who paid tribute to them in their writings. Later generations of Hanlons continued the family tradition into the twentieth century, performing for Barnum & Bailey and the Ringling Brothers, and the company still exists.

his cigar before the fire reached the little pale stripe—and in truth, that was less than nothing.

Less than nothing! Doubtless, for a notary, or a tax-collector. But how would that glib, sagacious and powerful artist, capable of appreciating the charm of an absolute and complete sensation, be able voluntarily to break and annihilate thus, with a cheerful heart, such a superhuman, immeasurable, continuous sensuality?

As I detest surprises, humorous anguishes and the brutality of *coups de théâtre*, and, in no matter what form they are produced, announcements of "continued in the next issue," I shall say right away that by savoring mouthfuls of the caressant and subtle smoke, and slowly sating himself on that etheric ambrosia, Etienne Silvant smoked the cigar all the way to the end, without giving any regret to all the wealth that he was disdaining, and stoically sacrificed thus the empire of the world. But perhaps it will not be useless to relate in a few words the things that passed through his mind as he did so?

Naturally, Etienne was not naïve enough to conceive what we call political ambition, and he went immediately straight to the goal, dreaming of sovereign domination in some vast Asian empire, where, standing before his throne, as motionless as absolute and omnipotent power, he could make peoples tremble by means of an imperceptible contraction of his eyebrow, while armies armored in gold, pensive elephants, chariots harnessed to tigers and battalions of amazons awaited his supreme caprice, and where he went to sleep in the evening putting his head into the mouth of his tame lion. There was something seductive about that, but in the final analysis, as a true Parisian[29] that poet, evoker of divine syllables, had a hor-

---

[29] At this point in the *Gil Blas* text a line of type is missing; the sentence is reconnected as it is here in the version of the text reprinted in *Contes féeriques*, but the first word employed in the *Gil Blas* version (*viveur*) is omitted from the reconstruction, suggesting that the author improvised the connection anew rather than simply reinserting the original line.

ror of affectation and of anything that could have assimilated his life to scene in a theatrical drama. And then, the cigar was so good to smoke that he let the fire devour the first stripe and continued smoking.

Then he thought about being richer than a thousand Rothschilds. But Etienne was a Shakespearean, knowing his *Timon of Athens* (in English) by heart. He saw himself as a machine for signing checks, devoured by opportunistic friends, parasites, imbecilic courtiers and valets, and the second stripe passed by like the first. So did the third, and this is why.

Etienne Silvant who, in order not to be ignorant of anything, as the worthy Théophile Gautier judiciously recommends, had drawn in studios from live models, knew how many women exist who are physically ill-constructed—not to mention their obscure intelligence—and whose configuration offends our ideas of symmetrical order by virtue of an incomplete harmony of proportions. Thus, after having dreamed for a quarter of a hour of being Juan Tenorio,[30] at the very moment when the cigar given to him by the fay Eryx was more delicious than ever, he rapidly perceived that such a dream would end in desiring…nothing at all!

Etienne had the good fortune to love and adore his mistress, Madame Estelle Chezely, who also loved him, by the greatest of miracles, and who was as proportionate as a well-made ode, simultaneously beautiful, pretty and good-humored, and who never said anything stupid because she did not know anything. Why would he have exchanged that cheerful and graceful companion for a thousand random and foolish women? No, he smoked, and smoked on, inhaling and expelling clear blue smoke with pure delight, and the fire devoured the cigar's third stripe.

---

[30] *Don Juan Tenorio* (1844) is a play by the Spanish dramatist José Zorrilla, one of the many dramatizations of the legend of Don Juan.

Then, finally, Etienne thought he had had something that resembled an idea. "To have," he exclaimed, "more talent than Victor Hugo!" But, suddenly chiding himself:, he said: "Imbecile! While we're alone, confess that you possess a talent quite sufficient to express your soul, such as it is, and that, powerful as they might be, fays cannot fabricate souls!"

That is how he came to smoke all the way to the end the beautiful leaves of golden tobacco, burning the fourth pale stripe like the others, and when it was entirely finished, experiencing no regret, because he had been completely happy, he said, in perfect consciousness of the case: "It's a fact that everything that a man can desire down here, personally, for himself, isn't worth as much as a good cigar."

"And," said a soft and murmurous voice in his ear, "that is true wisdom."

That voice belonged to the fay Eryx, who showed herself vaguely, fluttering in a ray of light, and then disappeared. I believe that she had had a strong desire to plant a kiss on her savior's forehead, but she resisted that desire because she did not want to cause any distress to the poet's mistress—in which she showed herself superior to many women. But otherwise, what point would there be in being a fay, intoxicated by the fresh scents of the forest and combing her blonde hair with a golden comb on the edge of a spring?

Catulle Mendès[31]: *A Poor Catch*

(Gil Blas, 12 September 1886;
reprinted in L'Écho de Paris, 13 April 1892
as "Les Mauvais trésors de la mer")

Alone on the enormous swell of the sea, a young fisher-men, letting his oars dangle, sighed:

"I'm finally weary of returning to my poor lodgings on the arid cliff-top every morning, after nights full of dangers and darkness; it's not a happy existence, living in the solitude of the Ocean and the solitude of the cliff. My only pleasure is going on Sunday to hear mass at the church in the valley and emptying after mass a tankard of cider outside the inn. O good fay of the marine waters, take pity on my poverty and my sadness, and by virtue of your clemency my deplorable fate might be changed."

As he spoke thus, the foam of a wave swelled up, took the form of a young woman, and became, still white, the fay of the marine waters, with long hair of golden seaweed.

"It doesn't depend on me," she said, "that you're not the most fortunate of humans. I wish you well, because of your youth and the beautiful songs you sing by night in the silence of the calms. But in what fashion can I help you? Nereid fay as I am, I only have power over the waves; all I can do is to give you a good catch."

---

[31] Two collections of fantasies by Catulle Mendes (1841-1909), including numerous *contes de fées*, are available in translation: *Bluebirds* (2017) and *The Little Fay in the Air* (2019); but there are numerous other such stories—including this one—in the pages of various periodicals of the 1880s and 1890s.

"I'm not asking for anything else, compassionate fay. I'll cast my nets, and all will be for the best if you grant that I catch..."

"What?" she asked.

"An isle A charming isle on which the most beautiful flowers grow and the best fruits ripen, a land of peace and delights, where I can live like a bird on its nest in a rose-bush...for I'm tired of living on the edge of that bleak cliff."

"Cast your net, then," said the fay.

He threw it, and shortly afterwards, not without some effort, he pulled out of the water a tract of land that was not very vast, of which one could make the tour in less than two hours, but which was the prettiest in the world.

You cannot imagine the enchantment of the young fisherman while he strolled in his domain. He would never have believed that such a delightful landscape could rejoice the eyes of a mortal. Beyond lawns undulating in the wind there were hills covered in roses, from which cascades gushed so luminous that they gave the impression of carrying diamonds and pearls; the sand of the pathways was so soft that it was a charm to walk on them barefoot; even the pebbles were caressant. Caves opened here and there, illuminated by stalactites similar to chandeliers and silver candelabra. There was not a single branch overhanging the pathways that did not offer an orange, a sweet lemon or a cluster of ripe grapes. You can imagine that the lord of that freshly-hatched land did not regret his bleak hut on the cliff-top and the smoked herrings that had previously provided his nourishment.

But two long months passed.

One day, when he was sitting on the sand of the shore, he cried out in a lamentable voice: "No, it's not a happy life, only to have for companions the roses on the hill and the turtle-doves in the woods. This isle is a beautiful abode, I wouldn't dream of denying it, but once, when I emerged from my hut on feast days, I encountered young women in white cornettes on the road. O good fay of the marine waters, take pity on my abandonment and my sadness, and by virtue of your clemency, my fate might be changed."

The foam of a wave did not fail to swell, and the fay of the marine waters appeared, with her golden tresses.

"In what fashion can I help you, young king of the isle?" he said. All that I can do is to give you a good catch."

"I'm not asking for anything else, compassionate fay, and all will be for the best if you grant that I catch..."

"What?" she asked.

"A woman! A young woman more beautiful than the most beautiful, smiling at my smile and amorous of my kisses. I shall put her heart in my heart as one hides a pink pearl in a warm silk case; for I'm weary of living without an Eve in this Garden that you have given me.

"Cast your net, then," said the fay.

He threw it, and shortly thereafter, effortlessly, he pulled out of the water a demoiselle prettier than a bird of paradise, dressed like the daughter of a king.

No words can express the delight of the young lord of the isle when he was the husband of such a charming person. Immediately he took her into one of the caves illuminated by stalactites, and he could not tire of kissing her lips, which were as fresh as a marine flower, or caressing her hair, which was as fluid and gilded as a silver stream. He loved her with such tenderness, alone with her among the flowers and the fruits, that the doves, cooing reproachfully, gave him as an example to the most indefatigable wood-pigeons. It often happened that she saw the stars blossom three times without her eyes having closed, except under his kisses.

If she had said: "Tear your breast with this stone and let all the blood run out, drop by drop, from your heart, in order that I can make a ruby necklace with it," he would not have hesitated for an instant and she would have obtained the desired jewelry immediately. Oh, what delights there were in the tenebrous depths of the woods and the mysterious brightness of the grottoes! You can imagine that the husband of the young woman who had emerged from the waves did not regret at all the time when he had wandered without a friend in the solitudes of the isle.

But an entire year went by.

One evening, when he was dreaming, walking slowly over the sand of the shore, he sighed in a melancholy fashion.

"Happy as I am, I'm not happy enough. No, it's not sufficient for me to have for a companion, among the roses and the turtle-doves, a demoiselle prettier than a bird of paradise, dressed like the daughter of a king. I grant that my beloved is as exquisite and as tender as possible, but once, outside the inn, I emptied tankards of cider with frank fellows who clinked glasses while singing. O good fay of the marine waters, take pity on me, and by virtue of your clemency, my fate, so worthy of envy, might become even happier.

The nereid fay appeared and said:

"Young husband of the most beautiful of women, what more do you want me to catch for you?"

"A friend!" he said.

"Be careful, happy man," she said, "and think about what you're requesting! You possess a beautiful demoiselle in a charming land. Perhaps you're wrong to request anything else. Many men who throw themselves into the waves in despair recount in our damp dwellings that the slyest of traitors is born on the same day as the most faithful of friends."

"I want a companion that I will love as a brother, with whom I can share the fruits and the flowers of this enchanted isle, and of whom, in exchange for the happiness that he will owe to me, I will only ask that he rejoice in mine!"

"Cast your net, then," said the fay,

He threw it, and shortly thereafter, with a joyful gesture, he took a young man of honest appearance from the water, who immediately leapt toward him, crying: Bonjour, comrade."

Sometime after that, on a stormy night, the young lord of the isle was wandering on the coast, howling:

"Fay of the marine waters, good fay, cruel fay, come, come to my aid. No woman is faithful, no friend is sincere. Give me, this time, I beg you, a good catch!"

The nereid fay appeared amid the turbulent waves, under the lightning, in the wind.

"What do you want to catch?"

"Good fay, cruel fay, is it true that in the abysms where so many warships sink, weapons are accumulated in great masses?"

"That's true."

"Enable me, then, to catch…"

"What?"

"An ax," he cried.

"Alas!" said the fay. But she added: "Cast your net."

He threw it, and shortly thereafter, with a furious gesture, he took from the water an enormous ax, which he seized with both hands and carried away at a run. Then his pace slowed down and, with the weapon raised, he advanced obliquely through the flowery bushes, bent over slyly, toward one of the charming caves illuminated by stalactites.

Paul Arène[32]: *The Valley of the Fays*

(L'Écho de Paris, 25 October 1891)

The little vale closed by rocks opposite the mountain and officially designated by the name the Valley of the Fays, after having once been, if the legend could be believed, as fresh and green as a paradise, was now the most desolate closed vale that could be seen.

This is why.

Apparently, according to a very ancient book that is no longer found in any library, in the time when France was called Gaul, the entire country for twenty or thirty leagues around was possessed by the Fays. They inhabited the rocks, the trees and the springs, and ran by night, without leaving any trace, over the fine sand of the pathways,

Unfortunately for them, one day a saint arrived, grim and clad in a wolf-skin, who built his hermitage there. He prayed and cut wood.

Troubled thus in their repose, forever hearing the sound of bells and the sound of an ax, the Gaulish fays were scared, and asked for mercy. They were so charming and so lacking in malevolence that the harsh Christian took pity on them and, renouncing further persecution, he assigned the aforementioned small vale closed by rocks to them as a place of exile.

Each installed herself as best she could, bringing what she loved the most, whether her mossy stone or her spring, her shady thicket or green clearing.

---

[32] Paul Arène (1843-1896) collected his fantastic tales in several volumes including *Nouveaux contes de Noël* (1890) and *Les Ogresses* (1891).

After that, people were astonished that an entire land, with mountains and ponds, woods and dense shade, rivers and cascades, could take up such little space.

At any rate, in that somewhat restricted domain, the fays were relatively happy. Their preferred dwelling was a grotto, into the hollow of which an abundant spring flowed, the clear water of which accumulated outside the grotto to form a lake.

To tell the truth, the priests of the surrounding area sometimes preached against them, but the people did not forget them, with the consequence that every spring, in order to render the fays favorable, but without ceasing to be good Christians, girls and boys brought them bonnets of flowers, rings forged in fine tin and scarf-pins that were thrown into the quivering water of the spring, with hearts full of hope.

That lasted for six hundred years, and would still be going on but for an imprudence on the part of the Fays.

It is necessary to know that in 1521—the year in which the event occurred—there was much talk of the Devil. Pillages by men of war and prey to plagues and famines, without recourse and without hope, the peasants, weary of praying vainly to God, had ended up turning to the Devil. And in spite of the edifying activity of exorcists and judges, and the fact that every Saturday, in the pig-markets in the towns and villages, at least one witch or sorcerer was burned, almost everyone went to the sabbat, and there was a great abundance of sorcerers and werewolves.

One day, when the Fays were sitting tranquilly in the depths of the grotto, dangling their feet in the spring, they heard voices, horns and galloping horses.

The fays said: "It's some lord of the castle hunting," and they did not take any action, being—alas!—habituated to such rackets offending their solitude.

But the din came nearer, which worried them slightly. Then there was a loud scream and the noise of a body falling into the water, which was suddenly tinted pink.

Having risen to their feet, they saw a naked woman, wounded in the side, who, after having plunged, swam toward them.

"Save me, good fays; I'm Rolande, the woodcutter's daughter. Thanks to this belt that my godmother gave me, I recently took the form of a roe deer in order to escape the pursuit of a wicked old lord who wanted to use my body in the woods."

The Fays would have been suspicious if they had been wiser, reflecting that witches transformed into animals resume their original form as soon as they bathe in fresh water or roll in the dew. They would also have been suspicious is they had listened more closely to the irritated voices of the hunters, who were beating the water with their swords, saying: "Where has the damned she-wolf gone?" with no mention of a roe deer.

But Rolande was beautiful. Her long hair, finer than the moss of springs, was shiny when wet, with mobile reflections of gold. They believed her without further enquiry. Fays have light heads, and however advanced their age might be, they remain credulous and curious, with an almost infantile soul.

Furthermore, in the evening, when the moon rose, the smiling Rolande, her wound already healed, declared that it was time for her to go to the clearing to meet her friends, Vert-Joli, Moyset and Saute-Buisson—which are, as everyone knows, the names of devils The Fays were not astonished to see her become a roe deer again, four times, by way of an amusement, and then revert to a plump naked woman by rolling in the dew that was pearling the grass on the edge of the spring, nor to see her break off a slender hazel branch, sit astride it, and depart.

"As long as she comes back!" they said.

The witch did not come back, but instead of the witch, Messire Sixte Le Grouin, the great judge of the province, appeared, with an escort of candle-bearers and exorcists. Having been told about the mysterious disappearance of a mortally-wounded she-wolf, and heard the story of a young pastor who declared that, while fortunately hiding behind a bush, he had seen naked women emerging from the water at midnight and flying in the moonlight, he blessed the spring and expelled the Fays.

It is since that day that in the Valley of the Fays, all verdure has withered and the spring no longer flows.

Perhaps it might be appropriate to add here the sad fate of that Rolande, who was not a woodcutter's daughter, as she said, but the wife of the lord who had wounded her, thinking that he was pursuing a she-wolf.

One evening, that gentleman, who was at the window of his castle, saw a hunter passing by whom he knew, and begged him to report on his hunt. Continuing his route over a plain, the hunter was attacked by a huge wolf, against which he first attempted a shot of his arquebus, without hitting it, and of which he could only rid himself by severing one of its paws with his large cutlass, which he put in his pocket while the wolf fled.

The hunter returned to the castle; his friend the gentleman asked him to to tell him about the hunt, which the hunter wanted to do, and, thinking that he was taking the paw out of his pocket he drew out a hand, one of the fingers of which bore a gold ring, which the gentleman recognized as his wife's.

The wife was found in the kitchen, warming herself, and hiding the stump of the severed hand under her apron. She confessed everything, and was subsequently burned.

That terrifying and veridical adventure is related in his *Discours*, which appeared in Lyon in 1610, by a witness worthy of faith: Messire Henry Boguet,[33] a mild man of great knowledge, zealous for the religion, who took a singular pleasure in burning witches alive.

---

[33] Henry Boguet (1550-1619) was a Burgundian judge, who published his *Discours exécrable des sorciers* in 1602; reprinted many times, it became a significant witchfinders' manual during the seventeenth-century panic.

Armand Silvestre: *The Tale of a Fay*
(L'Écho de Paris, 2 July 1892)[34]

For Jean Buffer[35]

I

I hope and I believe that the marvelous will one day take
a greater part in the works of thought. In lyric tragedy, a man
of genius has brought it back triumphantly, only taking up
again, in doing so, the tradition of the great Greek tragedies
that were not content with the human element but set it at odds
with the Divinity. Given the perfect illogicality that rules our
actions, nothing is less plausible, fundamentally, than that
which is real. That which is not has the advantage of elevating
the spirit while being no more absurd. Is not a dream a fact,
like the life from which, among the elect, it borrows half?
Why not take as much interest, or even more, in a pretty caprice of the imagination, as in something that has no interest at
all, like that which banal contemporary life offers us? People
shed real tears over such fictions every day at the theater.
What moves us is not entities themselves but the sentiments
that animate them. Those only gain by being immaterialized in

---

[34] In 1892, when this story was published, Armand Silvestre
(1837-1901) was at the height of his career as a civil servant,
and he was appointed inspector of Beaux-Arts. His tales were
collected in numerous volumes, and he produced two items a
week for the *Écho de Paris* with a remarkable regularity.

[35] Presumably a misprint, the intended dedicatee being the
sculptor Jean Baffier (1851-1921), a native of Berry, in the
folklore of which region he was intensely interested, and who
is mentioned in the story as its hypothetical addressee.

the most subtle essences. Long live the marvelous! Long live genies and fays! They repose in notaries and sportsmen, in housewives and little girls. Their fantasy is worth more than our wisdom. It has wings and sings, like birds.

And then, what assures us that these mysterious companions of dream do not really exist? Have you not seen forms passing over ponds on beautiful summer nights, and heard silvery laughter in the heather: exquisitely clad forms of white vapor, and laughter spilled like the obscure pearls of springs hidden in the grass, ready to be silvered by a ray of moonlight? Are the woods not populated by delightful phantoms, toward which our arms reach out, while the soul weeps within us, stirred by memories? Who knows whether something is not hidden behind those phantasmagorias in which universal life is quivering?

We are told every day that beautiful women love fools. Does that not revolt reason more than learning that the pretty Yvette, the heroine of my tale, had received from the fay Urgande,[36] her godmother, a philter with a very curious power? It sufficed to drink a few drops of it for those whose presence was desperately desired to appear immediately. What an admirable gift for a young woman who was destined to love and was often traversed—in the moral sense of the word—in her amours. For she was the purest creature in the world, like all demoiselles whom a fay deigns hold over the invisible baptismal fonts that abundant ivy hides and from which the chalices of convolvulus flowers pour out the regenerative water of morning dew. You can imagine that those superior persons— the fays, I mean—do not take that trouble for future sluts. Oh, the mysterious does not disturb itself for imbeciles! It has its elect, like everything that comes from Heaven.

Where did Yvette and that fay live? Absolutely anywhere you like, but it pleases me that it was in Berry, in the landscape where the divine George Sand so often evoked

---

[36] The fay Urgande, or Urganda, originated in the Spanish imitation of French romance *Amadis de Gaule* (1508).

those supernatural figures in which the poetic superstition of peasants still delights, in the valley of black shadows she has described so marvelously, where the farfadets commence dancing in the grass as soon as the stars agitate their silent golden castanets in the azure; for there is music that only spirits hear while patented tradesmen are snoring authentically in the conjugal alcove.

Oh, it is a wretched music that sounds the appeal of Saint Cuckoldry at the bedside of his instrumentalists! Ho ho! Let us turn away our ears, which grow on hearing it like those of the late Midas, that eater of gold, in order to hear, in the neighboring valley of Gargiles,[37] in the dying echo of vielles and bagpipes, the lovely canticles that the sprites sing in the moonlight, while the fay Urgande, coiffed in dragonflies with transparent wings, with arm-rings made of the living emeralds of beetles, pours lustral water from the corolla of a flower over the forehead of little Yvette and slips into her cradle the lovely philter that you know, contained in a delightful rock-crystal phial, with the manner of making use of it written in a Mahometan language that she alone understands. For, at the same time, she is giving her god-daughter a singular gift of divination for all that others learn with such difficulty in school. And all of that happened while Yvette's father was snoring and her mother was meditating cuckolding that fake bumble-bee one day. For families—the fact is notorious—never suspect what the fays do for their children.

II

How Yvette had grown since that memorable night, as if sunlit by the moon! She had grown up, and at sixteen she was the most delightful young woman in a land where pretty girls are not in short supply. She was of medium height, with chestnut hair of a warm and changing tone, the shadow of which

---

[37] The area now known as Gargilesse-Dampiere, where George Sand once lived.

put amber reflections on to the polished ivory of her forehead; with a regular nose whose nostrils quivered like the wings of a pink butterfly; with a little, delectable fleshy and mocking mouth; but above all, with eyes of a mystical blue, enclosing in an azure droplet the infinity of oceans. And there was the supple grace that her figure made as the beautiful flesh curved precociously over her hips, where the virginities of her bodice melted in a voluptuous torrent. She was mischievous in character, but nevertheless resolute, having divined that amour is the only thing in life.

There was no lack of suitors around her—for the good motive, of course, for I have said that Yvette was sage. And there was some merit in that, being sensually endowed as few people of her age are. Among those wind-blown organists who swooned while sighing noisily as she passed by, the one with whom her family was most taken was the tax-collector Mauvesse, who had a situation; but the one she preferred in secret was the handsome Pécuchard, who was neither so laborious nor so well-educated, but had a fine figure and a joyful character, while Mauvesse was rather badly built and as serious as a canon on duty. Mauvesse was skillful, however, and insinuating, and knew how to talk to his society, so well that the pretty innocent Yvette had taken him into her confidence regarding her love for Pécuchard and the secret of the mysterious philter of which she was the possessor: a culpable indiscretion if ever there was one, for you would not believe the extent to which we wound the fays by recounting to others what they have done for us. All of you who have these supernatural patrons, honor them in secret and jealous worship, far from the insipid curiosity of crowds. Otherwise, they will abandon you, and your dreams will be akin to butterflies with broken wings.

Mauvesse, who, while knowing that he was not loved, had his plan, listened to all that in order to take advantage of it. Needless to say, he had conceived a terrible hatred for the handsome Pécuchard. He would have liked to break his bones and then trample on the phosphoric broth; but the other was a strong as a Turk, and Pécuchard was as prudent as an advocate.

The idea of receiving an abominable thrashing maintained Mauvesse in respect before his rival. But when he was alone, he gave him imaginary beatings, foaming with fury and throwing futile punches in the air, "Take that, wretch! Take that, thief! Take that, villain!" He knocked him down in image, beat him up in effigy, and his victim's person, filled with bruises, burst like an overloaded bladder. He peppered Pécuchard with slaps and kicks that it would have been so sweet to deposit on his cheeks and shins, limiting himself in the reality of actions to discrediting him as much as he could with Yvette's parents—which was not difficult, since all their wishes were for him, Mauvesse. Thus, he had obtained that Yvette was forbidden to see Pécuchard.

As she suffered greatly from that prohibition, she remembered the omnipotent philter, and every night, while drinking a few drops, she evoked the beloved in mysterious rendezvous in which the illusion of kisses came to her mouth, and she abandoned herself entirely, knowing full well that it was only a dream and that her virtue could not suffer in those supernatural delights.

III

Meanwhile, having divined everything regarding the source of her trouble, she had dreamed in the simplicity of her soul of bringing about a reconciliation between Mauvesse and Pécuchard, who would appeal to the generosity of his rival and his loyalty, begging him not to oppose, futilely and without profit for himself, the happiness of two people who loved one another and whose hearts nothing could separate. She had written in secret to Pécuchard, to ask him to take that step, and the latter—who was a simpleton, like all elite souls—had put to his best clothes in order to visit his enemy and disarm him by means of frankness and true dolor.

That was to misunderstand the rascally Mauvesse. That day, precisely to economize the kicks and punches that he could not succeed in landing, utterly stifled by so many suppressed blows, to such an extent that he could no longer make a movement without unleashing something at someone and then confounding himself in lame excuses, Mauvesse had an idea infinitely cleverer than that of the candid Yvette. He would filch from the latter the little crystal bottle in which the philter was contained and would drink its contents to the last drop, Thus, the person that he most desired to see, Pécuchard, would appear before him in imagination and he could administer a monumental beating, discharging his athletic capital on his shoulder without running the slightest danger, since apparitions, as everyone knows, do not have the custom of returning the blows that one gives them.. Many tranquil people are like that. Mauvesse was well aware that apparitions cannot feel the slaps and kicks either, but that did not discharge him in the least of his burden. It would relieve him greatly to lash out; he would certainly feel better afterwards.

O marvelous power of the philter! He still had the taste in his mouth when Pécuchard stood before him, respectful of the fay's order, with his best hat in his hand. Oh, Mauvesse did not waste a minute. With a kick he sent the hat flying and he punched the phantom with both fists. But to his great surprise, the phantom retaliated, grabbed him, knocked him to the ground, and trampled his belly, so well that he lost consciousness, with a vague sentiment that he was in a jam. That was because it was Pécuchard in the flesh, who, in order to obey Yvette's delicate thought, had arrived at the psychological moment.

Seeing the cordial fashion in which he was welcomed by the man to whom he had come to hold out his hand, Pécuchard had responded in the same tone. Moreover, that succeeded for him, for Mauvesse, crippled for life and his complaint to the tribunal ridiculously dismissed, wilted even as an aggressor, was no longer a possible husband and Yvette became, by the force of events, Madame Pécuchard.

"But tell me then, my dear Baffier, the philter must have been powerless, or Mauvesse would have seen two Péchuards at once?"

"That's because, my dear fellow, you don't know the habits of spirits. They do not disturb themselves in order to appear when their place has already been taken." I will add, for the sake of more clarity, that Yvette's mother, having perceived that her daughter was getting drunk on that liqueur, had substituted pure water for it in the rock crystal phial that very morning.

Now, confess that all that is no more implausible that what we read in the newspapers every day, and the choice of Monsieur Maignan for the medal of honor at the last Salon, where the glorious Henner had exhibited and to which Roybet had sent two masterpieces.[38]

---

[38] The first reference is to the prolific Albert Maignan (1845-1908), who won the Medal of Honor at the Salon of 1892; best-known for his historical paintings, he also dabbled in symbolism, most notably in *La Muse verte* (1895), depicting a poet overwhelmed by the "fée verte" (absinthe), which Silvestre had not seen when he wrote the present story. Jean-Jacques Henner (1829-1895) was an enterprising and innovative painter fond of religious and mythological imagery, but most famous for painting nudes. Ferdinand Roybet (1840-1920) returned to the 1892 Salon after a long absence; although he did not win the Medal of Honor that year he was made a chevalier of the Légion d'honneur, and he did win the Medal of Honor in 1893. The two masterpieces to which Silvestre refers are presumably his portrait of *Juana Romani* and the group study *Propos galants*.

Antoine de L'Estoille : *Argentine*

A Norwegian Tale
(Contes du Nord, 1892)[39]

I. In which a fay is bored

At the entrance to a large grotto opening somberly over a blue gulf, a fay is gazing at the icebergs descending from the pole

It is the time when the men of the North go back up the rivers of the west in their boats.

"How bored I am, how bored I am," she says. "If I were a woman and I had a friend I would go to weep over her heart, but I'm only a fay. I have no tears, and my friends have no hearts..."

She sits down on the spangled sand licked by the azure waves; her hair the color of ears of wheat hangs downs all the way down the ground, her periwinkle-blue eyes shine like sapphires.

Her pink foot is playing with her green slipper; she is dreaming, her hands folded over her knee.

Then a chubby, plump, rubicund being in a blue satin doublet with black stripes appears, out of breath.

---

[39] Antoine de L'Estoille (1835-1894) published his early literary work, including the antiquarian *conte de fées* "Le Meunier de Carnac" (1866; tr, as The Miller of Carnac") as "Louis de Lyvron" shortly after retiring from a military career, when he made the acquaintance of Catulle Mendès and other Parisian writers, and was peripherally associated with the Parnassian Movement. Most of his fantastic fiction is collected in translation in three volumes published by Black Coat Press in 2020.

"But it's Grésil!" she exclaims, "the sniffling monarch of the steppes."

"You said it, Argentine; I'm Grésil, the king who commands the spirits of the earth, as Perce-Neige commands the spirits of the ice,[40] and I've come to ask for you. Your silver thread is under the ice, it's true, but it's in the ground, so you don't belong to Perce-Neige; you're mine, and I want you for a wife."

Argentine is about to laugh…but she thinks that her smiths and her elves are far away, in the depths of the grotto, and that Grésil has a merited reputation for being angry and brutal, so she responds to him rapidly; "Since you want to marry me, it's necessary for you to prove your love to me; go and find Perce-Neige for me."

"In her polar palace?"

"Yes; when you return you'll have permission to kiss my fingertips."

"I'm on my way…"

He swells up like a balloon and rises up to the crest of the cliffs.

"When he comes back," said the fay, "he'll have found Perce-Neige, who'll defend me."

Soon, two large heads with bristling moustaches emerged from the sea. Those two rounded heads were the heads of two seals harnessed to a coquille Saint-Jacques. Perce-Neige descended from it.

"Greetings, Queen," said Argentine, bowing. "Good day, Sister," she added, throwing her arms around her.

Perce-Neige is pretty, but she does not resemble Argentine. Small, slender and brunette, her smooth tresses have no reflections; her eyes, with lids slightly raised toward the temples, shine like velvet; her lips are red and her cheeks gilded.

---

[40] The French common noun *grésil* signifies hail, and *perce-neige* is the flower known in England as a snowdrop

Perce-Neige is a strawberry from the Northern thickets; Argentine is a peach from the gardens of the Orient.

When only Finns lived in Norway under leather tents, in the lands of the Orient, in a city surrounded by walls of copper, there were twelve men equal in strength and in courage, so tall and so handsome that they were said to be gods and named the Aesir. The city was pierced by twelve golden gates, in order that each of the heroes could go in and out as he pleased.

They were the first among men, and their neighbors were jealous of them; when they were drinking together in their marble palace, around a round table, on twelve similar chairs, the jealous men killed their wild boar and fallow deer with arrows. So, one evening, after a long feast, they said to one another: "Let's go where we can hunt in peace."

The next day they went out through their twelve gates, each having his lineage behind him.

Then they cut the copper walls with swords and each of them took one of the golden gates in order to make it into a shield.

They loaded the fragments of the walls on to carts and they marched northwards on their horses with black legs. They passed like a river of milk.

When they arrived in Norway—it was in spring, they had passed over the sea on the ice—they said: "This land is beautiful; its mountains sparkle, its lakes are as blue as the distant sky, its forests murmur and its waterfalls sing. Let's stop."

Their golden shields shone so flamboyantly that the bewildered Finns fled, crying: "They're the sons of the sun!"

But the Aesir, rude with the strong, were gentle with the small, they loved birds and flowers, sylphs and fays; when they departed, the sylphs, who slept there in the calyxes of roses, and the fays, who hid there in the stars of brambles, said to the rose-bushes and the brambles: "Grow so high and so dense that no one can approach the holy city any longer.

The rose-bushes branched like elms and the brambles interlaced like the mesh of a net.

Then the dreamy sylphs and the laughing fays said to the wood-pigeons; "Take us on your wings and let's go to rejoin them.

On seeing them, the fays of the North fled with the reindeer to the pathless solitudes....

When the leaves reddened in the crowns of the beeches, and the spray of the waterfalls sparkled like little rubies, when the mist silvered the reeds of ponds, when the long glaucous blades glided in the blue fjords, the wood-pigeons said to the elves whose flowers withered and the fays who were cold: "Let's go spend the winter in the lands of the sun."

Only the youngest of the fays, the one who was born out there on the eve of the departure, did not want to go; she had no memories.

Then the brunette daughters of the pole came back from the pathless plains, and Perce-Neige, their queen, met her on the shore.

"Since you only like Norway," she said to her, "be our sister. I'll give you a silver palace where the flowers will never wither."

"I'd like that," said the blondest of the daughters of the Orient.

That is why she is called Argentine, and why, in the midst of her brunette sisters, she resembles a sprig of honeysuckle on a carpet of myrtles.

Argentine told Perce-Neige about her troubles.

"In sum, I'm bored," she concluded, "And...I'd like to weep."

"In spite of my advice, then, you've gone into the world of humans?" said the queen, sadly.

"I only went there once, eighteen years ago. From the edge of a forest of firs, all white with snow, I saw a child as beautiful as daylight in a cradle lined with swansdown. He was cold and I carried him quickly into my grotto, and...."

"And now?"

"He's still as beautiful as daylight.

"I understand then. You love him."

"If I were a woman, perhaps he'd love me…and I would certainly love him…but I'm only a fay."

"Friend, as long as we remain in our domain, we're immortal, but if we love in the land of humans, we become women.

"I could cry then when I'm sad!" exclaimed Argentine, clapping her hands. "Look; can one see Noël without loving him?"

She showed her a handsome adolescent.

He advanced, smiling; the brunette Queen of the North launched forth in her shell.

II. In which we learn who Noël is...

Eighteen years before that day, Otto the Valiant, whose maple-wood boat flew like a seamew, had left Emma the beautiful in his castle.

As he quit her he had said: "The laborer reaps the field he has sown; the sea is the field of the men of the North; the red boats are our plows, the blue swords are our scythes; it's harvest time, I'm leaving. I'll bring you back golden rings, and pearl necklaces as a toy for the child. I'm departing without dread; my name is written on my door, and no one would dare to touch what belong to Otto."

Emma accompanied her husband to the shore. She had buckled his breastplate of scales, she wanted to untie the cable that moored the boat, because the old songs say: "She who buckles the breastplate will unbuckle it, and she who unties the cable will tie it up again."

Otto's companions were waiting for him; there were a hundred, perhaps two hundred; they were the elite of the northern warriors.

On seeing him so strong among the strong, Emma said to herself: "Who would dare to touch what is his?"

With tears in her eyes but confidence in her heart, she went back to sit down in the hall paneled in fir-wood, next to a cradle lined with swansdown.

The summer has passed, autumn is finished, the geese have fled the frozen ponds, the wolves have come in packs; Emma is weeping.

Where is Otto the Valiant? Has the tempest broken his boat? Has the mud of the river entangled it? Is his cadaver rolling beneath the glaucous waves? Is he sleeping under the reeds?"

Where is Otto the brave?

His boat is dancing on the waves like an iridescent bubble, his boat is gliding over the sea like a duck-feather; it is far away, far away where the sun sets. Upright at the curved prow, leaning on the dragon's head that rears up open-mouthed, Otto is still as handsome as a fir-tree, as white as an eider, and as strong as a salmon. He is so strong that his boat is full of golden rings; he is so white that the foam seems gray on his arms; and he is so handsome that the daughter of the sea is singing before his boat: "Otto, Otto, if you wanted…I have a palace of emeralds decorated with sapphires."

"You don't have Emma's eyes," replies the Northern warrior.

"Otto, Otto, in the depths of a wife's eyes, one reads: *Perhaps*; in the depths of mine one reads: *Always*."

Leaning on the red dragon, he dreams about Emma's eyes, as clear as a spring, and Emma's blonde hair, as delicate as spider-silk; but the undine sings so sweetly that her song lulls him, and the boat follows the undine into the depths of the west.

"Otto, Otto, if you wanted…I have emeralds in my palace, and pink anemones."

"In my castle I have a fine white carnation," replies the Northern warrior.

And he cries to the helmsman: "Steer for Norway!"

The boat rears up like a charger under the bit; like a docile charger it turns. The rigging stiffens, the sail stretches, and the joyful men ply the oars.

Otto can no longer see before him the undine with the ivory shoulders; he is thinking about the white carnation that he has left back there, on a swansdown cushion.

"Harder! Harder, companions!" he shouts, while pulling the oar.

"What is this white carnation, then?" wonders the undine. "If I had it in my palace, perhaps he would come."

Like a seamew, the boat flies. The coast is blue in the distance; it shines in the moonlight. It is Christmas Eve.

Then the undine stands upright on the waves; she must have that white carnation. In the radiance that bathes her she glides over the shore, she climbs all the way to the castle, the black silhouette of which is standing out against the steely sky.

A window is shining at the top of the tower; a woman is leaning over a cradle.

"There," she says, "are Emma the blonde and the white carnation that Otto cannot forget. When I have that beautiful carnation in my palace he will come in search of it.

"Woman with blue eyes," she shouts. "Otto is on the shore."

The blonde Emma shivers and runs to the window, from which the shore and the sea can be seen in the distance. Over the bay, of which the moon makes a mirror, the black boats are gliding.

Without kissing her son, and without taking her cloak, Emma runs to the shore, and the undine takes away the beautiful white carnation.

The undine swims in the moonlight, but the moon is rising toward the fir-woods and the pale radiance makes the shore distant.

Soon, out of breath, she sighs: "I'm a daughter of the waves, I stifle on land. Like the azure-tinted jellyfish that the sea abandons in the hollow of a rock, I shall die if the sunlight touches me, and this radiance is carrying me away."

Toward the firs the radiance rides; between the trunks it glides, on the stiff needles it is shredded.

The undine utters a cry; her shoulders are bleeding and the beautiful white carnation escapes her arms...

The moon rises into the sky; behind the mountain the radiance descends, carrying the undine away to the endless snowy plains.

Under a juniper bush, in his swansdown cradle, the white carnation is still asleep.

In the depths of the wood the hungry wolves are howling. Here they come.

Then the earth opens up beside the juniper bush, and a fay emerges from the narrow crevice.

The child utters a plaint and the fay sees him, as dainty as a carnation.

"What's the point of looking any further?" she says. "At the first step I've found a flower as beautiful as one can imagine."

Into the opened earth she carries the white carnation; the bells are ringing for Christmas.

That is why Argentine's beloved is named Noël.

III. In which Noël chats with his godmother

"What do you want, Noël?" the fay asks the adolescent, who is gazing in surprise at the huge seashell sinking into the gulf.

"I've come to drink from the spring."

"You don't find the water insipid? Men, your brothers, drink hydromel from golden cups."

"Is it good?"

"It appears so.

"I'd rather drink this beautiful running water from your hands. I'm very thirsty, godmother."

"Don't call me godmother any longer."

"What should I call you?"

"I don't know."

"You don't know whether hydromel is good, and you don't know what name it's necessary to give you. Let's stay as we are, godmother, let's call one another what we call one another."

"Men fight against monsters and giants."

Noël smiles; Argentine has made a nacreous cup with her hands.

He's certainly the son of a knight, thinks the fay. *He smiles at the idea of combats; when he has a sword, he'll want to make use of it.*

Noël is still thirsty, but she touches the wall of the grotto with her finger. The granite wall opens up and she draws the glutton into an immense forge, in which bearded dwarves broader than they are tall are extended around anvils, sleeping in their otter-skin capes.

"On your feet, idlers!" cries Argentine, stamping her foot,

Awoken with a start, the dwarves run to the forges, to the hammers and to the bellows, and the foremost smith, picking up a handful of jewels, says to his irritated mistress: "Look, we've been working hard."

"Forge me a sword for Noël," replied Argentine, without looking.

"In gold?" asked the dwarf.

"A sword for killing giants," said Noël, negligently

"You'll also need a very warm tunic, which rain cannot penetrate," the fay interjected. "While they forge, let's go see the spinners."

As they went to see the spinners, in the utmost depths of the grotto, Argentine said: "I'd like to see you on a fine horse when your sword is flamboyant. Would that give you pleasure? Let's go to the abode of the spinners, then, to find a tunic that the rain won't penetrate."

Under Argentine's finger, the depths of the grotto open up, and they enter into a round chamber where a hundred spinners are chatting.

"To your spindles, gossips!" says the fay, frowning.

But the mistress runs forward, fine fabric in hand, and, placing it on the hair the color of wheat she cried: "How pretty you are under that!"

"It's true that you're very pretty under that," Noël approves, taking a step back in order to see better.

Argentine smiles and strokes the cheek of the dainty spinner, as thin as a reed and as brown as a rush. "You're good workers. Now it's a matter of weaving for Noël a very warm tunic, which the rain won't penetrate."

"So he wants to return to the human world?"

"Argentine wishes it," sighs Noël, "but she'll come with me."

Argentine does not want to depart with Noël for the human world, she wants to join him there, because she wants to be loved not as a fay but as a woman.

"You're a man, and you'd be afraid all alone!"

The spinner laughed.

"Oh, you think I'm afraid?" said Noël, piqued. "Well, I'll depart alone; but as soon as I've killed a giant I'll return, because, you see, godmother, I don't find water good when I don't drink it from your hands."

The dwarves have forged a beautiful sword with a steel blade, a gold hand-guard and a silver scabbard. The spinners have woven an asbestos tunic that has no colors and all reflections, a tunic mild to the eyes, rude to the touch, as supple as deerskin and as hard as a shield.

When he had donned the tunic and buckled on the sword. Noël said: "I'll kill a giant, since you desire it, that's decided, but how shall I find one? In that unknown world I'll be like a blind man."

"You'll soon find a guide," replies Argentine, slightly hesitantly.

If she had been a woman, she would have blushed.

"But how shall I recognize that guide? Will it be necessary to say to all those I encounter: *I've come to kill a giant; show me one, if you please*?"

Argentine does not reply. She is thinking.

"Godmother, Godmother, let's stay as we are; the giants haven't done anything to you. I love you so much, you see, that no godmother will ever have a nicer godson."

"Shut up, we're talking seriously When you arrive up there you'll find a squire, very thin, as befits a young man. Fie! The fearful fellow, who seeks a thousand pretexts to remain."

"I have no need to seek a thousand pretexts; I have a hundred thousand good reasons.—but the sooner I leave, the sooner I can come back. Adieu, Godmother."

The elves who bear a flame on the forehead, those who follow the seams of silver under the ground, had carved a broad stair inside the mountain. Noël went up the stairs two by two.

As soon as he disappeared into the somber path, Argentine clapped her hands.

In the blink of an eye, smiths and spinners, miners and hairdressers surrounded her.

"I need a suit of armor," she said to the smiths, "And hosiery," she said to the spinners.

The mouths of the fat dwarves opened all the way to the ears, and the eyes of the dainty spinners lowered modestly.

"Why laugh, ugly wretches? And why look like that, stupid sluts? I want to be the squire of the man I love."

"She loves Noël!" cries all of that petty society. "Hurrah! Hurrah!"

And the otter-skin bonnets fly into the air. "Hurrah! Hurrah!"

And the hammers of the elves ring on their foil. "Hurrah! Hurrah! She loves Noël! Hurrah! Hurrah! Oh, the beautiful wedding! Hurrah! Hurrah!"

And the dainty spinners, as brown as rushes, draw the pale burnishers with fingers dusted with silver into a mad round dance.

IV. In which Noël sees the human world again

Noël is in a fir-wood. In front of him extends a snowy plain limited by high mountains, which crown a castle with sharp turrets.

The shadow of large clouds running across the sky puts ashen trails over the plain; the mountain, with sheer slopes, resembles a chipped saw, and the towers taper like black tears.

"A nasty country," he says, "I'm turning back," when a young woman falls into his arms, exclaiming:

"I'm dying!"

As an enormous bear was trotting behind the young woman, Noël spread his arms wide and the lovely child slipped on to the snow.

He marched upon the wild beast, brandishing his sword.

Argentine's smiths are good smiths; the bear is laid out dead next to the fainted beauty.

It appears that women are fearful, Noël thinks; and he kneels down in order to lift the pale head. *But they're pretty*, he adds, on seeing the rosy color return to the cheeks. *Not as pretty as my godmother, but very pretty all the same.*

"Where am I?" sighs a soft voice.

"In the snow," Noël replies, "between a dying bear and a boy who admires you."

"Thank you, Messire," says the unknown woman, bounding to her feet.

"Are you afraid of me, as you were afraid of the bear?"

The beauty smiles slightly and blushes deeply.

"I don't know," Noël continues, "whether all women resemble you—you're the first one I've seen—but I'd like them to; you're good to look at."

The unknown woman blushed a little less and smiled a little more. "You've come from the land of the fays, then, Messire?"

"Just now."

She was no longer blushing; she laughed.

Two more young women, who arrived running, stopped, trembling, before the cadaver of the bear.

"Women are decidedly fearful," murmurs Noël, "but they're as pretty as fays."

"Oh, no," says the unknown woman. Then, addressing the newcomers: "I was about to be devoured when this knight..."

"I'm not a knight, I'm Noël. I've come to kill a giant; as soon as the giant is slain, I'll return whence I came."

"Be careful, Hildewige," whispers one of the young women, "he's an elf; see, his doublet has all the colors of the rainbow."

"He's a brave man," replies Hildewige, and, turning back to Noël: "Who sent you to kill a giant?"

"My godmother. I do everything she wishes, because I love her. But I also love you; I sense it. What is your name?"

"Hildewige. I'm the daughter of Otto, whose castle you can see over there."

"Are there any giants in your father's castle?"

"No."

"Too bad. I would have been glad to chat with you along the way, but I'm in haste to return to my godmother."

"I understand."

"I'll come back up to the earth in order to see you. I sense positively that I love you. That doesn't annoy you?"

Hildewige recommenced blushing.

"You aren't saying yes or no," Noël continues. "You're too pretty for anyone to cause you pain; say that you're not annoyed."

"No."

"Then it's settled; I love you—not in the same manner, but almost as much, as my godmother. I'll certainly come to see you one of these days."

A sleigh stopped beside them. Hildewige climbed into it with the two women.

"There's a tourney at the castle tomorrow," she says, taking the reins, "and I'll expect you," she adds, launching the shaggy ponies at a gallop.

Noël watched the sleigh fly away in the snow cloud.

"I'm sorry to see her go away," he said. "Almost as sorry as I was when I quit my godmother. I love her...that's astonishing. It's astonishing for me, who doesn't know anything, but it didn't seem astonishing to her. What am I going to do now? I can't always be running from Argentine's grotto to the castle. It's necessary that they live together. If the castle is nicer than the grotto, Argentine can come to the castle; if the grotto is nicer than the castle, Hildewige can come to the grotto. Since they both want me to love them, they have similar tastes; they'll certainly please one another."

The sun slid behind the mountain; the sleigh disappeared in the evening mist.

"Let's go to sleep," sighed Noël. "This snow is as soft as down, the little spinners have woven me a tunic that the north wind doesn't traverse, and that bear will make me a soft pillow."

He lay down, with his head on the bear's belly, and went to sleep.

V. In which it is understandable why Noël loves Hildewige

Eighteen years ago, when Otto went into the high room in the tower with Emma, the swansdown cradle was no longer by the fireside.

"Wife, what have you done?" he said.

Pale, her eyes haggard, the mother ran to the widow, crying: "The elves have stolen him; I've got to get him back!"

Then Otto remembered the daughter of the waves.

"I told her where my treasure was," he murmured. "What has happened is my fault."

He hugged the crazed mother to his breastplate, put a kiss on her eyes and departed, without taking the time to empty the cup that his cup-bearer held out to him.

His companions are celebrating his return; he is alone on the maple-wood boat, the red dragon of which is plunging its scaly breast into the foam. He returns whence he came, into the depths of the sunset.

His back to the mast, which is bending under the north wind, he cries into the darkness: "I am Otto, do you hear? Can you hear me, queen of the waves?"

But his voice is lost in the noise of the waves breaking heavily.

The boat quivers all the way to the keel; like a deer struck by a spear, it lies down on its side; Otto is on an iceberg tossed by the waves,

"They're going westwards," says the warrior. "They're going where I want to go."

And, fearlessly, he shouts into the darkness:

"I am Otto, do you hear? Can you hear me, queen of the waves?"

But his voice is lost in the noise of the wind whistling between the thin needles of the errant iceberg.

At daybreak, Otto sees on the summit of the floating mountain a giant with a white beard holding the tiller of a rudder. As he is never afraid, he shouts to the giant:

"Steer toward the sunset!"

Only Otto the Brave could speak thus, thinks the giant; *for a long time I've desired to measure myself against the strongest of men.* And letting go of the tiller he says. "We'll wrestle one another; the loser will be the slave of the victor."

"Gladly," Otto replies.

They wrestled until sunset, and then all night, and all of the following day. At the end of the second day, however, the giant, being thirsty, wanted to break off a fragment of ice, and his right arm let go of Otto's back briefly; the warrior recovered his breath and squeezed his adversary's sides so forcefully that he made him cry for mercy.

"You'll obey me, as I would have obeyed you if I had been vanquished," said Otto. "Resume your place at the tiller."

"Where is it necessary to go?"

"To the emerald palace of the daughter of the waves."

"You won't find her in her emerald palace any longer; the moon's rays have carried her into the snowy steppes of the endless plain."

"Then take me in that direction; it's necessary that I find her."

After a week, perhaps two, the iceberg ran aground in the depths of a narrow gulf bordered by frozen ponds.

"You can return where you were going," said Otto then. "I'm returning your liberty; I'm proud of having wrestled with someone as strong as you."

"Since you're as generous as you're brave," replied the giant, "I'll tell you a secret that humans don't know. On the far side of these lakes, in a forest of birches, under a stone slab supported by three others, there is a woman older than the world; ask her for what you seek; she knows everything."

Otto traverses the frozen lakes and plunges into the forest of birches.

He had been marching for a week when he was attacked by crows with steel claws and bronze beaks. He swatted them away with his hand as one chases away flies in summer.

He marched for another week, and a wolf larger than a two-year-old colt barred his route. He seized it by the ears and rubbed its muzzle in the snow.

"Wolf," he said, "I could strangle you if I wished, but I'll let you go if you take me to the old woman who knows everything."

The trembling wolf replied: "Follow me."

Otto followed him and they arrived at the entrance to a grotto. The old woman, crouching before an iron spinning-wheel, was spinning hair.

"I don't have the hair that you're seeking to spin," she said. "Go away."

"Listen. Old woman," said Otto. "I've felled the giant with the white beard, I've swatted your crows as one chases away flies, and I've held your wolf by the ears; if you tell me what I'm seeking, I'll give you my golden necklace."

"And if I don't want to?"

"I'll force you to speak."

"Madman! I'm Death!."

"I'm not afraid of death."

"You're going to fight me?"

"Instead of talking so much, let's begin; you have no sword so I won't draw mine."

"You're a brave man! Listen: return to your castle; when a rosebud opens there, amour will bring the white carnation you seek."

He left Death spinning with her iron wheel.

When Otto returned to the high hall, Emma was still weeping.

"Weep no more, white seamew, my sweet teal," he said to her, "weep no more. Give me a rosebud, and when the rose blossoms, we'll see the one for whom you're weeping night and day."

Emma was worthy of a brave man; she was like the white seamew, whose wings are not tarnished by anything, like the multicolored teal which only has one amour in its life; her heart was swollen by tears, but her lips smiled night and day...

When the maidservants brought the waiting warrior the fresh rosebud, Emma closed her large bright eyes. She was a white seamew, who opened her wings; a gentle teal who only had one amour in her life.

Emma soul went to the land without winters; while passing over a marsh whose reeds were rustling in the wind, she heard a voice.

The voice wept: "You who have wings, carry me as far as the waves that are singing out there; I am the daughter of the sea. The desiccated reeds are bruising my breast, the mud of the marsh is hardening my hair; I am the daughter of the sea."

"It is my tears," Emma replies, "that have burned the reeds, it is my sobs that have caused the mud to rise all the way to your hair; the one you stole will bring you back, if he wishes, to the singing waves."

Otto's heart sighed in the tower: "If a sword were not necessary beside roses that bloom, I would follow you, my white seamew. Remake our nest on high, my sweet teal!"

Today, the fresh rosebud has blossomed; Hildewige is a rose.

That is why Noël, who loves his godmother so much, also loves the blonde girl with such blue eyes; that is why the wild rose, which has flourished under a sword, has inclined without dread toward the stranger whose eyes are as blue as her own.

VI. In which Argentine regrets what she wanted

As soon as Noël falls asleep with his head on the bear, Argentine emerges from the shadow of a fir-tree. She is wearing the pretty costume of a page, half-yellow and half-black, a slender sword and an otter-fur cap with an eagle feather. In order to resemble a page more closely, she has cut her hair.

"I no longer want to be a woman," she sighs. "Women are all liars and coquettes. She's brazen, that Hildewige! He must love me, in order not to have followed her to the castle. He was right, this morning; let's stay as we are. I'll take him back very quickly, and tomorrow he'll think that he had a dream."

She is leaning over him when she straightens up abruptly, putting her hands to her cheeks.

"Did the flap of my cloak touch you?" says a little shrill voice. "I regret it, but it's your fault; I had such momentum that I couldn't stop."

It is Grésil.

"I carried out your commission, but when I came to collect my salary, I found the house masterless and your servants laughed in my face. Hee hee," he continues, on perceiving Noël, "I'm beginning to understand. There's a fellow that it's necessary not to leave asleep under the stars; I'll drape an alcove for him so comfortable that he'll no longer want to emerge from it."

"You're forgetting who I am." Argentine interjects.

"And you're forgetting that you're no longer in your own domain. On the land where I reign, you have no strength and no power. If you're interested in this fellow, swear to marry me incontinently, or he'll serve as breakfast for the wolves tomorrow."

So saying, he shakes his mantle and the snow begins to swirl.

"Noël!"

If you wake him up, I'll blind him—look!"

And the snow falls more thickly

"You always want to cause me pain; you don't love me, as you claim," sighs Argentine.

"You're no longer at home; you're where I'm the master; I prevail over you."

Argentine is in the cloud that serves Grésil as a palace.

"You can see that my palace is too large for me alone," sniggers the chubby elf. "You can stroll around it at your ease."

"And he'll die in the snow!" sighs the fay.

"Indubitably."

If a fay could weep, tears would stripe her cheeks, she has so much chagrin. She has so much chagrin that her lips say what her heart is saying: "I love you dearly, Noël."

"Blow! Blow hard!" cries the elf.

Genii, swollen like balloons, send whirlwinds of snow over the forest.

"I'll be your wife," cries Argentine, "if..."

"If?"

A white radiance fills the gray palace, and Perce-Neige appears, mounted on a swan.

"If I wish it!" says the Queen of the Pole.

"You're queen in your abode, but I'm king here!" growls Grésil.

"You're a villain and a liar."

"What?"

"Have you, yes or no, asked for me in marriage?"

"I have asked for you."

"And what was my reply?"

"Go take a walk."

"Have you taken a walk?"

"That's all I've done."

"You have, therefore, as a smitten suitor, obeyed my orders. Here's my hand."

"Are you serious?"

"I don't like questions. My court awaits yours. If a single one of your subjects—my subjects, I mean—is lacking, we'll have words. Go and get suitably dressed."

"Perce-Neige, I render you your promise."

"I've said yes; you've said yes. Yes, it's too late."

"It's too late!" sighs Grésil, and he goes out, grumbling.

"Oh, my sister," says Argentine. "you're sacrificing yourself for me?"

"The marriage isn't made yet. An eider had seen you carried away; he warned me, I came immediately. But where were you going in a doublet with a sword at your side?"

"I no longer want to be a fay, since a Grésil can abduct me. When I'm Noël's wife, he'll defend me."

"Every being obeys its destiny," sighs Perce-Neige. And stamping her foot: "Grésil! Grésil!"

"I'm running," says the elf.

"Slowly...I like quick people. Take Argentine back whence you took her."

"But..."

"I don't tolerate observations. Go quickly, and come back the same way."

VII. In which Noël finds a squire

The sun rises—a pale sun—and Noël wakes up.

"Those spinners," he says, have woven a fine tunic; I didn't feel the cold. I'd gladly have breakfast. Where can one have breakfast on earth? Argentine promised me a thin squire to serve me as a guide, but I don't see him. I ought to have accepted Hildewige's hospitality yesterday..."

He was about to head toward the castle, the black towers of which were visible, when he perceived a dainty page.

There's the promised squire, he thought, joyfully. But he ran forward, crying: "Godmother!"

"Greetings, Messire," said the dainty page.

"That costume suits you," Noël replied, circling the page. "Truly, truly! But one thing astonishes me!"

"Do you need a square to hold your horse and furbish your sword?"

"Why have you cut your hair?"

"I was wearing a helmet, Messire."

Noël smiles. "Come on, Argentine..."

"My name is Muguet."[41]

"You're joking?"

"A small person should have a small name."

_____

[41] The French common noun *muguet* refers to the flower known in English as a lily-of-the-valley.

It's another idea she's had, Noël thinks. *It's a sequel to yesterday's; since it amuses her, let's pretend not to recognize her.* "It's agreed, Muguet," he said, finally, "You're my squire. To seal the bargain, come and kiss me."

While kissing the dainty page, who hoists herself up on tiptoe, he laughs. "Do you know my godmother?" he says.

"I don't know, Messire."

"She's a crazy little fay."

"That'll be why a fay said to me yesterday: 'Go forth, Muguet, and when you see a handsome knight, be his squire.'"

She's making fun of me, Noël thinks. *My turn, now...* "Muguet, you've arrived just in time; you're going to take a message to the castle that is standing out blackly against the snow; you'll find a beautiful demoiselle there..."

The dainty page shivers.

"What's the matter with you? I'm not charging you with a disagreeable mission. Hildewige is good to behold, and, coming on my part, you'll be well-received."

"Where did you meet that beautiful demoiselle?"

"Curious child! Let it suffice for you to know that I saved her life."

"Already?"

"Already. You're sighing? You would have liked to see that? Have no fear, in my service you'll see many more. I wanted to spend my time slaying giants, but on reflection, I'll spend it saving beautiful demoiselles. We'll amuse ourselves a great deal, friend Muguet. But here she is,"

Hildewige was approaching in a sleigh.

"I was wrong not to believe Perce-Neige," sighs Argentine.

"Greetings, Hildewige," says Noël.

"Good day, Noël," replies Hildewige.

Hildewige! Noël! They greet one another as if they had grown up together, thinks Argentine.

"I wanted to revisit the place where I was so frightened," says the young woman. "I didn't think I'd encounter you here, but I hoped to find you when I returned; my father is expecting you. Did you sleep here, then, in the snow?"

"And I slept there very well, dreaming about you."

"Is this your page," she interjects, indicating Argentine.

"He's nice, isn't he?"

"He looks like a girl."

"You think so?"

"You must give him to me; he seems better made for playing the viol than wielding a sword.

"What do you think, Muguet?" asks Noël, laughing.

"I don't want that!" cries the page.

"My father, to whom I recounted my adventure, would like to thank you," said Hildewige. "When I told him that you had a fay for a godmother..."

"For a godmother!" cries Argentine, sharply.

This page isn't a page, thinks Hildewige.

She returns abruptly to her ponies and departs at the gallop, after having blown a kiss to Muguet.

"She has also seen that you're not a page," says Noël. "Let's sit down in the warm, between the bear's paws, and talk seriously."

He draws her to him gently, on the soft fur.

"What do you want?"

"Nothing," Argentine replies, bowing her head. She has so much chagrin that she does not perceive that she is weeping for the first time.

"You're annoyed with me," Noël continues. "You think that I find Hildewige pretty. Don't deny it! Certainly I find her pretty, and I love her already, but I don't love her in the same way that I love you"

"I'm only a fay!" sobs Argentine.

"If you were a woman, do you believe that I'd love you more? Since yesterday, I no longer understand you, and when I rack my brains trying to understand, it fatigues me. Hold on! She's asleep...isn't she pretty? She's even prettier than Hildewige."

Then an old woman followed by a wolf larger than a two-year-old colt appeared.

"Noël," said the old woman.

"You know my name?"

"I know everything."

"Since you know everything, tell me what Argentine wants."

"She wants to be your wife."

"You mean my fay. She can't be my wife, since she's a fay."

"When she wakes up, she'll be a woman."

"I don't know whether it's necessary to say *so much the better* or *too bad*. My head is hurting! What gave her the idea of sending me to travel the world in order to follow me here? We were so comfortable down below!"

"Let her sleep and go to the castle; it's necessary that she doesn't see you when she wakes up."

Noël hesitated, but he thought that if she woke up a fay, she would find him very rapidly, and if she woke up a woman, she would wait for him.

"I'll watch over her," said the old woman. "Take my wolf."

"If anything happens to her, I'll strangle you," said Noël.

The old woman would have smiled if she had been able to do so; she sat down in the snow, and Noël headed toward the castle, holding the wolf by the ear.

VIII. In which many things are explained

In the great hall of the castle, at the foot of a platform on which Otto and Hildewige were sitting, a large carpet had been extended to serve as lists.

On the steps, the castellan's old companions were crowded silently between their wives and daughters; at the back of the hall, the servants of both sexes were heaped up; the bare-chested champions were waiting. But Hildewige did not give the signal; she was hoping to see Noël.

171

Hildewige is nicknamed the Rose of the North.

She is not one of those pale roses that lean over, shivering; she is a mossy rose with gleaming leaves and nacreous petals. She has the fine hair of Emma the beautiful and the glaucous eyes of Otto the strong; when she puts on her skates, her greyhound can hardly follow her over the ice of the lake, and when she takes the tiller, the dragon with the great wings seems to be playing like a seal between the rocks of the coast.

She has the gentle smile of Emma the beautiful and the proud gaze of Otto the strong. When her white fingers spin wool, her heart sings the beautiful poem in which the blue steel of swords rings, in which the sound of oars striking the long waves of the North Sea can be heard.

Her heart is like a spring in a granite hollow, like a clear spring whose bed can be seen, and sand over which the shadows of clouds and the shadows of the wings of gyrfalcons pass without leaving any trace.

Like the blonde virgins who sing the Eddas she would have liked to follow the brave men who reap the foam of the waves to distant shores, but she has the heart of Emma the beautiful; next to her pensive father she remains the swallow that twitters in summer, the cricket that laughs on the hearth in winter.

But time is passing. In order to say to the men "Do well!" she is rising sadly to her feet when Noël appears, holding the huge wolf by the ear.

Otto shudders; it seems to him that he recognizes the wolf of the old woman with the iron spinning-wheel.

Before such a brilliant assembly, Noël ought to be shy, but nothing of the sort; he cuts through the servants and the warriors with his head held high, marching straight toward the platform.

He bows to Otto, smiles at Hildewige, and says to the wolf, indicating an empty place near to the cushion the color of dawn on which the virgin's feet are placed: "Lie down there."

If he's the person that I believe, thinks the old man, *He's entering my castle like a ray of sunligh*t. And addressing Noël: "You're going to wrestle; I'm wagering on you."

"Me too," says Hildewige.

In the midst of the warriors, Noël is like an ash-twig among knotty elms.

"We'll take the bet!" cry the men of the North.

"Your swords against a kiss," says Hildewige.

Remarking that the wrestlers have bare torsos, Noël takes off his tunic, and as he does not know where to put his sword, he hands it to Hildewige.

The men smile, but the old man, seeing that golden hilt-guard and that silver scabbard, on which birds and flowers are enlaced, murmurs: "He's the person I'm waiting for; only an elf could have forged such a sword..."

"Let's go; do well, Noël!"

Noël does not know how to wrestle; when the first man leaps forward, his arms extended, he takes the two arms by the wrists and parts them as he would have parted two sprig of gorse barring his path.

The warrior tries to seize him but he lifts him up gently and, holding him in the air, he says to Hildewige: "What is it necessary to do with him?"

"Give him to me," replies the virgin gaily.

"Here he is!"

And he sets the warrior down between the paws of the wolf, whose muzzle creases.

When he turns round, the lists are empty.

Otto cried: "It's him!"

Noël did not understand why everyone was astonished by such a simple thing.

He had put his tunic on again and buckled his sword.

"You're my son," said the old man.

"You're my brother," said Hildewige.

"You'll be our chief," said her suitors, glad no longer to have him as a rival.

"Excuse me!" Noël exclaims. "I'm very touched, but I don't understand anything of what you're saying."

"Has a fay," the old man interjected, "kept you under the waves in an emerald grotto?"

"A fay found me under a juniper bush and I grew up next to her in a seam of silver. It's necessary, in order for you to inform yourselves, to go and find the old woman who knows everything; at this moment she's guarding the sleeping Argentine."

"I have no need, my son, to seek any longer. You are Hildewige's brother. Kiss her."

"Gladly. This castle is a fine castle; brave men fill it; I'll go fetch Argentine."

"I'll go with you, Brother," says Hildewige.

The rose now has a solid support, thinks the hero of the North. *I can go to rejoin the beloved of my youth, and rediscover on high the happiness of old.*

To the servants, he says: "Children, set the table..."

To his guests he says: "Friends, sit down around me; I have fought bravely; I have the right to repose."

IX. In which everything recommences

Hand in hand, they marched over the white snow.

"I shall love your fay," said Hildewige. "She's a pretty sparrow, and I shall make her a lovely nest."

"Her dwarves," said Noël, "will forge you a golden ring, and among the brave men who love you, you shall choose."

"I don't want a golden ring, I want a maple-wood boat, which will hold all three of us."

"To go where, my sister?"

"To go forward."

Hand in hand, they marched over the white snow.

"You were not mine yesterday, today you are mine," said the old woman, breaking one of Argentine's hairs; "I shall spin on my spinning-wheel the days that remain to you. Will they be long? I don't know—what does it matter to me? I shall spin the days that remain to you."

She fled, rustling like a dry leaf.

Argentine woke up, and called to Noël.

The she saw before her a white reindeer, which said to her. "Since you're only a woman now, I'll take you where Noël is coming to search for you.

"Let's go," Argentine replied.

While they were chatting, hand in hand, the great wolf had run away.

When they arrived in the forest they no longer found the old woman, and nothing remained between the bear's paws but the bonnet with the eagle feather.

"Oh, my brother!" said Hildewige.

"Don't torment yourself," Noël responds. "She's a little jealous. She's sulking somewhere nearby... Argentine! Argentine!"

"Perhaps the wolves have come?"

"Wolves don't eat fays. She's sulking, I tell you. Argentine! Argentine! She doesn't know who you are; she's sulking. But she's jealous; she'll be at the castle this evening. Perhaps she's already there...? She's certainly there...let's go back quickly."

The young woman took away the cap.

On the back of the white reindeer, Argentine dreams, and the more she dreams, the more the past seems to have been a dream that is gradually fading away.

Was I a fay? She could almost doubt it. But she knows that she loves, and she is going to where Noël will come.

Having arrived on the edge of the sea, the reindeer stopped.

"I can't take you any further," it said, "but if you're not afraid, I can see a salmon that can take you over the sea."

"Since I'm going to where he will come, let the salmon carry me."

As it quit her, the reindeer said: "In your husband's house, it's necessary to have the footfalls of a mouse and the hearing of a hare."

The salmon swam toward Denmark.

When Hildewige and Noël went into the great hall, the table was laid.

"Console yourself, my daughter," said the hero of the North; "the woman who knows everything said to me: 'When the rosebud blooms, amour will bring you the handsome white carnation. The woman has brought you to me in order to love me, you will find her again.'"

Then he sat Noël down to his tight and Hildewige to his left.

"Friends," he said then to his guests, "Noël will be what I was, because the grafted apple tree cannot yield a wrinkled apple." Then, addressing Noël: "You must not forget that it is necessary never to ask for what cannot be done; if you want to be the pilot, it is necessary to know the reefs; if you want to be the sword of your men, it is also necessary to be their shield. Remember, my son, that the strongest hydromel is made with the sweetest honey; if you want to be obeyed, command mildly..."

The hero of the North spoke thus for a long time, while his guess assuaged their hunger. When no one was any longer touching the dishes, he stood up, and after having hugged Hildewige and Noël, he went out without saying where he was going.

On the back of the salmon, which is speeding like an arrow, Argentine dreams, and the more she dreams the more the past seems to have been a dream that is gradually fading away.

She is going to where Noël will come, she no longer knows anything else.

Over the green sea the salmon glides like an arrow; having arrived at the sand of the shore, it stops.

"I can't go any further," it said, "but I can see a mare that can take you where Noël will come to look for you."

While the young woman, who is twenty years old, and only one day old, mounts the dappled mare, the salmon says to her: "In your husband's house, it's necessary to be like amber, which burns without leaving any ash, and like salt, which preserves the summer catch for the winter."

While the mare traverses the endless plains it is as if Argentine is emerging from a dream, not knowing whether she is awake or still asleep.

After having crossed forests and rivers the mare stops beside the dense thicket of rose-bushes and brambles that encircles the city of the Aesir.

"I'm returning whence I came," it says. "In your husband's house, be like the plain that gives us wheat, like the hill that gives us honey."

Then a fox yaps;

"Follow me; I've hollowed out a path through the brambles, a winding path between the thorny stems of the white rose-bushes. Follow me, young woman, into your husband's house; you shall be as lively as the grouse and as brave as the quail."

The sated guests had taken their leave. Noël was alone with Hildewige under the ash-wood beam of the high hall, by the fireside where the beautiful Emma, the beautiful dead woman, had rocked the cradle lined with swansdown with her foot.

"What will you do now?" said Hildewige.

"Search for her until I have found her."

"I would go with you," replied the daughter of the dead woman, "if I were not for the old man the staff that moves aside the stones of the road, the mirror in which he sees the days of old.

"Brother, bring us your bride; she will be received in our house like the warm breeze of May; she will be fêted like the first catkin of the willow."

X. In which what has been seen before is seen again

Argentine has followed the fox into the narrow path under the brambles, the somber path beneath the flowering rose-bushes; she is in the city of the Aesir.

The past is no more, for her than a fading dream; she is twenty years old and only one day old. She has forgotten No-ël's name but she remembers that someone is coming to search for her, and that memory is in her heart, like a drop of dew in the calyx of a anemone.

"That's not a fay," said the sylphs. "That's a woman."

"It isn't a woman," replied the wood-pigeons, "it's the Norwegian blonde who has come to search for a ray of sunlight in her cradle."

"She's still our sister," said the laughing fays. "She's still Argentine, the dreamer with blue eyes; she is welcome in the city of the Aesir."

The fays had brought her to the palace without a roof, where the wood-pigeons build their nests in the marble friezes, where the twelve heroes sit down every year on the twelve seats around the round table.

The Aesir were gathered there, talking about the past before full cups. Behind them, standing against the wall, their great golden shields were flamboyant, like twelve suns, illuminating the room.

On seeing her enter, Thor with the heavy hand said to Odin the one-eyed, who is presiding at the table: "You who divine everything, can you tell me what I am seeing?"

Then Balder, the hero who sings like a swan, said: "It's the flower of spring, grown down there on our tombs."

But Argentine replied: "A fox guided me, a mare brought me, a salmon carried me, a reindeer abducted me, and someone I'm waiting for ought to come to look for me here. Greetings, heroes!"

Then Odin, having reflected, said: "Let's squeeze together, so that there's room for her."

As there were only twelve seats around the table, Odin put his bronze helmet with great silver wings on the floor beside him. It was higher than the seats,

Balder made a cushion of his brilliant scarf, put it between the two wings and sad to Argentine: "Sit down, white ermine of the land of snows. Sit down among us, the most beautiful of our daughters, the freshest flower of the land that we gave to our sons."

Then Thor, the smith, saw that the helmet was too high. And he put his hammer under Argentine's feet, like a footstool.

It was a fine feast.

Odin, who divines everything, having reflected, said: "It's Noël, the son of Otto the Brave, who will come to search for you."

Then Balder, whose cup was empty, took the tortoiseshell harp hanging from his belt between his blue sword and his jade dagger, and he sang the great deeds of Otto, the hero of the North. Then he sang the amorous laments of the daughter of the waves and the chagrin of Emma the Beautiful when she no longer found the swansdown cradle by the fireside. When he said how the white carnation had been found under a juniper bush in the snowy forest while the bells were ringing for Christmas, Argentine cried:

"I remember now. Before being a woman I was a fay; but I love him today even more that I loved him yesterday."

And Odin the wise said: "In your husband's house, you shall be the lamp that drives away the thief, the ember hidden beneath the ashes, which reignites the fire."

The stars fell behind the mountain, and the Aesir got up in order to go to join them.

Argentine remained alone with the wood-pigeons, the sylphs and the fays in the marble palace.

XI. In which Noël sets forth

Argentine, Noël thought, *is certainly in the grotto. She's sulking, but she isn't annoyed; she will have left the door to the crystal staircase open.*

In the depths of his heart he was a little sad, but he could not help saying: "It's a good day; I've rediscovered a father who is a famous hero, a sister whom all the brave men are disputing; I've discovered that the strongest are not as strong as me. If that little fool hadn't turned her brain upside down, my father would have blessed us, Hildewige would have kissed us, and, the dinner having been served, we'd be married...."

"And by now, instead of retracing this path through the snow for the fourth time, I'd be helping Hildewige arrange my sparrow's nest coquettishly."

A pack of wolves was devouring the cadaver of the bear; they did not disturb themselves.

Where the crystal staircase had opened the day before, he saw nothing but a white carpet, without a crease or a wrinkle.

She's definitely annoyed with me, Noël thought. *She's left me to freeze in the snow.*

A terrible anger took hold of him. Seizing a wolf by the tail, he swung it around like a sling and struck the others with it, which were looking at him, bristling. They fled, howling.

And he cried: "I no longer love her; she's a fool, and wicked. I'll choose a wife among the beautiful demoiselles that lowered their eyes at the table...and if ever she takes it into her head to be jealous, I'll..." He threw the cadaver of the wolf a hundred paces away. "If she ever decides to behave like Argentine..." He wept hot tears. "But she won't be jealous and I'll love her dearly, as I would have loved you if you'd wanted, Argentine..."

He would perhaps have wept more if a cloud of hail hadn't whipped his cheeks.

"Argentine! Godmother!" he murmured. "Be kind; I'm no longer angry with you. Open the grotto for me; the weather on earth is frightful. I'm the son of a hero, I'll be a hero myself, since a grafted apple-tree can't bear wrinkled fruit; I'm the brother of a sister whom the brave dispute, and I love you more than all of that. Come on, Godmother..."

It was not Argentine who appeared but Grésil, in gala costume.

"Have you seen Argentine?" Noël asked him

Ah! He's still here, that youth, the cause of my marriage, thought Grésil. *I was looking for Argentine but I find him; I prefer that. Wait, wait...!*

"You're asking for Argentine?" he finally said.

"Yes. I've rediscovered my sister, but Argentine didn't know that Hildewige was my sister, and she was jealous...you understand? She was chagrined, and..."

"She's consoled herself; I'm returning from her wedding."

"That's not true."

"Do you believe that I'd be traveling the world in a satin doublet if I weren't returning from a wedding?"

"That's true," sighed Noël...and he fainted.

I'm going to be able to avenge myself! thought Grésil. *Without Argentine, I wouldn't be the unfortunate husband of a true devil. What shall I do with this youth? Since she loves him, I'll marry him off...*

Grésil spread out his white mantle and wrapped Noël in it.

When Noël came round he was in a large plain, on the edge of a lake with desiccated reeds, the warm water of which was fuming; teal were swimming there.

"Thank you, Grésil," sighed Noël. "You've understood that I could no longer live, and you've brought me to the only place where I could drown myself in such cold weather."

And without thinking, without thinking about the old man, or Hildewige, he threw himself into the clear water.

The lake was deep, he arrived breathless in a green grotto where an undine was weeping.

The undine recognized the white carnation and uttered a scream.

"We'll weep together," said Noël. "The woman I loved has forgotten me."

"If one died of amour, I'd be dead," sighed the undine.

She took him in her arms and rose up to the surface again.

Thanks to the doublet woven by the dainty spinners, Noël had only wet his hair; its curls, burnished by the water, were dangling over his shoulders.

It really is the white carnation, thought the undine; *I thought I was seeing the man I loved when, in the spry of the waves, at the prow of his red dragon, he went bare-headed where the wind pushed him.*

Noël, still slightly stunned, admired her; with her aquamarine eyes flecked with gold, her ivory shoulders and her hair brilliant with reflections like a new sword, she was as beautiful as moonlight.

"You're the living portrait of Otto the Brave," she told him. "You're not one of those one forgets."

"Alas!"

While they were speaking, the lake froze,

"Was it the flame of your eyes that warmed it up?" Noël asked.

"It was my tears. For twenty years I've been weeping night and day for my emerald palace. If you wanted to carry me to the nearest shore, I'd guide your boat and show you the paths that lead to the land of gold."

"My beloved's hair was so shiny that I find gold dull; if I had heaps of it I'd trade it for one of her hairs."

"You're not one of those one forgets; return whence you came and let me weep, since you don't want to take me away."

"Argentine told me, when she loved me: 'Noël, never make anyone cry; tears burn the hearts of those who cause them to flow.' I don't want you to weep..."

He carried the daughter of the waves away in his arms.

For weeks, and then for more weeks, as a falcon carries a dove, over the snowy plains, through forests, he carried her. The nacreous arms of the undine were wrapped around his neck, her fine hair brushed his cheeks, her heart beat against his heart; but he only thought of Argentine.

And was the daughter of the waves thinking again about the man who had disdained her in the mist of the sunset?

The heart of a woman is like a gulf; no one can fathom its depth. On Noël's breast, the undine allowed herself to be cradled as if on the waves, for weeks, and then more weeks, like a seamew asleep on the green wave.

But without wearying, night and day, she sang to him what the waves sing to the keel of ships, and the cutting edges of oars, and when Noël reached the shore, he knew what the reapers of the sea know.

On the edge of the sea bewailed for such a long time, before unknotting her arms, the undine hesitated. If he had not been thinking about his beloved, Noël might perhaps have felt the arms tightening around his neck; but he was only thinking about Argentine, night and day; he put her down gently where the waves died in a pink fleece of foam.

As she plunged into the sea, the undine said to him: "The woman you love will be like a pearl, which dies when its master no longer wishes to wear it."

"Where shall I go now?" said Noël.

He raised his head and saw, on the mountain, the pointed turrets of Otto's castle.

If what the undine said is true, he thought, *Argentine will have returned there...*

For weeks, and yet more weeks, he had been listening to the songs that render the heroes of the North strong; he was no longer a child, he was a man.

"A woman belongs," he said, "to the man who can take her; amour is the harvest of glory; I want the woman I love; neither the waves nor the earth can hide her."

He climbs with a firm step toward the castle perched on the high cliff, like a fishing eagle.

XII. In which Noël finds Hildewige and Otto again

Hildewige is under the vault of the first courtyard; she is coming back from the hut made of bark chips where the witch reads the future on a reindeer-hide drum.

In a dream she had seen Argentine and Noël in a marble palace filled with wood-pigeons under a flamboyant sky, where roses bloom in winter and summer.

She told the wise woman what she had seen in the dream and the wise woman threw a white pebble, a black pebble and three grains of wheat on to the drum covered with signs. The white pebble responded "Soon," the black pebble responded "Never," and the grains of wheat responded "Perhaps."

She is returning home pensive.

"The signs of the future," she says, "are not written on drumskins, the words of the future do not fall from the ringing of little bells; the future is what the brave make it, the future is a blank skin that one etches with one's sweat, a bell without a clapper that sounds under the sword. I shall say to the old man, who is leaning like a mossy fir-tree: *O my father, my cherished father, I would like to sleep on your knees like the she-cat that guards the hearth, but it's necessary to find Noël. When I've found him, I'll come back very quickly, and you will be in your house like an apple-tree laden with apples that eve-ryone envies.*"

She arrives in the middle of the courtyard as Noël emerges from the vault.

"Have you seen her?" he asks, before greeting her, before sending her a kiss with his hand.

"No, Brother, but Father has seen the old woman who knows everything; he will tell you where she is."

"Since we know where she is, we'll bring her back here."

Noël is no longer a child; for weeks he has heard the songs that render strength; those songs are speaking in his heart, and their refrains are flowing in his veins.

The old man is sitting by the fire, but his spirit is far, far away, in the land of clouds, whether the gentle teal has built its nest.

Why is his spirit alone near to her? Why, since he is thirsty for death, does he not drink from the ivory cup?

Because the old woman with the iron spinning-wheel has said to him: "The rosebud needs a sword for support, and Noël is only a rush in a rapid river; can he contend with the current that bears him away?"

When Noël entered the vast hall, the old man saw that he was no longer a child, but a man.

It only requires a week, he thinks, *to ripen barley; it only requires a week to redden the berries of the service tree.*

"Father," Noël says to him, after having placed the wrinkled hand on his head, "I would like to be the cup in the depth of which you will rediscover your memories, but amour has burned me and I am nothing but ash. When I bring back to your roof the woman I love, you shall have a golden cup, as fresh cup, for your old age."

"The old woman has told me, child," the hero of the North replies, "that it is necessary for you first to make the giant with the white beard cry mercy."

"If the thing can be done, it will be."

"But a pilot is necessary to guide your boat; the giant is sailing on an iceberg in the Sea of Darkness."

Then Noël sang what the waves say to the keels of boats and the cutting edge of oars, and what the wind weeps to stiffened rigging.

"Who taught you those songs?" asked the old man.

"The daughter of the sea that I carried over my heart for weeks, with her arms around my neck."

Then the old man got up, as straight as a pine and as strong as an oak. "Hildewige," he said, "bring me the largest cup, full of hydromel."

He emptied it in a single draught, as straight as a pine and as strong as an oak, "Noël," he said, then, "give me my sword."

As straight as a pine and as strong as an oak, he cleaved the bench with a single stroke.

And he said: "I am not falling apart piece by piece like an old boat in the mud of the port; like the red dragon with wings outspread, I am breaking on a reef..."

He was dead.

XIII. In which the city of the Aesir is seen again

Argentine is living alone with the wood-pigeons, the sylphs and the fays.

The wood-pigeons bring her wheat, one grain at a time, the sylphs give her honeycombs, and the fays, while playing, pick up oranges and peaches for her in the evergreen orchards. Her days are long.

She sits on the marble steps pensively, trying to remember the days of old, but the past is nothing for her but a forgotten dream; she is no longer a fay but a woman.

"Beautiful friends," she says to the wood-pigeons, "if I had your wings, I would fly from sunset to dawn, night and day, until I had found the man for whom I hope."

The wood-pigeons reply: "Wait! He will come."

But she is no longer a fay; she can no longer understand the language of the wood-pigeons.

Why did the reindeer abduct her? Why did the salmon bear her away? Why had the mare brought her?

"Spring is commencing," coo the wood-pigeons. "Sylphs, it's necessary to depart; the larches must be verdant out there; fays, it's necessary to depart."

"If we leave her," the sylphs reply, "who will give her honey?"

Then a chariot drawn by two cats descended from the sky. It brought Freya, the protectress of lovers.

"Argentine," she said, "It's me who bridled the reindeer, it's me who sent the salmon and it's me who saddled the mare; I'm the goddess of love. You must weep, as I have wept, if you want to live forever."

Having spoken thus, the blonde goddess, whose eternal tears fall in golden pearls, ascended again into the sky, and Argentine said to the wood-pigeons: "Fly away, so that I may weep."

The wood-pigeons have gone, bearing the sylphs and the fays away to the lands of the North.

XIV. In which Grésil is seen again

Why has Grésil married? He has none of the pleasures of marriage and all the annoyances; he is only the humble valet of his better half. It is forbidden for him to idle at the foot of cliffs because he crumples the saxifrage there; he must not linger in the forests because he fades the violets there.

He can only wander at his leisure over deserted shores and pathless plateaux.

One morning, he was running between the sunlit sand and the utterly black sea—it was in April—when he perceived a boat dancing on the waves.

"Let's distract ourselves a little," he says.

He blows, and the waves crackle under the hail, the hull groans, the mast bends, but the boat continues its route directly.

A vigorous helmsman is holding the tiller, he thinks. *It's necessary that it capsizes; I'm too bored!*

He blows so strongly that the yard-arm dips into the water, but the boat holds straight to its course. Then, furious, he launches forth.

A woman is holding the tiller, and Noël, leaning on the dragon of the prow, is gazing at the waves insouciantly.

"It's you!" howls Grésil. "You're standing up to me! Wait!"

He blows so forcefully that the torn sail flies away and the tiller breaks in Hildewige's hands.

The sharp rocks of the coast were very close. Grésil could already see the man he hated broken against the cliffs when the undine appeared in front of the boat. She placed her hand on the timbers and the boat stopped like a horse under the weight of the bit.

"Where are you going?" she said.

"I'm seeking the giant with the white beard," Noël replied.

"I'll take you to where he is."

While the undine, with her hand on the timbers of the ship, which is following her meekly, glides over the water, Grésil returns to his palace of clouds.

He finds Perce-Neige there.

"Where have you been?" the fay says to him. "You're never at home."

"I've been for a stroll. Am I not master of taking a stroll when I want to? You pretend to be my wife, but I don't know. If we're united let's separate. I'll take back my liberty and I'll render yours to you."

She touches him with her crystal scepter, and his misty mantle turns into a block of ice, under which he groans, crushed. His servants and his subjects come running; the scepter touches the vaporous walls of the palace, which congeal, and they are all prisoners around the immobile elf.

"I love you too much to let you wander the world," says the laughing queen.

"Oh, my cherished spouse," gasps the elf, "I'll always obey you. Return my liberty, and I'll be your slave."

The queen touches the mantle and the walls of ice with her finger, and they become clouds again.

"You see what I can do," she says. "Go in search of Argentine."

The elf departs over the snowy land.

The boat cleaved the waves over which ice-floes were floating, and the undine sang to the attentive Hildewige the poems of the sea where palaces are hidden beneath the seaweed and pearls fall in cascades into nacreous basins, in the depths of blue abysms.

They had been traveling for a week, perhaps two, when they perceived the giant with the white beard on an errant iceberg.

"Giant," Noël shouted to him, "I've come to wrestle with you. I'm the son of Otto the Brave."

"I can't refuse what you request," replied the giant. "If I'm vanquished I'll be your slave, but if I'm the stronger, you'll be mine."

And the contest commenced.

Hildewige, standing in the prow of the boat, and the undine, hanging on to the timbers, watched anxiously.

The contest lasted for a long time. Only Otto the Brave was strong enough to defeat a giant; Noël was vanquished.

"You're my slave," said the giant, "but I'll be generous, as your father was. You'll be free if the beautiful young woman who is weeping on the boat brings me two golden apples."

"I'll bring them to you," replied Hildewige. "Be patient, Noël."

Noël wept, not in chagrin but in shame.

"You're a rude companion," the giant said. "When you have your adult strength, we'll wrestle again. The beautiful young woman is certainly worthy of being your sister; she'll bring the two golden apples and we'll try our strength as two friends."

While the undine pushed the boat, Hildewige dreamed of the land where the golden apples ripen, and Noël listened to the giant telling him the secrets of the first day,

Grésil was searching for Argentine throughout Norway. Not having found her, he went to search further afield.

XV. In which Hildewige encounters the Viking fleet

"Do you know," said Hildewige, "where the golden apples ripen?"

"I don't know," the undine replied. "I'm the daughter of the Northern seas; but I've seen them shining in the hands of Vikings returning in summer from the lands of the west. You're my sister, Hildewige, my beloved sister, and I want to free Noël; we'll follow the route of the fleets and we'll end up finding the tree of the golden apples."

One morning, at sunrise, Hildewige perceived boats.

"Who are you?" shouted a warrior as handsome as the day, from the leading boat. "Who are you, who are traveling against the wind with neither oar nor sail?"

"I'm Hildewige," the virgin replied. "I'm the daughter of Otto the Brave."

"Otto was my father's companion," said the Viking. "They mingled their blood in the cup; they loved one another. You are as beautiful, Hildewige, as Freya the blonde goddess; if you want to climb into my boat, you shall be queen and I shall be king."

"Viking, I won't climb into your boat; the boat is the house of the laborer of the waves, and a virgin should only enter her husband's house. I'm going to the land where the golden apples ripen."

"It's far away, that land, and the sea is an untamed mare; you have neither sail nor rudder; you'll be its plaything."

Then the undine raised herself up, smiling; she had seen Hildewige's cheeks blush when the hero of the North spoke to her.

"Viking," she said, "I am the pilot of Otto's daughter."

And the boat without a sail and without an oar glides like a salmon between the black boats full of valiant warriors.

"Companions," says the Viking, then, "you have sworn to follow me as the reapers follow the man who goes into the field first. Today, I'm no longer a reaper; I'm a hunter pursuing a roe deer; I release you from your oaths."

The fleet continues its route toward Norway, and the Viking follows the boat without oars pushed by the daughter of the waves.

That Viking is the bravest of the heroes of the North; in his house he has heaps of gold and piles of silver, amassed at sword-point.

Then Hildewige' cheeks take on the hue of the eglantine of the woods, and the undine sings while pushing the boat:

"Fortunate the woman loved by a brave man! Fortunate the woman whose house has a sword for a bolt!

"Fortunate the mother loved by a brave man! Fortunate the woman whose children have a shield for a cradle!

"They have no need to release dogs into the enclosure by night; they have no need to put thorns in the gaps in the hedge; a blue sword guards them, and the scintillating flowers of a shield stop thieves better than hedges of plum-trees."

Hildewige thought: "If Noël had a brother, there would be two turtle-doves in the nest of two hawks."

For weeks they had been sailing toward the sunset when a warm current, azure in color, caressed the undine's flanks.

"I can't go any further," she said. "This sea is no longer my domain; unknown routes are opening before me."

"I've followed these routes!" cried the Viking. "Climb into my boat, Hildewige; you will be my sister."

"A man who is afraid of nothing never lies," said the undine. "Sit down without dread in the shadow of the brave man's sword; I shall return to where Noël is captive, and I'll tell him that you'll return, bringing his ransom."

A woman, thought Hildewige, *is not like a rose, which allows itself to be picked by whoever wants it.*

And she climbed into the Viking's boat.

Hildewige is sitting at the foot of the mast, between the warriors with white arms.

Then the Viking, in order to abridge the hours, and in order that no one will hear his heart speak, picks up his maple-wood harp The bold reaper with the red scythe has read, during his sleep, the runes engraved on the tongue of the Dragon, the god who makes verses vibrate.

He has picked up his maple-wood harp, and while the warriors ply the heavy oars in cadence. He sings:

"Mistress of the house, open the door to the one who is knocking; his feet will not sully the sanded floor; his feet have never touched the mud of roads.

"Mistress of the house, open the door to the one who is knocking; for weeks he has not slept beneath a roof, and his heart is only a rock polished by the waves.

"Mistress of the house, it is not a beggar who is knocking; he had golden rings and silver necklaces, bracelets of coral and enameled belts.

"Mistress of the house, it is not a thief who is knocking; he has only harvested his field, but his field is limitless, it is as long as his sword.

"Mistress of the house, my furrows are always sown, the crop always ripens there, and the waves of the ocean are the cattle in my cowshed..."

While he sings, the bronze shields ring against the planks, the ash-wood oars dip into the sea devoid of ripples, and Hildewige's heart beats gently.

The sun was flamboyant; a burning wind inflated the sail; the warriors were asleep; Hildewige was holding the tiller.

Then a streaming, emaciated, breathless being appeared, sitting on the yard-arm.

"If you are the elf of these unknown seas, what do you want?" Hildewige said to him.

"Alas, I'm Grésil, the elf of Norway. Under this fiery sun I'm dissolving into water; let me hide for a moment in the shadow of your sail."

"Where are you going, so far from home?"

"To search for Argentine."

"We're also searching for her."

"It's necessary for me to find her; my wife wants it. Never marry, young woman... In the shade of your sail I can breathe a little... Never marry, believe me; I'm no longer anything but a shadow, no longer anything but skin.... Never marry; now I'm cooked, and if I return to my palace I'll freeze."

"I recognize you," said Hildewige. "Noël has mentioned you to me."

"I can only go away, then—but I was so comfortable!"

"If you want, we can travel together. Inflate the sail when you've got your breath back, and we won't tell Perce-Neige that you tried to drown Noël."

"I'll inflate your sail night and day; since you're going in search of Argentine; when you've found her, I'll have found her too. But don't say anything to my sweet wife... Don't marry, young woman."

While the warriors sleep, the elf inflates the sail and the boat flies so rapidly that in the morning it runs aground in a peaceful cove, where the green trees are shining with golden apples.

"Wake up, Viking," the virgin says, launching the docile boat over the fine sand; "wake up, we've arrived; I can see golden apples shining on green trees ."

XVI. In which Hildewige and Noël continue their voyage

While Hildewige is going to the lands of the sun in search of golden apples, Noël is on the iceberg with the giant with the white beard. But the giant has not forgotten Otto the Brave, and he does not treat Noël as a slave but as a companion.

"You'll soon be free," he tells him. "Hildewige will certainly bring your ransom, and then we'll wrestle again, and the victor will remain the friend of the loser."

That giant was of the race those whom Vainamoinen, the god of Finland, had expelled from Lapland a long time before the coming of the Aesir; he sang to Noël of the days of Creation, and Otto's son engraved the songs in his memory, after those that the undine with the blue-green eyes had taught him.

He now knows how the world emerged from an egg laid by an eagle on the knee of Vainamoinen; he knows why Imarigen, the eternal smith, being unable to find a wife to his liking, forged one of silver. He knows why the luminous Aesir have exiled from the heavens the gods of vague form, who are still wandering, deformed and monstrous, in the mists of the North.[42]

Noël is no longer a child, he is a man. He is a man who has not allowed the fresh flower of his youth to fade; he will be as great as those who only have one amour in their life.

The hours are long for him on the iceberg, which is floating in the eddies of the Pole; he is always looking toward the sunset. On the sea, where white icebergs pass by like gulls, he is searching for a black dot.

But the icebergs, like gulls, come and go, and he does not see his sister's boat on the sea.

---

[42] These details are taken from Elias Lönnrot's synthesized Finish epic *Kalevala*, but the eternal smith is there named Ilmarinen.

One morning, while the giant is still asleep, he sees two moustached seals drawing a large seashell. Perce-Neige emerges from it.

"What are you doing here, Noël?" says the astonished queen. "Are you no longer searching for Argentine?"

"I was searching for her, beautiful queen, but today I'm a prisoner. The giant has defeated me, and I must give him two golden apples for my ransom."

"Then you're free," relies the fay. "I've brought Immer golden apples from my garden; you can give them to him."[43]

"Alas, beautiful queen, the apples that he wants ripen in the lands of the sun; they can't ripen in your garden."

"You don't know, child, that my palace is mirrored in a blue sea that never freezes, in a warm sea where the whales come to nurse their infants. Over my palace on high the sun only sets once a year, and while it shines for six months, oranges ripen in my crystal greenhouses."

The giant woke up. "Be welcome, Perce-Neige," he said. "What have you been doing for such a long time?"

"Immer, I'm married. I've married Grésil."

"When we were gods, I was known as 'the Wise'; it's said that one chooses badly when one has been searching for too long."

"It was necessary. I'm taking Noël away; here are two golden apples for his ransom, and here are two more for the good advice that you're going to give us, father of wisdom. We're looking for Argentine—where is it necessary to go?"

"It's necessary to go to where Freya, the blonde goddess, has a temple surrounded by a golden chain; it's necessary for you to ask her to bring you the one whose wings have been broken by amour."

Having said that, the father of wisdom said to Noël: "Your ransom is paid; would you like us to wrestle again now, like two friends."

---

[43] The name given to the giant, Immer, is German for "forever."

"I'd like that," Noël replied.

And the contest commenced. But the songs had inflated Noël's heart, their refrains were flowing in his veins, and he was no longer a child. After having wrestled for a week, he said to the giant:

"I believe, Immer," that we're as strong as one another.

"I believe so too," said the fay. "Clasp hands like two friends."

They held out their hands, and Perce-Neige said: "Now it's necessary to go to Freya's temple without delay."

"What about Hildewige?" Noël replied.

"I'll wait for her, while chatting about the past with Immer, who still knows what other people have forgotten. Mount my seashell; my seals will take you to the round beach where, under the gray ash-trees, a golden chain surrounds the temple of the goddess of love."

Noël climbed into the huge seashell.

While the seals were drawing Noël, the Viking's ship, full of golden apples, was heading for Norway.

It soon reached Immer's iceberg, the undine pushing it again. The days seemed short to the blonde virgin; the Viking's eyes were bright and their gaze slid over Hildewige's cheeks like a kiss.

XVII. In which Noël enters Freya's temple

The bells of the periwinkles were ringing in the spring, the wood-pigeons were arriving, carrying on their wings the dreaming sylphs and the laughing fays.

After having caressed the round heads of the seals that had brought him to the beach. Noël is wondering what path to take when a rustle causes him to raise his head.

"Oh, wood-pigeons, beautiful wood-pigeons," he says, "you who are come from afar, have you seen my beloved? She resembles the chamois of the rocks, the squirrel of the woods, the ermine of the snows. Her cheeks are pink apples, her lips strawberries, her teeth white currants; when she speaks, one thinks that one is hearing a pearl necklace; when she moves her head, one thinks one is seeing a golden shield shining.

"The blonde chamois, that lovely squirrel, that chaste ermine," the wood-pigeons reply, "can only be the one who is waiting in the city of the Aesir."

"That's her," say the sylphs.

"And here's Noël!" exclaim the fays, letting themselves slide like raindrops over the wings of the wood-pigeons.

They surround Noël.

"You're as dainty as mice," the child who has become a man says to them, "on seeing you I thought I was seeing grains of wheat flying from the hands of the sower in a ray of sunlight. If you have seen the one who has caught my heart on the hooks of her eyelashes and the net of her hair, tell me."

"When she wept night and day over her troubles, we said to her: 'Has your Noël wings like a butterfly, then? Does he know a thousand songs, like a nightingale? We understand now why she was weeping night and day; it's a bard that she loves, a butterfly of the flowers of dream, a nightingale of nights of amour. If you want to rejoin her, you who can, like the Master, give a body to your dreams, it's necessary to create a horse with wings, with feet like a swan's in order to swim, a horn on the forehead in order to defend her and a silken mane in order to carry her..."

"I'm not what you say, I'm only Noël, and very sad; I'm looking for the temple of Freya, the friend of lovers."

"It's over there in that ash-grove; follow us," coo the wood-pigeons. "We're the chicks of the good goddess."

Noël follows the wood-pigeons; under the green ash-trees he sees a golden chain surrounding a great stone circle. In that circle, strewn with silver sand, there is only a sword leaning on the trunk of a rose-bush.

Noël stepped over the golden chain fearlessly; he had no soot in his heart. He marched over the silver sand without leaving footprints; he had no mud on his feet. He parted the branches of the rose-bush without soiling them; his hands were unstained. And he read the runes engraved on the blade.

The runes said:

Amour is the harvest of tears, the grain of the brave, the bread of the strong.

Then I must be loved, thought Noël.

But he did not see Freya,

I shall see her soon, he said to himself. *The father of wisdom told me so, and a worthy man does not lie.*

He went to sleep at the foot of the rose-bush.

Noël has a beautiful dream; he is in a silent city where twelve palaces are aligned around a marble palace. He climbs the steps of the temple, and at round table, on a cushion the color of the rainbow, between the silver wings of a bronze helmet, he sees Argentine sitting, surrounded by twelve heroes.

"Do you know the man who is coming in Argentine?" says the one-eyed hero who is presiding over the feast.

"It's the man for whom I'm waiting," replies the fay who has become a woman.

"Oh! Godmother! Godmother!" cries Noël.

It is a beautiful dream.

Then he is in the silver grotto, in the midst of the spinners as brown as rushes as the squat dwarves with otter-fur caps; the spinners have hands full of brilliant veils made of silken fabrics; the dwarves are weighed down by necklaces and bracelets in beautiful red gold, and elves with flames on their foreheads are carving the final step of a crystal staircase.

Argentine says to him: "Will you never regret the fay when she is your wife?"

It is a beautiful dream, but the most beautiful dreams come to an end; Noël wakes up.

He is in a fir-wood, the branches of which are sparkling in the sunrise, and next to him, on the moss, in her page's doublet, Argentine is asleep; her hair has grown again, it is the color of wheat.

I wasn't dreaming, Noël says to himself. *Freya has returned the woman I love to me.*

Argentine wakes up.

"Have you slept well, Muguet," he asks her, laughing.

"I don't know, Messire," replies the dainty page, throwing her arms around him.

They had been searching for one another for such a long time that they could embrace!

XVIII. In which Noël returns to his house

The pointed turrets of Otto's castle were shining on the mountain.

"Let's go home," said Noël.

"I'd never dare in this page's doublet... If only I had my cap, it would hide me a little."

"Don't look for it; Hildegarde took it away on the evening when you were jealous. Let's go, Muguet; you wanted me to be a knight, and every knight must have a page."

They walked, chatting gaily about the future and the past; Argentine was a woman with the soul of a fay. Noël was telling her how he had found the undine when Hildewige appeared at a bend in the path; the Viking was beside her, and all the castle servants were behind her.

"We were coming to meet you," said the Northern virgin, running to Noël. "Be welcome, Master. And you, Muguet, come and embrace me; your mistress is waiting for you, her spinners have brought her marvelous robes and her dwarves have forged so many rings, so many bracelets, so many belts and so many necklaces that the great hall is full of them.

"Brother," the Northern virgin continued, indicating the Viking, "here, if you wish, is your brother. He's a worthy man, Muguet; I've slept alone on his boat for weeks, lying in his shield. If you want to remain a page and travel the world, he'll gladly take you."

Oh, Hildewige, Hildewige!" murmured poor Muguet.

"But while the two brothers chat," Hildewige continued, "You can accompany me; Argentine is waiting for me to fasten her necklace."

"Oh, what a dainty page!" say the companions of Otto the Brave.

"He has a woman's hair," their daughters respond, "and hands so small that they could never hold the hilt of a sword."

"Let's walk quickly," said Argentine. "What if sometime were to guess...?"

"No one will ever guess," said Hildewige, smiling.

They walked so rapidly that Noël found them waiting for him on either side of the door. Argentine had put on a dress inlaid with silver, and bowed, blushing.

"But where has Muguet gone?" he said

"Your page, my brother, is a scatterbrain," Hildewige replied. "He said to me just now: *My master is getting married; he'll no longer travel the world. I love traveling, myself.* And with that, he left."

"That beautiful fay resembles someone we've seen before," said Otto's companions

"Might she be the sister of the slender page?" whispered the women of the castle.

During the meal, Hildewige told the story of her voyage in search of golden apples; she had just related how she had found Perce-Neige on the giant Immer's iceberg when a seamew flew in through an open window. It was holding two identical necklaces in its beak.

"I recognize the white messenger of the daughter of the waves," said the Viking. "Brother, one of those necklaces is for your bride, the other is for my beloved.

"Is she very beautiful, that undine?" Argentine murmured in Hildewige's ear, very softly.

"You'll see her at our wedding; Perce-Neige has invited her." Then, addressing Noël: "This, Brother, is what the queen said to me on Immer's iceberg: 'I'll expect you; Grésil will come to fetch you. His palace is large; you'll be at ease there with all your guests.'"

"We'll leave right away!" Noël exclaimed. "Do you want to, Viking?"

"Let's go and dress, then" Hildewige interjected.

While the two brides were putting on their wedding dresses, the two men talk about the future, cups in hand.

"What shall we do?" says Noël.

"If you wish, we can go together to harvest the waves," replies the Viking.

"My beloved is a flower of the lands of the sun," Noël remarks. "I'm afraid that her cheeks might fade in the fog."

"Personally, I have no fear of that for Hildewige. She's Otto's daughter."

The sky darkened.

"Here's Grésil," said the Viking. "Let's go and fetch our brides."

XIX. In which everyone goes to the wedding

Grésil's palace passed over forests and plains. It traveled rapidly; the elf was in haste to arrive, Perce-Neige having said to him: "I believe that we're not well-matched spouses; when we've married these young people who love one another, you can take back your liberty and I'll take back mine."

Grésil does not feel well; he would be amiable if he could.

In the great hall with walls of down and a floor of ice, he hastens to look after his guests; he turns round in order to sneeze, and his sniffling subjects have been forbidden to cough.

While passing over the birch forest, Argentine sees the fays of the Oriental gardens chatting with the sylphs.

"If only we had them at our wedding!" she sighs.

Then Grésil, ever gallant, stops his palace and Argentine says to her former sisters: "Would you like to come to my wedding? I have this cloud for a carriage. Would you like to come with me to Perce-Neige's palace?"

The fays clap their hands—they dream of nothing but dancing. The chilly sylphs, seeing that Argentine has bare arms, take a chance and go with her,

When they were all reunited, the hall of Grésil's palace is almost full, and as it was rather cool, in spite of the down lining the walls, the parquet being slippery, everyone begins to dance.

"When I'm divorced," said Grésil, losing his head in the midst of the twirling roses, "I'll choose a companion among these cheerful fays." And he, the grave Grésil, sketched a minuet; his stupefied servants did not know what to think, and his chubby elves whistled dance tunes.

Finally, they arrive at Perce-Neige's palace: a marvelous palace, all crystal and amethyst.

Between high cliffs crowned with glaciers, a warm sea of a darker blue than the sky, slumbers indolently. It is the polar sea, for which men have been searching for such a long time, the sea into which the great river of the ocean flows.

The queen's palace is on a salt cape as brilliant as a ruby; its domes taper into pointed bell-towers and it broad, scintillating porticos emerge from waves that lick them.

Swans, eiders, mallards, teal, gulls and seamews design living flowers over the azure gulf, flower-bed with sinuous pathways, the rockeries of which are furnished by brown whales.

For six months the sun rotates without setting, like a fiery wheel, crumbling the glaciers, and when it sinks abruptly behind their dentellate summits, a yellow radiance springs from the motionless axis that our errant world carries through the sky. Its rays break into spangles, are rounded out into domes, are draped in curtains, crackling and inflamed, and the long night of the pole is nothing but a firework display with rutilant rockets.

Then the sun seemed motionless, crazy cascades leapt over the rocks, and the window-frames were opened in the immense greenhouses where orange-trees flourished.

The fays uttered cries of joy, and the sylphs glad to find the flowers of distant lands, said: "Next winter, instead of going so far, we'll come back here."

Perce-Neige was waiting for her guests under the porch of the palace.

"Be welcome," she said, "dreamy sylphs and laughing fays. Be welcome, heroes of the North. You, my sisters, kiss me, and you, Grésil, go and put on an ermine doublet in order not to freeze us."

The table was laid under the crystal cupola starred with gold, in an immense hall draped with bearskins, the parquet of which allowed the sea-bed to be seen, where jellyfish as blue as periwinkles were swimming among pink daisies and seaweed the color of blood.

The table was immense, but the guests were so numerous that everyone could speak to the ears of two neighbors. The Aesir had come with their tall companions with bright eyes and fine hair, The giant with the white beard clinked his cup with Odin's, and the vague gods of the first days, forgetting their defeat among the brave men of today and the heroes of yesterday, believed as they gazed at the brides in their golden diadems, that they were seeing the twin sisters who sowed the still-warm earth with lilies-of-the-valley in the dawn.

The dreamy sylphs and the laughing fays were, at that table, like flowers in a forest, and the daughter of the waves with ivory shoulders, among those brown breastplates and golden shields, seemed like a pearl on the pommel of a sword.

The queen had only one ruby on her white dress and a single snow-rose in her black hair, but her eyes were so brilliant and her cheeks so fresh that Balder the poet, sitting opposite her, said, smiling: "If I were a blue butterfly, I would burn my wings on her curved eyelashes; If I were a gray squirrel, I would surely steal two vermilion apples."

Under the crystal floor, great whales passed with velvet sparkles, and playful seals performed mad round dances.

The midnight sun put sprays on the summits, diamonds on wings, rubies on cups and coral on lips; it was a fine feast.

Then Balder, the immortal poet, took up his tortoiseshell harp, and the quivering strings sang under his fingers like fir-trees in spring, like a cliff in autumn, like the ripening wheat and like the fading hay. At those chords, falling like fresh dew and rising in ardent flames, veins swelled, and Odin the wise said to Noël's beloved:

"You will always be the firefly of the gardens of the Orient, the ermine of the polar snows; you will be Norway, the embalmed rose of the North. You will always be the beloved, the one who will never be forgotten, the mother of handsome reapers with sonorous scythes."

Then, the undine with ivory shoulders having got up, Thor of the heavy hand said: "Among us, you are like the narcissus between tall reeds; it is necessary that you we can see you." And he placed her on his golden shield.

On the golden shield sustained by the Aes, her arms outstretched, the daughter of the waves sang:

"I shall push their foamy boats, between the reefs I shall guide them, and in the days of winter and the nights of summer I shall sing, Norway, your immortal youth, your radiant beauty.

"The sea will be for them the ever-fertile field, the ever-tuned harp, the ever-open book, the ever-laden tablecloth."

"Climb up next to her," said Thor to Noël's beloved.

The woman who had been merely a fay only yesterday climbed up on to the golden shield.

"Hurrah for Norway!" cried the Aesir, the sylphs, the fays, Otto's companions with the unchipped swords, the virgins with heavy tresses and the Viking with white arms.

"For me, you will always be Argentine" said Perce-Neige.

"And for me, always my godmother," added Noël, smil-ing.

Georges de Peyrebrune[44]: *The Fays*

(Giselle; Les Fées, 1892)

There was once…a king and a queen.

It was in the remote times when there were true kings and veritable queens—which is to say, those mysterious and almost superhuman elite beings whose quasi-divine origin is lost in the darkness of the centuries and who, on the redoubtable foundation of their royal ancestry, governed their peoples without ever having seen them and without the latter ever have contemplated their august and sacred faces.

Enclosed in the triple enclosures of the gigantic walls of their giant palaces, built on the summits of hills and puncturing the skies with their gilded cones, like spearheads, while the tall pilasters of enormous porticos seemed to lift up the white curtain of the clouds, those kings—the only ones worthy of the title—lived and died in the eternal monotony of their Olympus without ever quitting it, except, clad in iron masks, for distant wars. And they maintained thus, with a proud sanctity, the ancient and hieratic majesty of their ancestors.

Whereas fêtes or tourneys summoned princes and peoples to the vicinity of the ramparts of the palace, the, the doors only let out the small society of servants and minor functionar-

---

[44] Georges de Peyrebrune (1841-1917), the illegitimate daughter of Françoise Judicis and an Englishman named Johnson, who took her name from her birthplace, Pierrebrune, arrived in Paris after the Franco-Prussian war, where she met the writer and editor Arsène Houssaye, who obtained publication for her first novel in the *Revue des Deux Mondes*, after which her career went from strength to strength, although it did not prevent her from dying poor. Her first collection of tales, published in 1877, is impossible to find.

ies. The remainder showed themselves above the granite of the walls and the dazzling marble of lofty terraces surrounding the ivory tower, perforated like a Byzantine campanile and erected on the top of pilasters, which enclosed, in its niche of golden cloth and the constellation of gems that shone thereon, the slender and completely invisible majesty of the veiled queen.

And, on scarcely glimpsing her, like a star at the zenith, the kneeling people shivered in fear.

Thus kings ought to reign.

However, human life unfolded for the very powerful princes of the realm of Evir with the joys and terrors common to all mortals; for, neither the shiny bronze of heavy closed doors nor even the grim gods engraved and painted on the flanks of propylaea arrested the inevitably entry of the miseries of existence, and the subtle breath of bewildered passions passed over the ramparts victoriously.

If, from the redoubtable vision of vast palaces and their giant walls enclosing mysterious cities of a sort, one crossed the enclosures, the ditches and the towers, traversing the quadrilateral of courtyards paved with gleaming mosaics, one reached, miraculously, the jasper portico guarding the intimate threshold of the quasi-tabernacle in the depths of which their royal majesties lodge; if, provided with a charge that permitted parting the formidable and sacred curtain behind which kings live and sleep, and the frightened eye were able to contemplate their faces, this is what it would see:

First of all, very small as if lost in the immensity of halls hung with crimson and gold, a dainty little girl, tall and pale, with long hair falling in blonde tresses, the naïve face of a Gothic virgin, sitting stiffly in her bright robe embroidered with sunflowers and fringed with topazes. The pectoral of her royal tunic resembles a golden breastplate. Also gold are her cathedra, raised up at the top of numerous steps, and the awning that covers it. That resplendent throne is situated under the arch of an ogival bay open to a sky gilded by the fires of the sunset, and behind it is displayed the distant vision of horizons lost in an immense desert, which unfurls the dazzling brightness of its golden dust endlessly.

That little girl, similar to the virgins of a missal, is the queen, and she has just given birth. However, her gaze is sad and her mouth has a crease of mute distress. And beneath her long and gaudy pearl-encrusted dress, the bird of paradise that God has placed in that frail cage—her heart—is beating violently. It is palpitating, that gentle, wounded heart. For close by, leaning his elbow on her chair, tall and proud, stands the king, who does not love the dainty and beautiful queen, even though she has just given birth. He married her, in accordance with the prevailing custom, by virtue of a treaty of war, while the bride was still in her cradle.

When she was taken to him, scarcely nubile, he found her to be not to his liking, and neglected her shortly thereafter. He abandoned her to the duennas and the eunuchs in order that she would be well-guarded, only allowing her—a child herself but a queen nevertheless—to watch children playing, pages and damsels who cheered up the solemn silences of the great palace of Evir with their irrepressible frolics.

So, sitting all day long in her high cathedra and lost in the stiff brocade of her enormous dress, the neglected little bride remained pensive and sad, with occasional sudden bursts of pretty laughter when some page took pleasure in diverting her in order to pay his court. One of them, moved to pity, knew the best ways of distracting her. He only appeared to live in order to serve her passionately. She looked on him kindly. And who could blame her? The little queen sometimes, while thinking of him, went to sleep consoled.

The powerful king was unhappy himself. Yes, possessing everything, he was miserable, for he could not obtain the amour of a haughty princess who lived at his court.

Tall, proud and bold, riding her hackney with the audacity of a heroine, with the commanding gesture and the imperious disdain that befits queens, the latter seemed to the king to be much more suited to sit by his side than the frail and timid child that fate had imposed on him.

And see how well he reasoned, for the young page who loved the queen so much thought the same, agreeing that things would have turned out more logically if the lady of the court had been paraded on the golden throne while the blonde little girl who reigned wearily had come to play games with him, and belonged to him, in all honor, as a wife.

The queen thought, for herself—silently, unable to say so—that not being loved by a king is perhaps a lesser evil than that of loving a handsome page. And her heart, poor bird, sometimes languished in mortal dolors and sometimes beat its golden cage urgently.

So, on the day when the king was leaning a nonchalant elbow on the throne where the queen was sitting palely, there were noisy celebrations throughout the realm of Evir. The crowd was pressing on the granite walls around the palace and its voice rose all the way to the summit of the terraces like the rumor of the ocean. At the four points of the horizon the brass of trumpets sounded alternately. The entire city resonated to the silvery din of cymbals, while bells rung at full tilt howled through all their bronze mouths.

And the crowd, with eddies like waves, brayed endlessly the name of the kings of Evir; for a prince had been born, the first of the young royal couple, and thus would be continued the dynasty of that ancient race, whose origin was lost in the darkness of the centuries, like that of the gods. Sure at least of still having a master whom it would be glorious to obey, the wise Evirean nation delivered itself to joy in acclaiming its prince and blessing the heavens. In addition, the king had been doubly liberal, for a son had not arrived alone, but accompanied, like a twin flower, by another fragile and delicate body, of a daughter.

Whereas the little prince was dark in his complexion and his eyes, and even the down on his little head, the unanticipated little princess was as blonde and pink as the dawn, for which reason she was named Aurore. Her birth had extracted a smile from the discolored lips of the poor martyrized mother. She thought that if the king took here robust son from her, he would surely leave her the paltry girl, as one leaves a doll in the hands of a child; and her reverie was already adorning her with amorous graces. Oh, if she, at least, could one day be happy!

She obtained from the king—tenderly inclined toward her momentarily—that in order to ensure the future happiness of the infanta, all the fays of the mythical religion of Evir would be invited to her baptism.

The king did not believe in the myths with which antique faith governed the souls of his people, but he lent himself gravely to the religious practices informed by tradition, and the priests who guarded the secret of words and evocative magic formulae were protected by him with marks of profound veneration. So, having granted the queen's wish he summoned the mages; the latter invited in their turn sorcerers, conjurers, fakirs, Brahmins, spiritist mediums and evocateurs from the depths of India, Egypt and Syria; and the order was given to prepare for the magical enchantments.

The queen had not asked for anything for the young king, so the latter, lying on a gold shield, received the imposing baptism of arms. The interlaced palms that extended over his cradle were sword-blades. His frail hand, after having touched the scepter, was attached to the hilt of a sword. Thus was presented to the people and to the army the future leader of the realm of Evir. He was named Rhamses.

But it was in a nest of rose-petals that Aurore was presented to the baptism of the mages; the softest flower petals were heaped up like down in a basket of silver filigree studded with fine pearls and the little princess, like a satin doll with enamel eyes, was curled up there, as naked as a little bird newly emerged from the egg.

She was then carried processionally through the galleries of the palace all the way to the immense hall with large bays open to the golden backcloth of the sky, where the queen was sitting stiffly on her cathedra, in her brocade mantle, with a crown of her head, pale between her long blonde tresses, which hung to either side of her archaic visage of a virgin in a missal.

Her dreaming eyes, so soft and blue, had scanned timidly the sparkling crowd accumulated around her throne. For an instant they had reposed—oh, very indifferently—on the haughty princess whom the king loved and who resisted him, and who, cheerful, proud and also coquettish, enjoyed the martyrdom of her royal slave. Softer and sadder, however and how tenderly veiled, those divine eyes had paused on the languid face of the handsome page who loved her so much. Oh, the great dolor that passed through the soul of the little queen, immobile and fixed in her pompous pose, thinking that it would always be necessary for him to live thus, tortured, guarding a hopeless amour in his heart.

In order to collect herself she lowered her eyes, slightly moist, toward the cradle of roses where the naked little doll lay, her eyes now closed, and her heart, invaded by maternal love, was numbed somewhat in that contemplation.

The king whose elbow was leaning nonchalantly on the royal throne, leaned back, in order that his liberated gaze could devour, without being distracted, the radiant beauty of his beloved princess, so cruel in her amused refusal.

Then the theorbs vibrated, the incense burned by the mages clouded the constellated vaults, and a great silence fell.

Through the odorous smoke, the blue tint of which embellished the bright faces of richly-adored women similar to immortal houris, the unique circular movement of their raised arms was visible, as if they were trying to draw into the orb of their magic circles, by means of their attractive force, the scattered falling fluids of sidereal forces, and thus impart to them, by means of a rapid cohesion, a tangible form.

Soon, in fact, furrows ran through the opaque smoke, like serpentine lightning-flashes in the cloud. Vague forms emerged, immediately deformed and then renascent. The spiral of vapors rising from the fiery tripods mutated, toward the vault, into the appearance of light bodies that rolled and blurred hectically, as if in a panic of impotent flight. There was a rip in a rapid blue light, from which a whiteness suddenly fell, like a wounded bird, which floated, with a vague sound of wings. Quickly, unfurled like the display of a vast diorama, there was a dazzling mixture of palpitating colors, fulgurant in a magical mutation, which fixed the eye in a blank stare.

Then, in the center of an enormous bloom, the multicolored flames of which spun in an endless whirl, a group of divine forms—the fays—flowered like the nascent petals of that immense rose, their floating tresses overflowing around them in a cascade of golden light.

Leaning back, hand in hand, as if for a round-dance of bacchantes, they circled ever more slowly and more visibly, even allowing to show, amid the iridescent vapor that veiled them, the dazzling whiteness of their projected breasts.

Finally, in the silence of the theorbs, the vibrations of which died away, a voice was heard, faint and musical, like that of a distant nightingale. It was a fay speaking.

"Darling," she said, pointing her finger like a pink dart toward the child sleeping in her bed of flowers, "You shall be beautiful; so beautiful that no one in the world will be able to see you without dying of amour."

"Good," murmured the king. "I know now who Aurore is going to resemble."

A second fay detached herself, seductively, and whispered in a languid sigh: "You shall be good, kind, tender and sensitive, so compassionate that, in order not to see anyone suffering, you will grant to anyone all the gifts requested of you."

"Good," sighed the queen, who sensed the imploring gaze of the handsome page passing over her closed eyes.

A third spoke, if one can describe thus something which more closely resembled the song of breezes passing over reeds. This one promised knowledge. Another accorded the magical gift of the arts, and another that of grace and charm. Another granted her the cleverness, strength and audacity that makes heroines. And each of them, in passing, extended her open hand, and radiance flowered from her slender fingers.

Slowly, the multicolored rose shed its petals, the flames of which stirred in an endless unfurling. The divine and nacreous forms, and the flamboyant tresses of the fays kneading from golden light, gradually reentered and melted into the blue spirals of the incense smoke. Only one luminous dot was darting a crackling tongue of vacillating fire at the fuming center of the semi-extinct rose when a sudden explosion ripped apart its blazing corolla, from which a woman emerged more beautiful, whiter and purer than the snowy marble of a Hebe. This one bore in her hand, like the stem of a lily, a wand decorated with pearls and opals, the sharp scintillating tip of which was carved in facets like a crystal fish-bone.

The new fay learned over Auotre's cradle and said, pityingly: "I've arrived just in time for your happiness, child so poorly endowed!"

"What?" cried the king.

"What are you going to do?" moaned the gentle queen.

"Does she not have all gifts?" murmured the crowd, enumerating them: beauty, grace, mildness, goodness, charm, talents, knowledge, and even heroism! What was she lacking, then?

"She lacks," replied the fay, "the precious faculty of being able to enjoy all those gifts without each of them become the source of the worst dolors for her. What! She will be beautiful, knowledgeable and as charming as grace itself—which is to say that she will attract to herself the passionate heart whose prostration would strew the earth before here little victorious feet; and, the supreme misery, she will, at the same time, be so sensitive and compassionate that it will be necessary for her to weep—oh yes, weep, Madame la Reine—as much to the dolors to which she will give birth by her refusal as for the weaknesses of her own languid soul, as soft and tender to amour as an open flower is to the kisses of the east wind!

"What a martyrdom that life would be, for such a poorly defended heart! Everything, external or personal, would be a subject of pain for it. All the scattered evil of the world would wound it eternally. It would suffer for the most infimal suffering of beings; it would writhe in anguish for human terrors and would swoon merely in knowing about the immolation of animals, ready to die of horror at the cries of those victims of torture...

"Then, nothing around her would be able to charm her. She would pass, slowly and sadly, dragging those fatal gifts, a hundred time accursed, not daring to raise to the heavens her beautiful mortal gaze, enveloping the divine grace of her body, hiding it like the excessively close splendor of a solar hearth, and hesitating even to place her foot on the ground, where innumerable living things swarm, fearing, with a tender emotion, perhaps wounding an invisible being.

"What good would it do her to have received from my imprudent sisters so many marvelous attractions, and be thrown by them into the hectic intoxication of their waltz, if I had not come: the absolute principle of moral strength?

"And in doing this I am obeying, not pity, which is unknown to me, but the magic formula of the most savant of your mages. So here I am."

Standing tall, barely touching with the tip of her naked foot the burning heart of the rose, fuming like a cup of incense, the fay inclined her white body slowly in a nacreous curve and slowly extended toward the sleeping Aurore the scintillating tip of her wand, with facets sculpted like a crystal fishbone florid with pearls and opals. Then, with a swift gesture, she touched her heart.

Then, straightening up again, she started to rise in the blue spirals of the aromatic smoke clouding the vault. At the same time she dissolved, melting into a pink mist in which a tangle of gold floated.

Still scarcely visible, she murmured these words, which fell:

"Aurore, you shall be happy, for you shall be insensible. Your heart, as hard as rock crystal, will never know either pity or love..."

"What! cried the king. "She will never love, nor be compassionate to those who die of love for her?"

"Never," replied the fay, vanishing with the last floating mist.

"Too bad," pronounced the king sadly, contemplating passionately his beautiful and haughty princess.

"But, paling again, in the depths of her cathedra, outlined against the golden backcloth of the sky, the virginal blonde queen who was suffering so much, without looking at her page, murmured:

"So much the better!"

Jean Lorrain[45]: *Tiphaine*

(L'Écho de Paris, 24 February 1893)

For Henri de Régnier[46]

Tiphaine, at midnight on the edge if ditches
Was wandering by moonlight, and the pink heather,
Raising its flowers on its stems, kissed her hands.

The valets in service had taken away the dishes, the venisons as well as the honeyed buckwheat cakes, the pages had brought the greyhounds from the kennels, and in the high-ceilinged hall, barely illuminated by the torches suspended in the rings in the wall, it was the time when the old seigneur, with his elbows on the arms of his waxed wooden stall, plunged into bleak remembrance of the past.

Outside, in accordance with the season, there was all the enchantment of moonlight over the fields of green wheat and

---

[45] Jean Lorrain (1855-1905) was one of the later recruits to Catulle Mendès' coterie of newspaper writers, but swiftly became one of the most prolific, notoriously aiding his productivity by drinking ether and mining the hallucinations that he suffered in consequence for imaginative inspiration. Translations of his fantasies can be found in *Nightmares of an Ether-Drinker* (2002), *The Soul-Drinker and Other Decadent Fantasies* (2016) and *Masks in the Tapestry* (2017).

[46] Henri de Régnier (1864-1936), who became one of the leading Symbolists of the *fin-de-siècle*, was still in the first phase of his career when this story was written and had not yet published the collections of prose—translations of which are included in the sampler *A Surfeit of Mirrors* (2012)—that helped to establish his reputation.

heather of May, of the bellowing of squalls running over the crests of the waves, and sometimes flocks of blinded seagulls arriving with packets of rain and gusts of spray collided with the window panes; on those nights all of the wooden beams in the old town besieged by November were creaking lamentably, and the ironwork of the heavy doors resounded, and through the interminable corridors of the fortress there was something like the noise of anvils, and sinister groans: an entire sabbat of souls in distress, which made the watchman huddled in his lodge sweat with fear and kept the men-at-arms in service in the hall of the manor awake, with lugubrious thoughts within their skulls.

But whether the squalls were raging, sweeping the snow of December and the dead leaves of October into the ditches of the old domain, or the moonlight of June was playing gently over the round-path and discovering in eccentric moving silhouettes the wallflowers of the battlements, it was for old Bertrand Du Guesclin,[47] in winter as in summer. in spring as in autumn, the worst hour of all, the hour haunted by regrets

---

[47] Bertrand Du Guesclin (c1320-1380) was a famous Breton knight and oft-victorious military commander, who fought on the side of the French (and thus against Breton nationalists) in the Hundred Years War. For the last ten years of his life he was Charles V's Constable de France. In 1363 or thereabouts he married Tiphaine Raguenel, their union often being cited as an exemplar of courtly love in troubadour ballads, in which she is represented as beautiful and knowledgeable, especially in occult arts, whereas her notoriously ugly husband was illiterate. A depiction of the wedding of Bertrand and Tiphaigne by the writer and illustrator Paul de Semant (1855-1915) is still available as a print, and might have been the inspiration for the story. When he wrote the story, Lorrain could not know that a ruined house on Mont Saint-Michel would be falsely attributed to Tiphaine in the early twentieth century, and a skull fancifully imagined to be hers excavated in the early twenty-first.

and dreams of the past, the hour of specters, with that hostess of old men, sorrow, behind them, and in her shadow fear of the future; and there was also, in the meditation of the old melancholy hall of long vigils far into the night and the silence, the isolation of Comte Bertrand with his memories: the memories that sometimes surged forth with the face of long ago, with muted sandals, in the embrasure of some low door. And the somnolent old sire then had the vision of vague individuals with heavy eyes and sealed lips leaning on their elbows on the arms of the stalls of the perimeter, and the names of former companions in arms, once clamored in the fire of battles or stammered in the tender drunkenness of feasts, buzzed in his ears; and in the weave of the long tapestries figures of dream appeared, whose gestures and smiles he recognized, distant hours rising again from the past, with the flowers of youth in their hands, but their gold and silk tarnished now...and the old man awoke then, his long face hollowed out by deeper wrinkles, and putting his poor old hands together, he let a large tear run down his wan cheek, and sighed: "Tiphaine."

Tiphaine! And above the visions of iron and blood of his warrior years, red battlefields strewn with cadavers under angry skies, fiery and bleak, the sack of towns resounding with the jeers of the victors and the screams of slaughtered population, triumphant entries under the undulating pleats of banners, with steel shields at the elbow and lances in hand, to the sound of festival bells and flag-laden streets, forced marches in the moonlight and nocturnal ambushes in the rain in the quivering rushes of ponds...above all that, the mild and floating face of a young woman was evoked, a svelte lady of pensive grace with beautiful hands bearing alms; and the blonde Tiphaine, whose smiles and caresses had embalmed and rejuvenated his fortieth year, gradually reappeared before him.

As if captive between the blue trees of the tapestry, she smiled between the gnarled branches bearing the yellow apples of fabulous forests dreamed by the embroiderers; marvelous birds with dazzling plumage fluttered around her head, and it really was her bright eyes, translucent and blue, that were staring at him, as it really was her bare feet that where shining softly on the grass, in the tangle of enormous and sumptuous flowers.

Tiphaine! And in his heart of an old chief of partisans, he saw her again such as she had appeared to him the first time, sitting by a spring on the edge of an ancient forest.

It was one evening, a little before nightfall, and the shadow of the wood was invading the heath, where brief gleams were zigzagging in places, final reflections of daylight on the gilt of furze, dying away in the darkness. The air was so mild and so strangely poignant that Du Guesclin, then in his prime, almost had to do himself violence in order not to faint; it was then that he had perceived her. Sheathed in a long ash-gray dress, with a mantle of pink linen embroidered with anemones clasped over her shoulders, she was sitting still, her elbow on the rim of a rim of a small fountain in the form of a well; white forms were pressing around her with a silky sound, and in a flutter of wings the comte had recognized a flock of wild geese extending the simultaneous effort of their necks toward the unknown woman.

Although seated, she had appeared to him to be very tall, even gigantic, and, rude soldier as he was, he had stopped, hesitantly, before that strange crepuscular silhouette profiled, as if luminous, against that savage heath, magnified by the darkness.

He hesitated again when the unknown woman, having got up from the stone bench on which she was sitting, had greeted him by his name, in a voice so soft that he had imagined that he was hearing the water of the well speaking. "In future, handsome sire de Tombelaine," she had said, "I shall wait for you here every evening of my life, as I am this evening." And, all the geese having risen from the ground with little cries, the lady had appeared momentarily to be enveloped by a white turbulence of wings, with a sudden splendor of precious stones and gems in the yellow silk of her hair and the embroideries of her mantle fastened with rubies.

And every evening he had returned there, as if brought back by the hand to the edge of that flowery heath, where, simply by virtue of seeing the sun set again behind the lady's shoulders and her mantle of rose linen softly illuminated by the ultimate reflection, he felt as if a fruit were dissolving in his heart; and there were three months of tender rendezvous and delightful waiting, until the night of Saint John when, in the twilight of the great rejuvenated wood, it was given to him to go in quest, to the sound of lutes and flutes, of the beautiful bride, ornamented and adorned liked the reliquary of Saint Anne, to stand on the ruined threshold of the paternal manor.

Oh, that return through the thickets of the ancient forest, bathed in moonlight, the troubling incense of hawthorn and the unconscious caress of the mosses on which their feet lingered, and the profound gaze of periwinkles, as if awakened with a start, between the snaky coils of roots at the foot of the green oaks of the slopes; oh, all the enchantment of those haunted woods, that night of songs, music, silken banners and errant torches; and, through the ravines and the clearings, conducting the white-clad bride in her linen veil to the seigneurial domain of the husband.

And now, through the wools and the frayed gold of the long tapestries, he saw again the nuptial procession passing, the deacons in stoles and the priests in chasubles beneath the fringes of the awning, the sheets of light in the braided hair of the young women, friends of the betrothed couple, the long stems of lilies in their hands surrounded by green box, and the handsome squires leading dogs on leashes, and the soldiers with rude faces beneath morions garlanded as a sign of celebration, and the laughing pink-cheeked children holding sheaves of fennel, lavender and irises against their bellies, some of them emboldened astride the backs of a few mastiffs, and the trailing dresses of the ladies, and the hennins of the demoiselles and the caps of the musicians , and the bearers of candles setting the blue-tinted darkness of the forest ablaze with light, and the cavaliers clad in fur, and the flashes of moonlight on their stirrups.

Tiphaine! He saw her again as chatelaine in the dwelling, a saint in the chapel and a housekeeper in the gynaeceum, in the midst of her women, spinning wool and embroidering fine gold thread, and whether she was idling in the middle of the interior courtyard of the castle, paved with black marble, or she appeared at the corner of some country path in the tall shadow of ripe wheat, coming through the crops to meet him, accompanied by some juvenile page carrying a satchel or gifts of nature for the needy, it was always her great hennin of a noble and powerful lady that he saw surmounting that pensive and charming visage with lowered eyelids and a rosy ingenuous smile: her hennin, the color of saffron and honey, almost the hue of her tresses, the strange coiffure of a magicienne, with the double fall of veils that the slightest breeze agitated like two wings, and which always seemed to envelop her with he knew not what invisible flight.

And over her footsteps the brocatelle of her armoried robe snaked and rustled, sometimes disquieting.

Oh, that undulating train with the flexibility of a snake, as if it were belying the motionless prayer of the hennin, pointing like a bell-tower toward the sky! But he had lent an ear to the suspicious words of his old chaplain, and the pusillanimous monk had poured into his heart the poison of mistrust, the mistrust that withers amour and dries up good faith.

Bizarre, in fact, had been the encounter with that unknown woman in the troubled hour of dusk, in that solitary place, ill-famed because of the well once consecrated to the evil gods, nymphs and spirits that the Gospel had dispersed, and that sudden amour, like a malign fever, and the languors that had followed, the force that had brought him back every evening, involuntarily, even his name, pronounced by the lady in a seductive voice of speaking water, and that flock of geese, phantoms so rapidly evaporated in the darkness—all of that contained magic and charms, and he had struggled, captive of some maleficent amour, caught in net of a demon or a fay.

And, intoxicated with fear by the monk, he had been able to follow his fearful counsel and suspect the gentle and devoted lady. "By night she deserts your bed; she goes into the open country by means of ancient posterns that are thought to be sealed and, accompanied by a dwarf with a monstrous head, who parts the nettles and the wild herbs in her steps, she collects hemlock on the tombs of lepers and makes the mandrakes sing."

And, mad with horror and curiosity, he had wanted to see her and to follow her one evening, but he had not had to spy on her for long, for scarcely had they arrived on the edge of the village, on the very threshold of the arched door that opened on to the fields, when the beautiful lady had said, turning toward him: "Never again then, handsome sire de Tombelaine, will I wait for you every evening as on the eve of today, for the knell of death has sounded for Tiphaine; you have suspected me—adieu."

And while he agonized in anguish and terror, his hands flat against the wall of the little stairway, she had vanished into the white country of the moon; something like a sound of wings had quivered, and he had never seen her again.

Tiphaine!

Henry Gauthier-Villars[48]: *Miscalculations of Fays*

(*L'Écho de Paris* 26 August 1894)

Once there were two lovely children, one of whom was named Daphnis and the other Chloe, who knew nothing of life because they had received a very clerical education.

It happened that they got lost in a wood on the eve of their marriage while going through a forest and found themselves utterly destitute, no longer daring to walk in the dark for fear of going further astray. And as the night was full of mystery, Daphnis and Chloe trembled like innocents before an examining magistrate.

Suddenly, the moon rose, and enabled them to see that they had reached a deserted clearing, but soon there arrived, in single file, a ragged wolf, an ugly little ferret, a red-faced girl with a moustache, a splendid women who seemed sunlit, a fat man, a scullion, a woman clad in a donkey-skin, etc., etc.

Then the fat man advanced toward the couple and said: "Have no fear, we only wish you well. You're going to be married tomorrow and you're unaware of the philosophy of existence; we're going to teach you about it. It's your lucky star that led you astray into this clearing. Your heads have

---

[48] Henry Gauthier-Villars (1859-1931) became notorious after inventing the "house pseudonym" Willy for the young authors from whom he commissioned risqué novels for the family publishing company managed by his brother; those he commissioned from his wife Colette became a bone of contention when she elected to assert her authorship. He also attached that pseudonym, and others, to many of his own works, and the present story is unusual in being signed with his own name.

been stuffed with ridiculously optimistic dreams; you've been persuaded to believe in good fays who bring the plans of poor mortals to fruition. All that, my children, is a joke, and you ought to believe the exact opposite of that nonsense.

"Know first of all that there are no good fays; the wicked ones killed them all a long time ago. There are no more kings who desire children; on the contrary, the fewer they have, the happier they are. There are no other talismans than lock-picks for opening doors, and you'd be wrong to count on a wand that discovers treasure. Princes are no longer changed into animals; all that can be done is to change animals into civil servants. And for your edification, here is my story:

The Ogre's Story

"I have no seven-league boots, not even a bicycle, but only big shoes; far from devouring little children, I collect orphans; I give them to travelers to eat without asking for any payment. A little wretch called Poucet fell into my hands with his entire family; he had a ball in my house; he and his brothers teased my daughter without me doing them any great harm—children need to amuse themselves. Then, one ugly morning, when I awoke, there was no longer anyone there. They had all run away, taking everything, including my shoes. And furthermore, that swine Poucet had told horrific lies about me in order to ruin my credit with the suppliers. Never give shelter to vagabonds."

The ogre fell silent. The wolf spoke in his turn:

The Wolf's Story

"I was wandering n the woods, famished, when I saw Little Red Riding Hood coming toward me, who said: "My grandmother lives five hundred meters from here, a nasty old woman who causes me a lot of misery; little wolf, you'd be a dear little wolf if you were to wring her neck; she's very plump." Like an imbecile, I strangled the old harridan; in the

224

meantime Little Red Riding Hood warned the gendarmes to arrest me as an anarchist. I got twenty years in New Caledonia and the slut inherited her grandmother's savings, which she coveted in order to marry an apprentice hairdresser. Never try to avenge another's rancor."

The wolf fell silent. The beautiful woman who was yawning stretched herself and said:

The Sleeping Beauty's Story

"I was asleep in the castle. The prince came to find me, although I hadn't summoned him. I was waiting for Amour and was ready to love the first person who presented himself in his name. Alas, after a few days the prince was bored and started to yawn; he scarcely listened to me and let me know that he was tired of me; then he went to sleep. I couldn't wake him up, in spite of my caresses, and in his insulting sleep he dreamed about other women. Then I ran away, and even though I have a great desire to sleep again, I can't close my eyelids. My lovely dream has ended, and I'll never be able to avoid the reality that gouges my eyes again. I've been punished for having believed in Amour."

The scullion stood up.

Cinderella's Story

"Like unfortunate peoples, I've had a history, but it's devoid of interest. I sacrificed myself for my slatternly sisters; I amassed dowries for them, and they beat me. Then I fell in love with a shoemaker, who abused me in his turn, and my children imitated their father, for such is the destiny of women: to receive blows and look after the house while dreaming of adventures that never arrive. No godmother, fay or otherwise, protected me; mice gnawed my poor skirts and by way of slippers I only possessed clogs. The life of the household—what a fraud!"

A lord with a long beard cried:

225

Bluebeard's Story

"Have I been slandered sufficiently? I had seven wives; the first six left me to run all over the place with tenors. The seventh ran away with a contralto, after having carefully packed up the riches of my palace, aided by her two brothers and her sister; while those wretches were robbing me, Anne kept watch. In the course of the divorce proceedings I was charged with all sorts of crimes, and the legend is accredited. Young man, mistrust your wife. If I'd killed mine they wouldn't have ridiculed or robbed me, and I'd have an excellent reputation."

The little ferret advanced within the circle briskly.

Riquet à la Houppe's[49] Story

"Riquet à la Houppe at your service. You complain about slander? What I could tell you! I had money, hair and intelligence and I was turned over by a little simpleton as nasty as a polecat. I thought she was gentle and good, and believed she loved me, when she only coveted my title and income. Once she was Madame Riquet she ruined me, deceived me and tortured me; I ought to have killed her, because I couldn't live with her any longer. So, don't imagine that love transforms everything it touches."

A young woman took the floor

The Girl with the Pearls' Story

"I was so good and beautiful that a fay granted me the ability to spit jewels. My ugly and malevolent sister received the more enviable gift of being able to spit vipers and toads, so that everyone strove not to fall out with her. Being jealous, she denigrated me ferociously, unrelenting in casting discredit on

---

[49] aka Ricky of the Tuft.

my merchandise. 'Where did these jewels come from?' From some theft, doubtless; and then, they were fake, paste. The result was that my commerce collapsed and I had to quit the country. My sister bought the company for a hunk of bread, married the head salesman and lived happily. To succeed in this vile and base world, it's necessary to be wicked."

The booted cat explained how he had been stolen in the affair of the lands of Carabasville, after having had the imprudence to serve as a front man for his master, who had then made him take all the responsibility for the murder of the ogre.

The forty thieves had cheated Ali so comprehensively that he was still Baba.

Donkey-skin was leading a miserable life, dropped by the king's son, who regretted his misalliance with her.

The ogre summed up the situation: "Children, don't believe in tales of fays and buy Manuels-Roret instead;[50] cultivate your garden and throw stones into those of others; steal and slander, and you'll be happy."

The next morning, having found the path back to the paternal house again, Daphnis and Chloe decided not to marry. Anyway, they hadn't wasted their time during the rest of the night, and Chloe was now only a demi-virgin.

This tale has no moral.

---

[50] Manuels-Roret were a series of illustrated practical guides to various métiers and pastimes, launched by Nicolas Roret (1797-1660), which began publication in 1825 and reached the height of their popularity in the 1830s. They survived long after Roret's death, still circulating at the end of the century and continuing after the Great War.

Paul Margueritte[51]: *The Guardian of Bad Dreams*

(L'Écho de Paris, 11 February 1895)

For Stéphane Mallarmé

The King of the Lakes was prey to nightmares; that was an evil spell cast on him by the Nixies when he caught one of them in the deployment of a spavin with crimson mesh weighed with silver quoits. The captive nixy struggled like a fish, her eyes already vitreous, and her woman's face and body of green scales resolved into the soft gelatin of a medusa. She melted in his hands and spread out in the grass, so rapidly diminished that she could not be seized, and flowed away in ray of sunlight.

Since then, black or bloody nightmares assailed the king who violated the treaty; and he feared sleep as much as death. He stayed awake long after nightfall and only went to sleep to the sound of crystal flutes; brass horns woke him up at dawn. He no longer ate fish, nor hare, nor pâtés; those dishes made his soul too heavy; he no longer drank flame-colored wines, the intoxication of which was bitter and troubled. He even renounced brown narcotics, which plunged him into a bottomless Lethe, for his tomorrows took the place of nights, and it was then awake, with his eyes wide open, that the worst

---

[51] Paul Margueritte (1860-1918) was a hobbyist mime artist, who adapted many of his fantastic and proto-surrealist short stories from pantomimes and "charades" that he had scripted, but his novels—some of them written in collaboration with his brother Victor (1866-1942)—were conventionally naturalistic, in spite of the fact that he had signed the "manifesto of the five" in 1887, protesting against the Naturalism of Émile Zola.

dreams haunted him, to such an extent that he lived them, by necessity, mouth agape, like a man afflicted by stupor; a cold sweat, similar to tears, ran down his cheeks.

The king, who no longer went to bed without the light of several candelabra, in a room fanned by clusters of ostrich plumes, on a bed as fresh and soft as fruit pulp, took it into his head to be woken up by a very old woman, so old that she had not slept for ten years, and who scared children with her hollow and vigilant eyes in which a perpetual insomnia burned. He appointed her the guardian of his dreams.

Leaning over his face, she was to look out for somber reflections therein, the anguish that palpitates behind the eyelids, the unuttered screams that freeze upon the lips, signs more fleeting but no less revealing than sighs, moans and inconsequential speech. In doubt, for all the more reason, if she suspected his slumber, she was to extract him from it by placing her hand on his arm. And if she perceived that he was having lascivious dreams, she was to wake him up very rapidly, for such phantasms are followed by regrets.

She installed herself on a low seat beside the bed, and the king, after having turned from one side to the other for a long time, went to sleep.

He then descended into a well of shadow, and his entire body seemed to fall gently into a void. Floating, disparate images fulgurated before his eyes, and he found himself on a heath at twilight; the sun, low on the horizon, sent forth a pale light. He walked, and his shadow stretched out immeasurably, raised on stilts.

While walking he turned his head anxiously. A causeless anguish invaded him. He tried to explain it. Doubtless he had reached the limits of his kingdom, unknown lands where fountains of silver sprang forth and crystallizing liquids solidified into stalactites of all colors. The nixies did not live there, but redoubtable spirits that growled under the earth spat out jets of vapor and hot mud. The king was still walking and hot lava burned the soles of his feet. He had would have liked to pick a flower or to see an eagle fly, but it was a dead land. An infinite lassitude oppressed him, and the consciousness of mystery and fear penetrated him.

A large pond in the form of a seashell stopped him, from which hardened liquid had overflowed in pink and green drool. The bottom of the pond could not be seen, and the emerald liquid that filled it seemed to be boiling, for it was agitated by a continuous frisson. The king had stopped, and from foot to head his shadow was projected into the water, a brightly colored shadow that simulated life convincingly. He gazed at it. motionless, and it seemed to him that that when the water froze in winter his own reflection would be frozen in it, soon thickened, dense and compact, petrified as a statue. By moving, he would doubtless have broken the charm and deformed the rigid resemblance, but it was impossible for him to stir his little finger; and from one second to the next, his double, the king of crystal, congealed into stone, while around it the water remained fluid and retained its soft tremor. His terror increased. He divined—yes, he knew, clearly—that the maleficent spirits of the ground were on the lookout for him, Where to flee? Would the image not attest that he had passed that way? He wanted to destroy it, to strike it with his foot, but that foot, seized by the water-fay, he felt stiffening fearfully, like sap rising in the pores of a tree; the liquid stone reached his leg, his thought and his entire body. He was going...

The old woman shook him. The king's wrath was great, because she was so late pulling him out of that Gehenna. But she swore a great oath that he had never had such an even respiration and a visage as calm, so that she had only woken him regretfully, and rather with excessive zeal.

After which, having proffered terrible threats, he went back to sleep.

Now he was walking in a strange garden, where nothing flourished but eyes. Enormous white bulbs stuck out everywhere on long and frail peduncles, and in the midst of those bulbs, which resembled tulips that must have flowered in the ground, with their onions in the air, an immense flower-bed radiated in all directions, formed of circles of green, blue, brown, yellow and violet irises striped with gold and jasper, with black pupils in the middle. And all those living eyes, in which one discerned male and female gazes, the gazes of ancestors and the gazes of newborns, those of cruel cats, affectionate dogs, piercing lynxes, yellow owls and dull fishes, all those eyes, in the envelope of the sclerotic, gave the impression of sick children swaddled in white.

The king engaged in sandy pathways, and under his footfalls the eyes blossomed; some leaned over on their stems as his cloak brushed them. Many greeted him with a reproach, a smile or a malediction. There were chaste ones and provocative ones, churlish ones and demented ones, and those of beasts contained an intense mute dream. A tenacious haunting! The king would have liked no longer to be harassed by those thousands of pupils; he fled, but the maze of eyes opened before him, innumerable and renascent. By mistake, he crushed one of the bulbs and recoiled in horror; the flattened eye swelled again, elastically, and, with a little earth in the corner of its gaze, it pursued him with its stare.

He understood then that he had to pick one of those living flowers; he had to, and right away. He leaned over a delicate azure eye, the timid and charming eye of a virgin, and he pulled. The peduncle resisted, and as the eye suffered, contracting, the king saw it pale and agonize; he lurched slightly, in a flight of the soul, and to his invincible disgust, he saw the fluid of the eye become clouded. With supreme effort, he tore it from the ground, no longer a bulb with its tail but a delightful child sixteen years old who fainted in his arms and stuck her mouth to his to thank him. Unfortunately, she was blind.

He was not greatly astonished, and covered that fresh face, so fresh and so pure that one might have thought it that of a little girl, with kisses. He spoke to her without her listening; she was deaf. He hoped that she might speak, but she was mute. With that, quivering and arching her back amorously, she clung to him, melting into his embrace. Intoxicated by pity and tenderness, he got carried away, dissolving in tears of an unequalled suavity, which flowed from his being like a spring of sensuality.

The old woman had rapidly woken him up, shaking his shoulders.

He ground his teeth, seeing, instead of the exquisite virgin, that wrinkled face of a witch, and it would not have taken much for him to kill the guardian, but she moaned so lamentably that she thought she had done well, since he was weeping, that he turned his back on her in order to continue his dream

Dzz! Dzz!

The king heard a large fly buzzing somewhere. It came closer, buzzing more loudly, and fled with an abrupt swerve into the corner of the room, circling the candelabras. *Why isn't that impudent old woman chasing it away?* he wondered. Suddenly, he ceased to hear the fly, but he felt a singular tickling sensation in his nasal fossae and under the skin of the nose. Dzz! Dzz! The vibration of the fly rumbled like a drum. Great God, what was it doing there? And although he could not see it, the king distinguished a hideous phosphoric green fly of storm and sepulcher, with its abdomen swollen with eggs.

He would have liked…oh, what impotent rage, not to be able…!" He would certainly have the old woman impaled. And still, under his nose, almost in his brain, the fly was buzzing, exploring his utmost depths, reaching the after-palate. Damnation, now it was tickling the uvula. And the king, thus tickled, started to laugh: a convulsive and extraordinary laughter that never finished, rising in scales, making arpeggios, bounding in cascades and swelling in gurgles, twisting him in paroxysms so torturing that in the end he woke up.

The old woman, placid, with her arms folded, was looking at him, refraining carefully from interrupting such a joyful slumber. That, at least, was the reason she gave to the king.

He immediately had a bucket of quicklime brought, pincers and a beehive. On his instruction, the guardian of bad dreams was stripped of her garments, and in order that she should know the reality of the visions that she had not been able to foresee or dissipate in time, her legs were thrust into the lime, her eyes were plucked out and her face was coated with honey in order that the bees would eat it.

The king then made the excellent resolution never to sleep again, and the physicians prepared potions to that effect that were so efficacious that he did not close his eyes for a week, and went mad.

His successor made peace with the nixies.

René Maizeroy[52]: *The Knight and the Fay*

(Le Journal, 29 August 1896)

The fearful bells were breathless, exhausted and weighed down by fatigue, and over the hills and the deserted fields, in the great silence of Sunday, in the sad mildness of the declining daylight, the distant funereal knells resembled the weary voices of mourners drinking cider from door to door.

Disdaining the processions of pride, the protective lances that barred the horizon like the bars of a prison, the silken banners embroidered by women's fingers that were flapping, whipped by the wind and the horns sounding reckless challenges, alone with his sword—the faithful and sure friend that he kissed devotedly, like a virginal mouth, before and after battle and whose iron hilt studded with strange gems have the impression of being alive—the Seigneur d'Argouges had raced toward the high walls of schist and granite that overlooked the sea, and had only stopped his horse on the edge of the abyss.[53] The enormous stallion with a tangled mane sniffed the bitter odor of the reefs anxiously, reared up as if he had

---

[52] "René Maizeroy" (René-Jean Toussaint, 1856-1918), who also wrote fantastic newspaper fiction under other pseudonyms, including "Mora," was a soldier before turning to literature. One of his early novels was prosecuted for obscenity; he was once wounded—but only slightly—by Jean Lorrain in a duel.

[53] Robert d'Argouges was the protagonist of a lesser-known Norman/Breton variant of the famous legend of Raymond de Lusignan and the enigmatic Melusine; The Normandy-born Jean Lorrain also referred to the variant in question in his legendary tales for the *Écho*, as does the tale by "Jacques Fréhel" that follows this one in the present anthology.

heard the hoarse plaint of some monster, bleeding from thrusts of the spurs, and shook his gilt-fringed caparisons, whinnying wrathfully.

The track of the hectic ride appeared in the crimson of clover, in the bright gold of rape, in the quivering snow of buckwheat, in the thick grass of orchards dotted with pink apples, in the fields where crows were croaking, in the thatch where larks were singing, and in the dead leaves that were fluttering in the woods in swarms.

The Seigneur, standing up in his stirrups, his eyes filled with something like a reflection of torchlight, contemplated the red sails of enemy ships on the horizon, like the birds of disaster that soar above green gulfs, and his large warrior's hands, clenched, agitated convulsively, as if he were wishing for the power to attract them, seize them, crush them and shred them into formless wreckage—the debris of prows, the tatters of sails, disemboweled hulls and broken masts—in the foam of the swell.

The ships, as if waiting for the darkness in which they would drop anchor near a solitary strand, were moving back and forth, fluttering audaciously, illuminated by the oblique rays of the sun that had pierced the nacreous clouds. The sky, from which founts of light were streaming, had the magnificent aspect of a tabernacle, the altar of which was strewn with innumerable pink and mauve petals, changing feathers of turtle-doves and loose necklaces of amethysts, pearls and turquoises, decked with faded oriflammes. And vague forms were born there one by one, mysterious and tempting.

The Seigneur vociferated litanies of hate, howling like a hungry wolf on the lookout for prey, his masculine visage of an adolescent that no one can hold back or clasp to the heart, enveloped by radiance like a monstrance, was quivering like molten metal seething in a crucible. But he stopped suddenly, anguished. Soft voices—puerile, tender voices, like echoes in a forest when evening comes, and also like girlish laughter, like the plaint of a spring trickling through horsetails, voices in the sky—were calling to him.

The uncertain forms had mutated into the delightful bodies of women, some of whom had white wings like angels, and the others multicolored wings like butterflies. They floated around him, surrounding him with a puerile and joyful rounddance, dazzling him with their beauty. They murmured:

"Robert, would you like to be the victorious man who will crush like apples in a cider-press everything that dares to confront you, everything that might provoke you? Would you like the cellars of Argouges to be overflowing with treasures that would drive the miserly king of England mad with envy? Would you like to become the triumphant master whom bishops anoint, who has money struck with his effigy, who forgets the count of his cities, his manors and his hamlets? Would you like to be loved as no perishable man has ever been loved?

Then, separating, they went on, seductively:

"One of my sisters is smitten with your sturdiness, your blond curls and your virginity, handsome sire d'Argouges; would you like to become her husband forever?"

And, getting in ahead of the response that the pale warrior was about to make, a fay alighted gently on his saddle-bow, knotted her arms around the neck of the man she desired, embalmed him with her breath, which was scented like thyme and the last roses, her eyes staring into his, her hair scattered in the light, and sighed: "Would you like to be my beloved, my husband, forever?"

The stallion had calmed down, and although the bridle was hanging loose over his massive beck and the master had not spurred him again, obediently, as if guided by invisible hands, he launched forth toward the towers that loomed up above the woods, bounding over hedges and stream impatiently, as joyful as a herald of victory. The Seigneur gazed at himself in the limpid eyes of the fay, abandoned himself to long amorous kisses, bruised her, sustained her awkwardly, supported her on his thick armor, and one might have thought that he was garlanded on returning from a tourney with an armful of lilies and pale vervain.

The fearful bells were sobbing and gasping in the dusk, and the fay cried in a dolorous accent as heavy as the will of Destiny: "Remember what I say to you now, handsome sire d'Argouges; I shall keep all my promises. I shall delight you incessantly with my amour, but if ever you talk about death before me, I shall disappear as if a stroke of a scythe had cast me back into eternal night!"

And as the voices of amour had announced to him, one Sunday in autumn, Robert d'Argouges, ignorant of the shame of defeat, extending his dominating right arm like a scepter over cities, manors and hamlets, seeing nothing around him but people on their knees, bowed heads and hands that blessed, knew Paradise in the gynaeceum, where the immutably beautiful fay poured out the honey of divine caresses.

But in the fourth year of their bliss, on the evening when the laborers were lighting fires of joy at the crossroads, on the hills and on the cliff-tops, when the festival bells were singing from the angelus of dusk to the angelus of dawn, the Seigneur, who was returning from war covered in blood and burned, laden with futile beauty, when he reached the threshold where she appeared in a silver robe, as if woven from moonbeams, lifted her from the ground and carried her like a prey in his arms, had the misfortune to cry out:

"Ah, sweet Lady of my life, why does your mouth give me so much happiness that I should now regret dying!"

And the fay exhaled a long, sad plaint, melted away like mist between his rigid arms and disappeared into darkness; and the sire d'Argouges became, in a few weeks, a curbed old man, worn out like a staff on which some poor pilgrim had leaned for many years, perished, pronouncing strange words that chilled with terror the chaplains and petty clerics at prayer, and made the yellow wax candles of death vacillate between their trembling fingers...

Jacques Fréhel[54]: *A Tales of the Present and the Past*

(La Fronde, 23 February 1899)

Toward the end of the month of March in the year 700 Saint Aubert sent Scubilion, Gautier and Jehan d'Argouges, clerks in his abbey on Mont Tombaë to Mont Gargan, in order to obtain from the monks the relics of Saint Michel des Loups. The archangel had appeared to him, sword in hand, with the result that, seeing evidence of his will, he had dedicated the monastery to him that he had just constructed on the summit of Mont Tombaë, a somber and terrible granite cone six hundred meters high looming up in the middle of the forests of Seyssi and Koquelonde, the refuge of the last druid spared by the Romans, and a lair of wild beasts.

They set forth at dawn, equipped with their psalter and a pilgrim's staff. Scubilion was all pride and sanctity, Gautier modest fervor and d'Argouges poetry.

It was the Golden Age of the cenobitic life. Saints were sprouting in Gaul, as hard and vigorous as plants of the woods felled by Tiberius after the massacre of the druids.

Our clerks were walking gravely, like young men who can already sense the circle of a nimbus around their heads. The forest opened before them, immense and mild. The sky was pale and gray with blue depths. To the right and the left there was a uniform sea of motionless ferns and slender trunks, a calm and profound underwood.

---

[54] "Jacques Fréhel" (Alice Télot, 1861-1918) was a social worker responsible for the care of orphans, who wrote some works for children as well as being a member of the stable of writers assembled by the feminist newspaper *La Fronde* in imitation of *Le Journal*'s stable.

When they climbed an eminence they saw the treetops in the distance forming undulations, a broad swell extending and swaying toward mauve hills with smoothed angles. They breathed more easily on plateaux open to the sky than when descending into the mossy depths.

The perfume of violets filed the pagan forest of scarcely-fallen idols. It penetrated the coarse robes, and clung to the hands and nostrils, as if it were the dying respiration of Sessia, the vanquished goddess.[55]

Scubilion, a punctilious man, the son of a Jersey fisherman, reminded his brothers severely that it was the time when the monks of the forest, wearing cilices under their goatskins, were saying their prayers in their hermitages of Mabdanum and Kenfruth, and that it was appropriate to do likewise. He praised the good fortune of monasteries situated on the edge of the sea, which had the right to catch fish, collect wrack and finds, the right to take royal and fatty fish, surgeon, baleen whales and cachalots. Above all he loved shores and little osier boats lined with leather bobbing gently on the waves.

Gautier, with the profound eyes of seers, declared that he asked God incessantly to be able to domesticate ferocious animals, and that he hoped to encounter on his route the mon-

---

[55] The name Sessia is found in the writings of Tertullian as a Roman goddess of crop-sowing, but her invocation in connection with Bretagne is idiosyncratic. The story relates it to Sessiacum, the name of a mythical forest that once connected Bretagne with the island of Britain before being submerged— a notion elaborately developed in Leopold Quenault's scholarly fantasy *Les Mouvements de la mer, ses invasions et ses relais sur les côtes de l'Océan Atlantique, de la Méditerranée, de la Mer du Nord, de la Manche, de la Baltique, et en particulier sur celles de la Bretagne et de la Normandie* (1869), which the author had evidently read.

strous idol of Mendès that the faithful had recently cast down, in order to exorcize it...[56]

D'Argouges, smoothing his long blond beard, opening large eyes misted by dreams, said that he would love to see the goddess Sessia...

Sessia had given her name to the forest, then Sesiacum; she presided over the sowing of seed and had care of wheat.

The new-born spring shook its perfumes in the branches. The sweet songs of little birds fell from the treetops. An invisible spirit spoke in the murmur of the wind with a mysterious accent, and green plants with flexible stems swayed soundlessly.

"Be careful, d'Argouges," Scubilion fulminated. "These woods are fertile in ambushes. Saints need sands devoid of shelter, arid deserts with meager rosemary and desolate promontories. You are of a proud race that claims to be descended from a fay,[57] from some priestess infidel to temeritous vows.

---

[56] The reference to an "idol of Mendès" presumably has in mind the "goat of Mendes" employed as a symbol by the occultist Eliphas Lévi, borrowed from a mistaken passage in Herodotus (the deity of the Egyptian city of Mendes actually had the head of a ram, not a goat). Lévi's illustration was very frequently reprinted and was belatedly associated by nineteenth-century occultists with the "Baphomet" allegedly worshiped by heretical Knights Templar, whereby it entered the lexicon of modern Satanism. It is conceivable, however, that the author of the present tale also had in mind Catulle Mendès, the great pioneer and exemplar of the kind of newspaper short fiction that *La Fronde* was carrying forward and feminizing.

[57] As previously noted, the well-known legend of Raymond of Lusignan and Mélusine had a Norman parallel—dramatized in the tale by René Maizeroy that precedes this one in the anthology—in which Robert d'Argouges, a member of a notable family of the region, marries a magical woman encountered by a spring, who disappears when he breaks a verbal prohibition she had imposed on him but subsequently makes ghostly re-

Remember that! You are a good monk, but paganism is in the depths of your veins, like dregs. A villain like me is less at risk. Be careful, d'Argouges!"

D'Argouges lowered his eyes. A pink flame shone on his cheeks, and a sigh inflated his breast. He said: "It isn't my faith that is vacillating, Scubilion, but I can't help loving the souls doomed by idols and admiring all faith, even in error. So, when we meditate in the Cloister, I think about the times when Mont Tombaë, newly dedicated to the Archangel, was called Belenos, and when that gigantic rock served as a shelter for a college of new druidesses, suspended there like a nest of doves, but doves with the hearts of eagles. Is it not true that they were pure and that their prayers rose toward the Sun as ours rise toward God?"

A sarcastic expression passed over Gautier's lips. He responded, coldly: "It's difficult to belie one's blood. The harp of the bard and the burning fusions of poetry suit your spirit, more young than mortified. Human love attracts you and the very thought of woman has a dangerous sweetness for you. You have not put on that robe to love the grace of creatures."

D'Argouges had a charming smile. "I can only love that of Jesus," he said.

Scubilion commenced an interminable orison, until fatigue and hunger took possession of the ingenuous travelers. They searched for a propitious place in order to take their frugal meal and their siesta under the protection of God.

One did not take long to offer itself to them, where tall beech trees guarded a little spring. Russet leaves formed a noisy carpet; three mossy stones served as seats and a rock as a table. They took bread and cheese out of their satchels, sated their hunger, and, pulling their cowls down over this heads, they went to sleep on the moss without paying any heed to the wild beasts that were roaming the woods.

---

turns, crying the fatal word. The best known of several literary versions is *La Fée d'Argouges, légende du XIVe siècle* (1838) by Alfred Castel.

Scubilion dreamed that he was walking barefoot without wounding himself through madrepores, stones, shells and marine plants. He laughed on seeing the armored crabs, the silvery lepas and shells in the form of oval cups. He imagined that he could hear the voice of the rising Ocean, a grave, swelling song, the immense sigh of the wave, gliding over distant beaches.

Gautier imagined that he had replaced the idol of Mendès, and received the gift of miracles and transformations. Jesus had given him a wand, and he touched wolves on the head, and they sang the praises of God, following him in solitude. He also read the future and made peoples tremble, frightened by his revelations.

D'Argouges was filled with the charm of the forest. He heard the songs of birds in a celestial harmony. The perfume of flowers intoxicated him like aromatic smoke. He could not sleep and thought he saw shadows gliding through the tangle of willow branches. But a light step made the leaves crackle and, opening his eyes, he perceived an admirably beautiful woman a few paces away from him, who was cutting the bark of a beech with the point of a dagger.

"Ah!" said the poor monk, rubbing his eyes. "Am I dreaming?" And he uttered the war cry of his race, which was: "To the fay!"

She did not turn her head until she had finished her task, immobile in her white tunic, and he soon read with stupor on the trunk of the tree the name of Belenos, which means Sun.

She finally showed him her snowy face, in which an eternal youth shone; then, smiling softly, she said: "I am Sessia."

The forest quivered on hearing her name; the treetops inclined; multiple distant crystalline voices murmured: "Sessia! Sessia!"

"Come," she said to d'Argouges, "my forest no longer contains a fugitive Celt, a proscribed bard, a druidess without an altar, or a servant of Theut;[58] my forest no longer wants to live, and you are seeing its last day. Follow me!"

Devoid of will, with an automatic tread, Jehan stood up and marched in the wake of the white robe. His pale lips murmured a vain prayer.

The goddess said: "I protected the crops; by my cares the wheat germinated healthy and strong; the furrows owed their verdure to me; in summer I lost myself in the ears, I crowned my head with cornflowers; the granaries of the farms were overflowing and the laborer, baking his bread, blessed Sessia. I was good, little children knew my name; even the men of the sea bought me presents to their moorings and I consecrated the arrows of warriors; my power was known."

She put her hand to her forehead, where vervain was wilting.

"I had even renounced amour, so much did the benefits I could distribute satisfy my heart. Monks like you came and hunted my druids and my priestesses, the laborers misunderstood my gifts. So, I am going to take them away from the earth where the most beautiful wheat in the world germinates, and draw the green waves to me in order to make a shroud for myself. Where we are, there will be nothing more tomorrow than the sea and the sky."

She cocked an ear, with a distracted expression.

"Can you hear? Can you hear my trees, my grottoes, my rocks my reeds, my blades of grass and my first flowers, sighing before being annihilated?"

Sessia became pale and began to weep, and d'Argouges remarked that the tears rendered her beauty more striking than her smile, as if divine. He sensed his heart melting, and marched more resolutely behind her.

---

[58] The name Theut is deliberately ambiguous, probably uniting a variant of the name of the Egyptian god Thoth, important in French Occultist tradition as "Hermes Trismegistus," and the hypothetical god of the Teutons, patron of the Germanic peoples.

A signpost suspended by the roadside bore the legend: *Crossroads of the Precipice*, and another, a little further on: *Road to the Abyss*. The monk read those indications, but they did not stop him.

Scubilion and Gautier woke up shortly afterwards; they no longer found their companion. Before them, flamboyantly incrusted in the bleeding bark of the tree, was the hated name of Belenos, the last challenge of the druidess.

They resumed their march, sadly

Already, a furious storm was tearing clumps of ivy and moss from the trunks of the trees; the branches were colliding like Frankish bucklers, with a sinister sound. The wind started to blow tempestuously, a prelude to the imminent equinoctial tide. The frightened woodland birds, warned by their instinct, quit their shelters, flew away in a confused cloud with sinister cries, and came to settle in the mountains; packs of wolves, foxes and wild boar ran hither and yon, as if mad with terror.

The tide rose, immense, green and glaucous, breaking everything, crushing everything, rolling enormous blocks of stone over the largest trees, which it reduced to thin twigs. The sea advanced incessantly, casting down all obstacles. The wave rushed over the mountains, coiling and writhing like a gigantic serpent that was raising the tempest. Finally forced to obey the ebb, it withdrew, growling, full of menace for the next tide.

The sunlight, traversing the somber clouds, came to illuminate the desolate spectacle. Of all the immense forest of Seyssi, nothing subsisted but a group of islets, which conserved the name of Chausey, a few rocks here and there that the sea had not been able to uproot, marshes and ponds, in the middle of which Mont Tombaë raised its beautiful and severe structure, still streaming with frost.

On returning from Mont Gargan, Scubilion and Gautier—who were carrying devotedly the relics of Saint Michel des Loups in a precious enameled casket—believed that they had been transported into another universe when they no longer saw the spacious forest that the sea had invaded.

On the hillock of Lihou the body of Jehan d'Argouges was found, clutching in his arms the cadaver of a druidess in a white robe. At that spectacle, the two clerks turned their eyes away, making the sign of the cross.

At sea, a black line designed in the north-west the new islands already covered in algae protruding from the water in the midst of long fleecy waves.

Thousands of sea-birds and storm-birds were circling over the reefs. The cries of curlews and sandpipers had replaced the chirping of the blackbird and the nightingale.

Lucie Delarue-Mardrus[59]: *The Haunted Water*

(Le Journal, 3 March 1907)

Little Jeanne, with a large school-bag under her arm, was passing over the Pont du Carrousel one winter evening and could not help slowing down in order to look at a surprising spectacle: the lights of Paris reflected in the water.

Her heart beat faster. It was the first time that she had found herself there, at that belated hour; for it was only since she had been ten years old that her mother, a milliner, sometimes charged her with little commissions on her way home from school.

This evening, therefore, hasty and a little fearful, she was hurrying to the address she had been given, in order to get back quickly before complete nightfall. And now, suddenly, the twilight over the water stopped her. She had been instructed not to idle on the way; but a ten-year-old schoolgirl cannot have the seriousness of a true apprentice. In any case, little Jeanne was such a particular child, albeit docile and mild. As soon as early childhood it had been perceived that she was "not like the others." And although she went meekly to school and was marvelously healthy, her relatives only watched with a sort of muted anxiety the frail person with the overly large eyes living and developing in their midst, who did not talk or

---

[59] When the Normandy-born Lucie Delarue-Mardrus (1874-1945) began to write regularly for the *Contes du Journal* slot in 1902 she was married to the Egyptologist J.-C. Mardus, famous for his translation of the *Mille-et-une nuits*, but she was also an active member of Natalie Barney's coterie of lesbian poets. She continued supplying material to the slot long after she stopped writing short stories and simply serialized her (naturalistic) novels therein.

play, and whose confidence no one had succeeded in capturing.

How was it imaginable, for example, that the ordinary sight of the Seine and its reflections, known to everyone, could strike her to the extent of making her forget the time? No one in Paris would have had the idea of leaning over the balustrades of bridges and quivering, as in the theater, simply because the slow rhythm of the black Seine was lengthened or shortened by the yellow, red and green streaks that the various lights of the city and the navigation allowed to fall into the nocturnal waters.

Nevertheless, after a moment, recaptured by the eminence of reality, the child started running in order to make up the lost time. But it was to come back very late, the commission completed, and to lean over again in the same place, devouring with her eyes, insatiably, the illuminated water that hypnotized her.

A first idler, noticing the absorbed girl, stopped behind her in order to look at whatever she was looking at; and, as he could not see anything that could excite curiosity, he began craning his neck, advancing and retreating, more and more intrigued. On seeing that, other passers-by also stopped and looked in their turn. Women having been added to the men, coachmen having stood up on their seats and baker's boys having slipped through the packed ranks, within a minute there was a compact crowd on the bridge, which, behind Jeanne, began to whisper commentaries of all kinds.

Meanwhile, finally extracted from her reverie, the child ended up turning round. Then she saw around her, with a frisson of fear, three hundred faces occupied in examining her. And it was with the gesture of a little hunted animal that she recoiled when the first passer-by, in the middle of the crowd of others, began to interrogate her.

Bewildered by surprise and timidity, she blushed, lowering her head and twisting her fingers. Then she ended up stammering, nearly weeping: "I was looking at how beautiful it is on the water..."

Then the crowd was shaken by a great burst of laughter. And immediately, scornful and disappointed, the people dispersed, shrugging their shoulders and saying: "If it were a corpse or a barge run aground, one could understand! But stopping to look in the water...!"

And the majority among them concluded, with rancor: "She's crazy!"

Then the circulation, momentarily disturbed, was reestablished. Liberated from the troop that surrounded her, the poor little girl, white with emotion, went home without saying a word. But a neighbor had preceded her, who, at the moment when she came in, was recounting the incident to her mother. Scolded, punished, and even having received a few slaps, little Jeanne wept all night. And henceforth, there was a refrain in the house every time she was charged with an errand: "Above all, don't do anything foolish outside!"

Her mother, struck by that adventure and full of resentment, said to her almost twice a day: "Instead of having ideas that aren't like other people's, you'd do better to bring me good notes from school, like little Anna or little Marie..."

The result was that the timid culprit, perfectly convinced that she had been wrong, since the grown-ups affirmed it, strove in her ten-year-old heart to resemble her comrades and not to look at the water again when she passed over the bridge at twilight.

However, her instinct being stronger than her, after a time she could not help raising her eyes slightly as she crossed the river, and then looking. And always, when night was falling, the same phantasmagoria fluttered before her eyes.

It was, for her, something so marvelous, the multicolored fire that danced indefatigably in the water, that she wondered with amazement why everyone did not stop to contemplate it for hours. And she began to observe the faces of those who passed over the bridge in order to assure herself that they did not notice anything. But not once, even at the most beautiful moments, did a single person give the slightest glance to the fluvial splendor. Noses lowered, eyes bleak, they passed by. A few were chatting and laughing. None of them, whatever class they belonged to, accorded a second of admiration to that fête of the somber water stabbed by gleams, to that magnificent adventure of every evening.

And little Jeanne ended up saying to herself: *I can certainly see things that other people don't see; that's why they call me crazy.*

One evening, attracted irresistibly, and fearing the idle and sniggering crowd that, by virtue of a simple impulse of imbecility, flocked and mocked without knowing why, the child had the idea of going down very close to the water, on the bank, where the shadow is propitious to those who dream.

She went, in spite of the cold, to sit down in a corner, on a step, and her little imagination toiled.

It seemed to her, from the height of the step, that she understood better the significance of the obscure water inhabited by glimmers of three colors. The tales of fays that she had sometimes read passed through her mind. Did not the forms of the reflections resemble persons? And when a river-boat passed, trailing behind it a tress of light, it appeared to her that a troop of fishy beings, lively and scintillating, swam insistently around the hull of the boat like a shoal of luminous eels.

She went home that day quivering with a secret and inexplicable joy. And every time she had occasion to cross the bridge, she went down to the same place to sit down for a moment at the bottom of the same staircase, in order to gaze at her dear Seine living by night.

Now, it happened that a flood made the river rise so high under its bridges that the circulation of the boats was interrupted. Those were fine evenings for little Jeanne. The water covered half the ordinary staircase, as if it had made an effort to get closer to its fragile friend. And the reflections were so clear, now, that that nothing was any longer stirring the Seine, that the little girl expected incessantly to see faces appearing through the liquid shadows. She was soon convinced that, decidedly, all those beings of light standing in the middle of the little waves, whose tails were beating feebly, were nothing other than water fays of a sort, invisible to others.

That thought became even firmer in her mind when she observed, under the arches of bridges, in the depths of the river, colonnettes of fire that loomed up, so close to one another that one might have taken them for the pipes of a fulgurant organ. Were not those fleeting architectures of light the palace of those marine ladies, the fresh-water sirens that little Jeanne loved?

Her immense eyes detailed things one by one. She did not take long to remark, at the foot of a large brown barge moored a few paces away from her, a reflection of a particular kind. Isolated and green, it moved slightly in place, stretching its body of a precious serpent as if it were trying to make signs. It was so close that one might have thought that it was about to emerge from the water in order to crawl up the steps and coil seductively around the schoolgirl's feet.

And Jeanne began talking to the friendly water spirit in a low voice.

"You're Melusine, aren't you?" she breathed.

But there was no response except for the slight jiggling of the eddies, by virtue of which the mobile and indecisive green lady at the foot of the silent barge zigzagged like durable lightning. Without a doubt she was saying in her mysterious language:

"Come with me! I'll take you to my castle of reflections. You'll also know my sisters. Some are translucent and as red as fish in bowls, and others all golden. There are also some as green as me. Can't you distinguish any from here? There's an entire shoal lingering under the Auteuil-Austerlitz pontoon. If you come with us you'll learn to live submerged; you'll also be a beautiful evening mirage, shifting, mute and retractile. And when the circulation is reestablished, more rapid than river trout, you'll cleave through the water with us, in pursuit of the slender boats full of people who don't see us."

And as, sometimes, for amusement, boys threw stones from the bridge into the Seine, little Jeanne saw her fresh water sirens flee and disappear with the thousand scaly gleams of a frightened fish-pond.

And she said to herself: *It's necessary to refrain from scaring them...*

That is why, on the evening when she decided that it was time to respond to their signs, she took all precautions in order not to trouble the somber water around her.

She had taken advantage of a slightly longer errand with which she had been charged to return late over the bridge. Then she had descended to her usual place.

Undoubtedly, in the house, her mother was already anxious, not having seen her daughter return; but with the insolent laughter of a child, she was amused with all her heart in thinking of the pleasure she would soon have in joining the sirens' round-dances in their palace and fluttering in the dark water with the whimsy of a will-o'-the-wisp.

She looked around slyly to see whether anyone might notice her.

It's necessary that I pay attention, she said to herself, *for people would surely believe that I'll drown and they'd immediately come to prevent me from going with the ladies.*

Then, as everything was black around her and no one could distinguish her, she went down one step gently, and then two...

The icy water circled her legs. Her teeth chattered.

When I'm entirely in the water, she reasoned, *I won't be cold at all any longer.* And with a little mute laugh: *Since I'll be fire, like the others!*

Then, feeling the glacial circle reach her waist, with a single movement, she let herself go, her arms extended, hands forward, ready to seize, through the muddy and obscure water, the sirens invisible to ordinary eyes, and who, for so many evenings, had been waiting for her, each in her place, doubtless because she was a dreamy little girl without speech...

It was not until two days later that the body of the drowned child was found, under the large brown barge.

Thus the green siren had attracted her, in accordance with her magical promise. And those who, filing through the Morgue, felt sorry for the poor little item of wreckage, stiff between two banal cadavers, did not know that her heavily lowered eyelids had closed upon a joyous and dancing paradise of flame and water.

That is why none of them had the idea of looking, in the evening, in the direction of the illuminated Seine. Perhaps they would have perceived there, mingled with the fascinating reflections, the little fiery soul of the child poet. But people do not look at anything, or, if they look, they do not see anything—which comes to the same thing.

And all of them, on going home, astonished and tearful, repeated: "Such a young child!"

While the next day's newspapers concluded, unanimously: "The causes of the suicide are unknown."

André Beaunier[60] : *Gugemer*

(Le Figaro, Supplément littéraire du Dimanche,
4 September 1909)

This adventure did not take place yesterday. It dates from
the time of the fays, and the fays have been dead for numerous
centuries. When they were alive they were not seen very often,
and even the most cunning individuals who boast, in old
books, of knowing all the stories of those beautiful supernatural ladies probably never saw them. But their presence could
be divined by manifest signs. People attributed to their sovereign and capricious will the various incidents that intervened
suddenly in the course of destiny without anyone having anticipated them and without anyone being able to explain them
otherwise. They were the charming reason for all the strange-
ness that there is on earth. So, after the death of those miraculous individuals, people found themselves quite embarrassed
to interpret the daily prodigies of nature and life. They were
obliged gradually to invent science, which replaced the fays as
best it could, with less grace and with a less complaisant scru-
pulousness.

In the time of the fays, young Gugemer went out hunting
one day. He was armed with an excellent arbalest and his skill
in its employment was celebrated. Broad-shouldered and slim-

---

[60] André Beaunier (1869-1925) was better known as a critic
than a novelist, his offbeat fiction seeming too unusual to attract much critical praise; his philosophical novel *L'Homme
qui a perdu son moi* (1911) has been translated as *The Man
Who Lost Himself*. His shorter *contes philosophiques* were
never collected..

waisted, he went through the forest, keenly alert, and his twenty years shone in his blue eyes, which no stubborn thought had yet profaned. It was morning, the hour when the grass and leaves wake up, and white wisps of mist, like transparent scarves, were floating slowly under the trees, clinging to the branches, tearing apart in the bushes or holding steady above the meadows, suspended like islands in the light ar. As for the sun, it was rising in the distance behind the forest, and that other hunter was launching thousands of golden arrows from his ambush.

Gugemer was singing as he went. He was not singing anything in particular, but his heart was so joyful and innocent that it was flourishing in vague songs and madcap exclamations.

Suddenly, in the middle of the path that Gugemer was following, a hind appeared. It arrived in a single bound and then, instead of fleeing, it stood still and gazed at the hunter, Gugemer only hesitated for a second. He shouldered his weapon, took aim, and the bolt flew.

Gugemer saw that it was about to hit the hind, but then it seemed to rebound without touching her, and, turning about, came toward him. It struck his arm. The pain was so terrible that Gugemer did not think of being astonished, but he uttered a groan and fainted.

When he recovered consciousness the bolt was no longer in his arm; it had disappeared. He scarcely searched for it; but he verified that that the wound was hurting him, extremely.

Now Gugemer was brave, as it befits men to be, and squeamish, as they habitually are; he was desolate, and felt sorry for himself. There was already enough to displease him when the hind appeared again. She said to him: "Gugemer, your wound will only be healed when a pretty woman has suffered because of you."

And the hind ran away without giving Gugemer time to inveigh against her. In any case, the singularity of the episode imposed upon him and he had no desire to augment his misfortune for the brief satisfaction of a perilous impertinence.

"Very well!" he said.

From then on he searched for a pretty woman who would be willing to suffer because of him.

With his arbalest slung over his shoulder he went down toward the village, marching with difficulty and suffering more with every step he took. He encountered three young women, who were blonde and puerile. They were holding hands and their cheerful trio occupied the full width of a flower path bordered by oleanders.

As they were not grim, Gugemer called to them. He said: "Beautiful demoiselles, wait while I tell you a very surprising story."

They drew nearer. At first, his story amused them, like an ingenious boast; but they soon saw that it was all true, for Gugemer gave twenty persuasive details, with a sincere emotion. They adored its many peripeties, and when the hind appeared to Gugemer again they clapped their hands. But when the hind spoke, announcing that it would be necessary for a pretty woman to suffer for the hunter to be healed, they did not like that threat, and they ran away, running. Three seconds sufficed for Gugemer to see them, and then no longer to see them.

He remained crestfallen, and understood that he had lacked prudence, in revealing everything. He promised himself to be more circumspect in future, even hypocritical. And he resumed his route, moaning.

After some time he recognized a young nun who was walking rapidly, her eyes lowered, going to prayer. The shrill bell of a convent was ringing precipitately, lightly and briskly, appealing to the servant of the lord with a cheerful insistence, engaging her to hurry, marking and hastening the rhythm of her footsteps. The nun was starting to run when Gugemer begged her to listen to him. She was rosy and ravishing under her béguin; her broad and heavy robe did not fit her very well;

she resembled the slightly simple and very genteel Madonnas that the Flemings used to paint.

"Have pity on me," Gugemer said to her.

And he showed her his wound, which was certainly giving him great pain; but all the same, he moaned more than was absolutely necessary.

The young nun stopped then and came toward him.

"Poor young man!" she said.

She took him to a spring and bathed his wound with a subtle and amicable care; then she was able to find in a basket, in which there was also a rosary, a gospel and holy images, a piece of fine white cloth, which she used to clean and then to bandage the bloody wound.

"Alas, alas!" she said, with a sentiment of compassion so evident that Gugemer hoped to see her suffer because of him. But as he continued suffering, he realized that the saintly exercise of pity and charity brings its recompense with it, and is neither a fatigue nor a dolor.

Various experiments led Gugemer to think that amour was indispensable in such a circumstance; no pretty woman would suffer for him otherwise. Thus, the hazards of life gradually informed him of the elements of wisdom.

As he was in haste to see his wound healed, however, he first accepted a foolish tenderness that was presented to him. He had not chosen it—or, more exactly, he had not had the illusion of choosing it, for a sage would have been able tell him that one does not choose one's amours.

Gugemer was handsome and conceited. He had confidence in being loved more than he would love. The old pedagogue who had taught him Latin in Horace, Ovid and Propertius had revealed to him by that means that amour is a great torment. Gugemer anticipated that the little creature who testified so much amenity and so much complaisant good grace and familiar inclination to him would experience all possible chagrin—and in any case, he would see to it.

Contrary to his expectation, however, it was him who loved much more than he was loved. That happened without him knowing how, in so little time that he did not perceive it. He marveled at it later, but at the time he could not help it. The little creature, light and mischievous, gave him many occasions for chagrin, melancholy, jealousy and impatience; and he detested her, but much less than he loved her.

In brief, it was him who experienced all the sadness that an imperfect amour comports.

He tried to avenge himself and he said harsh things; but as the coquette did not love him she was insensible to his reproaches and his jeremiads, and to the spectacle that he offered her of an extremely unhappy heart.

Gugemer resolved then to be loved without being in love himself next time. He put all his zeal into it and took advantage of the lessons in cruelty that he had received, without asking for them, from the pitiless and seductive little creature.

He did not succeed easily in being loved thus—in being loved truly without loving. Either the beauty was frivolous or he commenced to be smitten himself. Then he feared a suffering even worse than that of his wound, and fled fearfully.

He acquired in those attempts a remarkable skill, a delicate subtlety. In addition, he became increasingly unsentimental. His egotism was refined, and also his malevolence.

Finally, he encountered his victim.

She was prettier than the stars of Italian nights, milder than the perfume of vervain, more tremulous than the foliage of an aspen, and dreamier than lakes between the banks that they reflect.

She saw Gugemer and loved him; and Gugemer knew that she loved him. He waited for her to love him more, and then he said to her: "I love you."

From then on, she belonged to him. He tormented her, but she was very fervent about him, she was not conscious of being tormented.

He told her that he did not love her. She could not believe it. In any case, she loved him enough to remain ecstatic forever.

He announced to her that he was leaving her. For a minute, she dreaded his absence, but then she decided that he would not be absent for her, whose heart was eternally impregnated with him.

He even beat her. Then she understood that he did not love her; but the cherished brutal hands, in wanting to touch her, were marvelous caresses for her.

However, after ferocious inventions, when she had understood that he did not love her, one day he kissed her mouth with a perfidious ardor, and she suffered from that loveless kiss to the point of dying of it.

Thus, Gugemer was cured of his wound. But when he saw his poor little victim lying inanimate, by his fault, he detested his cure and he felt compassion. He wanted to die too, because of his remorse and his regret.

The fay who had subjected him to those emblematic ordeals intervened. She resuscitated the amorous fool, and inspired a similar amour in Gugemer.

They were very happy. They had won!

FRENCH FANTASY
FROM BLACK COAT PRESS

( ) Marie Catherine d'Aulnoy. Tales of the Fays (2 volumes)
( ) Honoré de Balzac. The Last Fay
( ) Mme Barbot de Villeneuve. The Naiads / Beauty and the Beast
( ) Cyprien Bérard. The Vampire Lord Ruthwen
( ) S. Henry Berthoud. The Angel Asrael
( ) Aloysius Bertrand. Gaspard de la Nuit
( ) Charlotte-Rose Caumont de La Force. The Land of Delights
( ) Comte de Caylus. The Impossible Enchantment
( ) Félicien Champsaur. Pharaoh's Wife
( ) Comtesse D.L. The Tyranny of the Fays Abolished
( ) Antoine-Louis Duclaux, Comte de l'Estoille. Argentine
( ) Antoine-Louis Duclaux, Comte de l'Estoille. The Miller of Carnac
( ) Antoine-Louis Duclaux, Comte de l'Estoille. The Song of the Skylark
( ) Alexandre Dumas & Paul Lacroix. The Man who Married a Mermaid
( ) Marie-Antoinette Fagnan. The Enchanter's Mirror
( ) Paul Féval. Anne of the Isles
( ) Charles de Fieux, Chevalier de Mouhy. Lamekis
( ) Judith Gautier: Isoline and the Serpent-Flower
( ) Jules Janin. The Magnetized Corpse
( ) Gustave Kahn. The Tale of Gold and Silence
( ) Paul Lacroix. Danse Macabre
( ) Louis-Guillaume de La Follie. The Unpretentious Philosopher
( ) Etienne-Léon de Lamothe-Langon. The Virgin Vampire
( ) Etienne-Léon de Lamothe-Langon. The Mysterious Hermit of the Tomb
( ) Maurice Level. The Gates of Hell

( ) Marie-Jeanne L'Héritier de Villandon. The Robe of Sincerity

( ) André Lichtenberger. The Centaurs

( ) André Lichtenberger. The Children of the Crab

( ) Monsieur de Listonai. The Philosophical Voyager

( ) Jean-Marc & Randy Lofficier. The French Fantasy Treasury (3 volumes)

( ) Charles Lomon & P.-B. Gheusi. The Last Days of Atlantis

( ) Marie-Madeleine de Lubert. Princess Camion

( ) Charles Malato. Lost!

( ) Maurice Magre. The Marvelous Story of Claire d'Amour

( ) Maurice Magre. The Call of the Beast

( ) Maurice Magre. Priscilla of Alexandria

( ) Maurice Magre. The Angel of Lust

( ) Maurice Magre. The Mystery of the Tiger

( ) Maurice Magre. The Poison of Goa

( ) Maurice Magre. Lucifer

( ) Maurice Magre. The Blood of Toulouse

( ) Maurice Magre. The Albigensian Treasure

( ) Maurice Magre. Jean de Fodoas

( ) Maurice Magre. Melusine

( ) Maurice Magre. The Brothers of the Virgin Gold

( ) Catulle Mendes. The Little Fays in the Air

( ) Louis-Sébastien Mercier. The Iron Man

( ) Joseph Méry. The Tower of Destiny

( ) Hippolyte Mettais. Paris Before the Deluge

( ) Henriette-Julie de Murat. The Palace of Vengeance

( ) Marie Nizet. Captain Vampire

( ) Charles Nodier. Trilby The Crumb Fairy

( ) Pierre-Alexis Ponson du Terrail. The Vampire and the Devil's Son

( ) Pierre-Alexis Ponson du Terrail. The Immortal Woman

( ) Pierre-Alexis Ponson du Terrail. The Police Agent

( ) Edgar Quinet. Ahasuerus

( ) Edgar Quinet. The Enchanter Merlin

( ) Restif de la Bretonne. Discovery of the Austral Continent

( ) Restif de la Bretonne. Posthumous Correspondence (3 Volumes)
( ) Restif de la Bretonne. The Story of the Great Prince
( ) Restif de la Bretonne. The Four Beauties and the Four Beasts
( ) Marie-Anne de Roumier-Robert. The Voyages of Lord Seaton to the Seven Planets
( ) Louis-Claude de Saint-Martin. The Crocodile
( ) Nicolas Segur. The Human Paradise
( ) Nicolas Segur. Penelope's Secret
( ) Pierre de Sélènes. An Unknown World
( ) Brian Stableford. The Queen of the Fays (anthology)
( ) Brian Stableford. Funestine (anthology)
( ) Brian Stableford. The Origin of the Fays (anthology)
( ) Brian Stableford. Tales of Enchantment and Disenchantment (anthology + non-fiction)
( ) Charles-François Tiphaigne de La Roche. Amilec
( ) Simon Tyssot de Patot. The Strange Voyages of Jacques Massé and Pierre de Mésange
( ) Louis Ulbach. Prince Bonifacio
( ) Willy. Astral Amour